Don't
LET IT BE TRUE

Also by Jo Barrett

THIS IS HOW IT HAPPENED (NOT A LOVE STORY)
THE MEN'S GUIDE TO THE WOMEN'S BATHROOM

Don't
LET IT BE TRUE

Jo Barrett

AVON

An Imprint of HarperCollinsPublishers

DON'T LET IT BE TRUE. Copyright © 2009 by JoAnna Barrett. All rights reserved. Printed in the United States of America. No part of this book may be used or reproduced in any manner whatsoever without written permission except in the case of brief quotations embodied in critical articles and reviews. For information address HarperCollins Publishers, 10 East 53rd Street, New York, NY 10022.

HarperCollins books may be purchased for educational, business, or sales promotional use. For information please write: Special Markets Department, HarperCollins Publishers, 10 East 53rd Street, New York, NY 10022.

FIRST AVON PAPERBACK EDITION PUBLISHED 2009.

Designed by Diahann Sturge

Library of Congress Cataloging-in-Publication Data
Barrett, Jo.
    Don't let it be true / Jo Barrett.—1st ed.
        p. cm.
ISBN 978-0-06-124117-8
1. Rich people—Texas—Fiction.   2. Texas—Fiction.   I. Title.
PS3602.A77749D66   2007
813'.6—dc22   2008043380

09   10   11   12   OV/RRD   10 9 8 7 6 5 4 3 2 1

Houston is, without a doubt, the weirdest, most enter-
taining city in Texas, consisting as it does of subtropical
forest, life in the fast lane, a layer of oil, cowboys and
spacemen.

Texas Tourism Guide

One

Every woman in Texas has a dirty little secret. A secret that could destroy her reputation, crush her fragile confidence, and sully her good name forever.

The most common Texas dirty little secret had to do with strippers. Here's how that one went: Wealthy Texas oilman divorces first wife for second wife. Second wife bears children, dresses in expensive designer clothes, and builds impressive rococo-style swirling McMansion, complete with French chandeliers and full-time gardener. Second wife joins "society" and becomes philanthropic. She is photographed at all of the best events in the best clothes. Her friends are similarly wealthy, powerful, and stylish. Second wife's dirty little secret is that she met her wealthy husband while dancing the pole at the Men's Club in Las Vegas, or worse, Tampa.

Kathleen Connor King had two dirty little secrets. The good news was that neither of them had to do with stripping. The bad news was that she was poor.

This was secret number one.

The reason for this secret is that everyone assumed Kathleen was wildly rich. Everyone who was anyone in Houston, that is. She'd been born a King. As in "the Kings" from Houston. As in owning most of the oil in the surrounding counties. Which was more fuel than anyone could possibly imagine. Except maybe the folks over at Shell, Exxon, and Texaco.

Carrying the last name of King trumped everything else about Kat. It didn't matter that she was artistic and wore all the wrong clothes. For other girls—plain girls without King in their last name—this would equate to social suicide. But Kathleen was simply viewed as eccentric. Wildly rich and eccentric! How exciting, everyone thought. And so Kat was extended all the courtesies that the Houston socialite set could afford. Free tickets to the best events. The Houston Opera Ball, the Contemporary Arts Museum Gala, the grand opening of *this* restaurant or *that* boutique; and, of course, the most fashionable charity dinners.

Kat usually made a splash at each function, wearing clothes she'd picked out from Twice Around Texas, her favorite thrift store. She was a trendsetter, to say the least. No one knew it was because she couldn't afford the designer stuff. The other society women, in their Gucci, Hermès, and Carolina Herrera, fawning over Kat in her funky, vintage threads.

The sham continued right onto the society pages. The Guccis, Hermès, and Carolina Herreras always made sure to be photographed with her. To be seen in the society pages with their arms looped around little ol' Kat, as if they were best friends forever. As if they bothered to get to know her. But they didn't. As much as Kat tried, they didn't bother to understand her personality, her flair, her *art*.

This was why Kat was drinking an ice-cold Corona straight from the bottle. She was nursing a splitting headache. Even after two extra-strength Tylenols chased down with beer, the pain radiated across her temples like flashes of lightning.

Kat's headache had started earlier this afternoon. When the Guccis had suggested an afternoon of shopping at Neiman Marcus followed by Botox treatments at the medical spa in Uptown Park, Kat countered with African tribal dancing, which was free on Wednesdays in Hermann Park.

The Guccis looked at her funny, smiled politely, and said: "Oh, Kat. You're adorable, sweetie."

And then they skipped off to enjoy their shopping and Botox, leaving Kat to mull over a half-eaten Cobb salad.

Kat drank the rest of the beer, set the bottle on the floor, and considered her predicament. *I don't care to be in the scene*, she thought.

A part of her didn't care if Houston society found out about her dirty little secret. Sometimes, at charity events, Kat would fight the urge to jump up and shout, "Don't you people know that I'm poor!"

But she couldn't do this. She had to remain Kathleen Connor King. She had to keep the myth of her family name, the aloofness of all that wealth and entitlement alive. And why? Because of the Foundation. The foundation her grandfather—Cullen Davis King—had named after himself, and the one that Kathleen carried the torch for to this day.

The King Foundation was Kathleen's raison d'être, and not because she hosted the most powerful ticket of the year. But because deep down, despite the fact that Kathleen had been born with a silver spoon in her mouth, she had a heart of gold.

It was the most exclusive event of the year. It raised millions of dollars for the Pediatric Cancer Hospital. And it was hosted by Kathleen herself—the last remaining King in the prominent King family.

Using her last name like a weapon, Kathleen Connor King had single-handedly created the most famous fund-raising event in Texas. Each ticket cost (gasp!) ten thousand dollars. A table cost one hundred thousand. There were fifty tables. And Kat managed to sell out every year.

It was the reason that she suffered through society events and agreed to have her picture taken with the Guccis, Hermès, and Carolina Herreras.

It was the reason she was painting, this week. Her "jungle art" would fetch a few thousand dollars during the foundation's annual auction.

Kat dipped her brush in the can of hot pink boudoir paint and swirled it around the canvas, making the shape of a tree. She was painting a hot pink forest, in fact. Complete with hot pink birds and hot pink monkeys.

She scratched a fleck of dried paint from the tip of her thumb and wondered when Dylan would get home. She was feeling the feeling. Or, as her mother would've said, "hot between the thighs."

Two

The Colonial Funeral Home was exactly as Dylan imagined it to be. Grim and macabre, with fake flowers everywhere and coffins displayed like Cadillacs. Dylan tried not to breathe, but something smelled. It was one of those cover-up smells. Like when someone sprays lemon freshener over a recent cigarette he smoked.

It was sort of like that. Only worse.

Dylan imagined it was the smell of death covered up by ammonia and bleach and possibly a peach candle. He spotted a candle burning on a nearby table and leaned closer to take a peek.

Peach Frosting.

The candle was named "Peach Frosting."

Dylan shivered. He could smell peach from a freakin' mile. What a nasty, hairy little fucker. The peach.

He gulped back the sour bile forming in his throat and tried not to focus on the fact that he was freezing his balls off. Why did Colonial Funeral Home insist on cranking up the A.C.? Why couldn't it feel more like a log cabin, with a nice crackling wood fire and some warm apple cider for folks to drink?

Why did it have to be so damned . . . clinical? With all that cold air blasting from the vents, and all those coffins lined up in neat rows.

Dylan tried not to think of his father's body lying frigid and dead in the back room.

The funeral director, in his somber suit and discount store tie, was whispering something about "arrangements." Dylan was hardly listening. All he could focus on was Peach Frosting. The candle was called "Peach Frosting."

Dylan knew he'd never eat another peach as long as he lived.

"Many of our clients choose the music package," the director said, which caught Dylan's attention. "You get the coffin, the flowers, the transportation, and the music."

"You mean like a band?" Dylan choked. The idea of having a band at Butch Grant's sorry little send-off was enough to cast a smirk across his face.

"A harp," the funeral director said, raising a pencil-thin eyebrow.

"Jesus," Dylan said under his breath.

He needed to get out of this place. Pronto.

It had been two hours. Two hours of Dylan's life dedicated to the ungrateful Butch Grant, yet again.

Dylan peered inside one of the coffins. It was lined with red velvet and reminded him of a Halloween prop that a vampire would pop out of. He knocked his fist against the coffin.

"No harp. No bells and whistles." he said. "I want his ashes to be put in"—he pointed to an urn on a table next to the peach candle—"in one of those."

"That is a vase, sir. The urns are in the next room."

Dylan scowled and scratched his arm.

It was almost comical. Here he was. In a funeral home in Tanglewood, with the larger-than-life Butch Grant lying dead in the next room—and he'd just pointed to a flower vase as the vessel for his father's remains.

Nice job, genius.

He might not be a rocket scientist, but Dylan knew when to say when. "Tell me your name again?" he asked. The funeral director had mentioned it, but Dylan had forgotten.

"Ned Greely."

"Mr. Greely, I'm no good at this. Picking out this stuff is not my forte."

"It's a difficult process for anyone, Mr. Grant."

"Listen up. I need you to pick out an urn from the next room, put my father's ashes in it, and call me when it's finished."

The funeral director worked his bottom lip feverishly. This was obviously not how it was done.

Dylan stared at the floor.

"I'll pay extra," he mumbled.

"Of course, Mr. Grant. You must be very upset."

Ned Greely had a cold fish handshake, and as Dylan pumped the cold fish up and down, he felt a chill creep across his skin. His stomach flip-flopped and he gulped back the vomit that was steadily trying to come up his throat.

"Th-th-thank you for your help, Mr. Greely."

Dylan pivoted on his heel and strode quickly toward the door—the door with the little bell chime—the door that exited ammonia and bleach and dead bodies and peach candles.

Three

Dylan stomped on the accelerator and felt the sports car rocket forward down Interstate 10. There would be no tears today. He wasn't made of stone, but he wasn't stupid, either. Crying over Butch Grant would be like getting punched in the face all over again. Jeez. After too many whacks, even a dog learned not to care.

On the seat next to him was Butch Grant's last will and testament. Scrawled out in his dad's own chicken-scratch handwriting.

Dylan knitted his brows together. *Who the hell writes their will in red ink?*

He balled up the pages in his hand and tossed them in the backseat.

Gunning the accelerator, he sped toward the exit ramp for Shepherd. Past the ol' taco shack, the Chevron, the dry cleaner's. Finally, Dylan was back in his 'hood. The familiarity felt like a warm blanket.

He exhaled sharply and realized he'd been holding his breath. It was a miracle he hadn't passed out behind the wheel.

Enough is enough, he thought, shaking his head like a dog fresh out of the water.

He eased the car past the towering fountain gracing the front entrance of the Royal Arms Luxury Residences. The high-rise building was thirty stories of breathtaking metal and glass, boasting terraces with dead-on views of the Houston skyline. A towering behemoth of new money set stubbornly amid the whispering blue-blood Houston neighborhood that had frowned on such development.

The Royal Arms was the only condominium high-rise that had ever been built inside the 77019 zip code—the prestigious River Oaks neighborhood where Houston's old guard elite lived in sprawling mansions with gated, manicured lawns.

Dylan swung his car into the circular drive and waited for one of the valets.

"What's up, Achmed?" he said, stepping out and tossing his keys to one of the red-uniformed men. *Or was it Abdul?* They were all from Jordan or Syria, all earnest, and all their names tended to start with an A.

Dylan felt relief as he saw the gold name tag that confirmed it was Achmed.

Who could blame him for forgetting their names? He was one of the biggest tippers at Christmas, and he knew this because the valets always went the extra mile. One of the Abduls would even wash Dylan's car, as long as the big boss man, the Senior Abdul, wasn't around. The Senior Abdul liked to keep the lesser Abduls in check.

Dylan strode up to the glass doors and waited for Poor Eddie to buzz him in. Poor Eddie, the building concierge who sat behind an antique mahogany desk, sneaking Cheetos and Twinkies and Twix bars when no one was looking.

Dylan had nicknamed him "Poor" Eddie not because of his

wages, but because Eddie always had a sob story about his health. His knee had gone bad. His hearing. His teeth. Poor Eddie had an array of physical ailments. Each week it was something different. Dylan liked Eddie, but hated feeling obligated. Hated having to stand at the concierge desk while Eddie regaled him with another tale about his glaucoma, his high blood pressure, his prostate.

He wondered if this happened at the fancy Park Avenue buildings in New York City. Did those Manhattan Masters of the Universe stand around for twenty minutes while some building concierge driveled on about his goddamned cataracts?

The secret to getting past Eddie was to look hurried and preoccupied. Often Dylan would pretend to be on his cell phone as he hustled past the front desk. But today he was in no mood to fake it.

"Eddie," he said, nodding briskly as he strode through the lobby.

Eddie broke into a broad grin and rubbed his liver-spotted hand over his bald pate. "Mr. Grant," he breathed, with those deep pools for eyes pleading for Dylan to stop and chat.

Dylan winced. Eddie insisted on calling him "Mr. Grant." Eddie called everyone else in the building by their first name. And so, as Houston's rich and overprivileged new money crowd swooshed through the glass doors and past the entrance garlanded with a fresh flower bouquet every morning, Eddie would call them all out by name. Heralding the wealthy residents of the Royal Arms with his cheerful siren call:

"Morning, Karen."

"Morning, Charles."

"Morning, Tom."

But when Dylan walked by, it was, "Morning, Mr. Grant."

It has to be the car, Dylan thought. *That damned car.* The other cars in the building were nothing to sniff about, the valet lot always jammed with six-figure wheels. Porsches, Range Rovers, Mercedes, and not one but several Ferraris, but Dylan's car stood out from the pack. It was the worst kind of car, in Dylan's opinion. A car that screamed: *Look at me, everyone! Look at what I'm driving! I'm stupid rich!*

It wasn't his fault, of course. It was the fault of the younger Mr. Grant. Dylan's brash younger brother. He'd been trying to rein in Wyatt for years, but it was like putting a leash on a wildcat. His brother had done the unthinkable and just *left the car at the building*. Just left it for Dylan to take care of. Just left it for Dylan to drive. Just left it. Period.

Wyatt.

Young, rakish, partyin', good ol' boy—God bless him—Wyatt.

Wyatt Grant had left a brand-new Bugatti for Dylan to drive. A cool million dollars on wheels. A moving bank. A damned liability if you asked Dylan.

His younger brother had moved out to Las Vegas to "become a real estate developer," which Dylan knew for a fact meant that Wyatt wanted to get laid by hot, baby-oil tan chicks. In Wyatt's words, Vegas was a great place to "prowl for new skirt."

Dylan smiled at the thought of his brother. Had he not suffered so much hardship as a child, Wyatt would've been pure asshole. But because their father had been a disaster—a *Titanic* on two feet—Dylan had to give his younger brother a break. Wyatt never stood a chance. Not after taking a round of shotgun shells in the leg at the mere age of nine that caused the Younger to walk with a limp even to this day. Alcohol and shotguns didn't mix well in the hands of Butch Grant.

Good thing Dad is dead, Dylan thought.

Four

Kathleen knew there was a bottle of vodka hiding somewhere. She padded into the kitchen and proceeded to open all the relevant cabinets. Dylan didn't like to keep liquor in the house, which was understandable with the type of father he'd grown up with, but Kathleen enjoyed a little nip now and again.

"I see you," she said, as she spotted the miniature airplane-sized bottle. Stashed behind a box of Keebler saltines that were surely stale by now.

Kathleen twisted off the cap.

The drink of champions, she smirked—taking a swig directly from the bottle.

She rarely drank, but today had been one of those days when a person needed a little nectar to kill the pain.

Dylan will be home soon, she thought. She just wanted her raging headache to subside. She needed to be there for him. She needed to make love to her man. She needed to forget about dirty little secret number two.

Kathleen padded around the kitchen, waving the bottle of

vodka in the air like a wand, and considered her fate. What series of unfortunate events had led her to the doctor's office this morning? How had she come to be the last remaining person in her entire family?

And why—of all people—me?

The Kings had been plagued with the same Greek tragedies as those of other powerful clans, like the Kennedy family, and even the royal family in England.

It read like a bad movie . . .

Kathleen's mother had died from ovarian cancer when Kat was still in elementary school. Five years ago, her father had been killed in a gangland shooting at a mall in Dallas. Kathleen's younger sister, Meredith, had lost her life when she was just fifteen, the very day she received her temporary driver's license in the mail and jackknifed into an eighteen-wheeler on Interstate 10 during the typical teenager joyride.

Kathleen's venerable grandfather, Cullen Davis King, had some staying power, but even this great man had died in his sleep a few years back—of a massive heart attack.

There was no one left *but* Kathleen. After her grandfather's death, she lived and breathed the foundation. What else was there?

Kathleen checked the clock on the microwave.

He's going to be walking in the door any minute now.

She took another sip from the vodka, and then chunked it in the trash—underneath a newspaper.

Then she stripped off her clothes and waited.

Five

Dylan stretched his arms out wide and felt a pop in his back. *It's been ten minutes*, he thought. Eddie was rambling on. Glancing at his watch, Dylan realized he'd been listening to Eddie for not ten, but a solid *twenty* minutes. It was time to cut to the chase.

"How was your doctor's appointment?" he asked.

Poor Eddie shook his head grimly. He cast his eyes downward, rubbed his bald head, and lowered his voice a notch.

An Oscar-worthy performance, Dylan thought.

"Not so good, Mr. Grant. Doc says my cholesterol is out the roof. I've gotta start on the Lipitor. But my insurance won't pay . . ."

Dylan listened as Eddie trailed on. Something about Eddie's arteries.

Just then, Dylan spotted them. Hidden discreetly behind the FedEx packages at the concierge desk. A half-eaten bag of deep-fried pork rinds and the crumbling remains of a Snickers.

"How much for the pills?" Dylan asked.

"I don't know, Mr. Grant. Could be a hundred. Maybe more."

It used to be fifty, Dylan thought. He flipped out a hundred-dollar bill from his money clip and dipped it into Eddie's sweaty palm.

For such a sickly dude, Eddie was quick on the uptake. Fast as lightning when it came to pocketing a Benjamin.

Dylan watched as the cash disappeared into Eddie's thick commercial-grade trousers.

"Thank you, Mr. Grant," Eddie breathed. As if Dylan had just given him a kidney.

"Don't mention it, Eddie. I'd lay off the snacks if I were you."

Eddie pressed the button on a set of glass security doors. Dylan walked to the bank of elevators that would whisk him up to his sweet twentieth-floor pad.

That was fun, Dylan thought.

Dealing with Eddie had been a pain, but that wasn't the problem. Thinking about his father had gotten Dylan's blood pressure up and he felt his heart pounding firmly in his chest. Butch Grant had a way of reaching his cold hand out from the grave and squeezing Dylan's lungs, until his breath grew short.

As Dylan stepped into the elevator and stabbed at the button, he was suddenly overwhelmed by a smell. Cheap cologne. It was a cologne that reminded Dylan of the eighties. Of high school kids in Jeep Wranglers listening to *Head like a hole. Black as your soul. I'd rather die than give you control . . .*

Who the fuck is wearing Drakkar Noir in this building?

The answer arrived in a cloudburst. It swept into the elevator. And it was dressed to the nines.

It was Steve.

The Katrina guy.

Terrific, Dylan thought. *What next?*

Mr. Louisiana had been displaced by Hurricane Katrina, moved to Houston, and set up shop. Mr. Louisiana—a white guy wearing a black guy's clothes. Crocodile-skin loafers. A pin-striped suit too long for his body. Gold everywhere. He looked like a drug dealer or rap artist, this guy Steve. A white guy in a black guy's clothes.

Steve stuck out his knobby forefinger and punched the button to the third floor.

Figures, Dylan thought. Steve was the type of guy to enter a high-rent building only to get a low-floor discount.

Steve regarded Dylan, just as Dylan regarded Steve. They both stood in the confined elevator. Their arms crossed across their respective chests, staring each other down.

Elevator gunslingers.

"So," Steve said finally, breaking the ice that was building up. The testosterone raging inside the small enclosure.

"So," Dylan echoed.

"You made any money yet today?" Steve asked, all testosterone and balls.

Dylan glanced lazily down at his watch. It was two o'clock in the afternoon.

"Day's still early, brother."

Steve's eyes became like needles—perhaps because Dylan had called him "brother"—but then Mr. Louisiana allowed a chuckle to escape his lips.

"Aw, hell," Steve shook his head. "What business you in, *dawg?*"

Dylan winced. Steve talked like he was Ice Cube or Ice-T or Vanilla Ice, or one of the ices.

"Family business," Dylan said, trying not to breathe. The cologne was worse than a Mexico City nightclub.

Steve persisted. "You the doughnut guy?"

"Nah, man. I'm not the doughnut guy."

Nah, man? Dylan found himself talking the talk. The Steve lingo. He probably smelled like Steve, too. Drowning in Drakkar.

Jesus. This guy Steve is one infectious sonofabitch.

" 'Cause I heard a rumor this new *dawg* moved into the building who's richer than shit. I'm talking *loaded*. You know Whipley's? Those doughnut shops out on Memorial Drive. Hell, they're even serving kolaches now. They got everything."

The elevator stopped on Steve's floor, but Steve stabbed the open button with his nubby forefinger. Much to Dylan's chagrin, the door alarm started to ring.

Ding! Ding! Ding!

Mr. Devil-May-Care didn't seem to mind the noise, and kept his finger firmly pressed on the button.

Dylan hesitated. "I'm not the Whipley guy. I'm in oil and gas."

Being "in" oil and gas was Dylan's favorite tagline. It could mean anything. And usually, people didn't pry.

Of course, Steve the Infectious Disease wasn't most people.

"Lucky, dawg! I'd kill for some of that mailbox money. We should get together, you and I. Talk shop."

Ding! Ding! Ding!

"Gotta bounce, brother. Let's meet downstairs for coffee," Steve said. As if they were fast friends all of a sudden.

Not a chance, Dylan thought. He couldn't catch a break. As soon as he set foot inside the building, he felt like Bill Gates at a titty bar. Everyone flocked to him because of the damned car.

Dylan watched the elevator doors whoosh close. *A few more floors and I'll be home, sweet home.*

Six

Stepping inside the condo always took Dylan's breath away. The view alone was worth the trouble. Boasting a sweep of floor-to-ceiling windows facing east—smack-dab on the Houston skyline—it was priceless. Not to mention that the condo was made all the more dramatic with blond hardwood floors and soaring ceilings.

"What's up, buttercup?" cooed a sweet voice. Dylan strolled into his main living room and admired the view. She was naked, of course. Lying on one of her canvases. Right in the center of the floor.

Kat.

Good ol' Kat.

God, I love you, woman, Dylan thought.

She was his sweetheart, ever since she'd punched him in the nose in the fourth grade. Dylan had deserved it. He'd called her "Pudding Face." And she'd responded with a swift right hook that left him bleeding next to the jungle gym.

Yet something tugged at him. They weren't married, and the

subject had never come up. It wasn't like Dylan was a commitment-phobe. It's just that marriage itself seemed like a major headache. Heck, they'd been living together since college. What did a piece of paper matter?

Kat was always working on different projects. This week, she'd decided she was Marc Chagall.

"How did it go?" she murmured.

"It was a blast," Dylan said dryly. She was no stranger to death in the family. She'd offered to go with him to the funeral home, but he'd vigorously protested. *The last thing you need to deal with is something like this*, he'd told her.

Now Kat was trying to get his mind off things by being naked and pretending like he hadn't spent the afternoon with the grim reaper's close cousin—Mr. Ned Greely.

"I learned that a flower vase is not an urn," Dylan said.

"Oh, sweetie," Kat said. She continued painting in the nude, but looked up at him as if he were a wounded animal on the side of the road. Dylan had instructed her not to hug him, kiss him, or do anything when he got home that wasn't normal.

Pretend like it's any other day, he'd told her when he left for the funeral home. *Otherwise, I'm gonna lose it.*

"Don't give me those pity eyes," Dylan scolded. "You know I hate that."

"Do you want to *talk* about it?"

"Absolutely, one hundred percent. Let's spend all evening rehashing my father's wonderful parenting job, my fun-loving childhood, and the fact that his death is a tragedy not only to me, but to all mankind."

"Oh, sweetie. Get over here," Kat commanded him.

Dylan watched her roll onto her back and drip the paintbrush across her lithe body. Her breasts were small and firm—not the silicone balloons favored by his brother, Wyatt, and most other men whom Dylan knew. Kat was tiny, small-framed, and stubborn as a bull.

Kat flicked the brush in his direction, sending splatters of hot pink paint all over Dylan's jeans and the hardwood floor.

"Hey now! You're spilling paint all over the condo!"

"It's water paint, you nutcase," she said. "It'll wipe right off."

Dylan scowled as he approached her, staring down at Kat naked on her canvas.

"You painting your butt or something?"

Dylan knew it was a stupid question. But with Kat, you never could tell.

"Yes, I'm painting my butt," she said.

"Why?"

"Dylan Grant! Why on Earth would I be painting my butt? Do I look like a butt painter to you? This is a tree, silly. See the branches?" She traced her finger along the paint.

Dylan wondered why Kat was painting a hot pink forest.

"Trees are green, aren't they?"

She drummed her fingers impatiently against the canvas. "I'm waiting for you to get your ass down here and make a woman out of me."

Kat rolled on her back, flashed a come-hither smile, and gave him The Look. Dylan had come to know The Look quite well. It meant, *Let's have sex right this minute or else you're not getting any for the rest of the week.*

Watching Kat drip paint across her firm little tummy, he was more than happy to oblige. Hell, it had been a long day. Anything to get his mind off the recently deceased Butch Grant was a welcome reprieve.

He bounced around a minute trying to get his shoes off, then stripped off his T-shirt and kicked off his jeans one leg at a time.

Dylan slid down on top of her and cupped her breasts in his hands. He suddenly felt something wet slide across his privates. It was Kat. Rubbing her paintbrush back and forth.

"Hey!" Dylan grabbed Kat's little wrist and stared down at himself. He was now, officially, Hot, Hard, and Pink.

She tittered and wriggled her body underneath his. "That looks cute," she said. "Now stick it on the canvas!"

"I'm *not sticking anything* on any—"

Kat grabbed him and pressed his hardness against the canvas, right underneath the leaves she'd painted.

Dylan glanced down and allowed a fleeting smile to escape his lips. Leave it to Kat to get his mind off the unbearable.

"Thank you for providing my tree trunk," she announced.

It ended up being a large splotch that even Dylan had to admit, he was proud of.

Seven

Dylan was sleeping. Like a big bear. On her canvas. And his genitals were hot pink. It made Kat want to start laughing, but she didn't dare disturb him. *If sleeping were an Olympic sport, you'd take home the gold, babe,* she thought. He always fell asleep after sex. For at least ten, maybe fifteen minutes.

Kat tousled the big bear's hair and stood up. She shimmied out to the terrace in the nude, took a seat on one of Dylan's bulky patio chairs, and lit a cigarette.

She wasn't a smoker, per se. It's just that sometimes—especially in times of crisis—a cigarette tasted damned good.

Kat blew the smoke out slowly and thought about secret number two. She stared out into the distance and flicked her ash over the edge of the balcony.

Why me? she wondered.

Of all the women on earth, why did it have to be her?

Dylan knew secret number one. He was well aware of Kat's financial predicament. But secret number two belonged to Kat.

Kat regarded the cigarette with a frown and stabbed it out in the silver tray on the table. She stretched her arms above her head in a yoga pose known as "praying mantis," and took in a sharp breath.

What if they're wrong? she thought. *I mean, it's not like these doctors know everything.*

She tried to clear her mind and focus on her yoga teacher's instructions—*Na-ma-ste*—but the sound of a blaring horn startled her. Jumping from the deck chair, Kat peered over the wrought-iron ledge to the front entrance of the Royal Arms. Twenty floors beneath her, she spotted him. Blaring on his horn. Shouting and waving his arms frantically out the driver's side window. Waiting impatiently for the valets to come park his awful, wasp yellow Hummer.

Well hello there, Prince Charming.

It was C. Todd Hartwell. The building's rogue. A self-proclaimed Texas Casanova. Complete with eel-skin cowboy boots and smelly armpits. He was rumored to have fathered many children, slept with hundreds of women, and tried to bed Kat on every occasion he could muster.

Kat watched him angle out of the Hummer and slam the driver's side door in frustration. A red-uniformed valet ran toward him at full sprint. C. Todd had driven onto the building's front entrance flower mound, crushing the tulips and scaring up a few birds.

Kat shook her head. *Jesus. Grow up*, she thought.

C. Todd gave the valet a good tongue-lashing before ambling toward the front entrance. He must have had the sense of a trained bloodhound, because just as he reached the front entrance, he looked straight up—twenty floors at Kat. For a moment, they locked eyes. Kat watched him smile at her—the same snake charmer smile he always gave her. She realized, suddenly, that she was naked and her breasts were in plain view.

Oh! Shhhhit!

Kat turned and fled back into the apartment—and rammed straight into Dylan.

"Hey there. Easy, wild Kat. What's got you spooked, hon?"

"I accidentally flashed C. Todd, and it's not even Mardi Gras," Kat said, covering both breasts with her hands.

"Sonofabitch!" Dylan roared. He jerked Kat sideways and ran out to the balcony, his hot pink genitals flopping. It was enough to put Kat in stitches. She couldn't help it. She laughed uncontrollably. Watching Dylan lean over the balcony with all that hot pink flapping between his legs.

"Yeah, you better run and hide!" Dylan was shouting over the railing.

He heard Kat snorting with laughter so he whirled around.

"Look," she said, pointing at his hot pink surprise.

Dylan stared down. In his sleep, he must've forgotten about the hot pink paint gracing his pride and joy.

"Jesus, Kathleen! This better come off in the shower!"

Kat crossed her arms over her chest. Her visit to the doctor this morning had been quite enough drama for one day.

She began to tap her foot. Slowly.

Tap . . . tap . . . tap.

Kat's foot tapping was famous. It meant that her patience was tried, and that Dylan better march to the shower, or else there'd be hell to pay.

Tap. Tap. Tap.

Every woman in Texas had a signature move. Kat's foot tap was like the Bataan death march.

She watched Dylan sulk off to the bathroom. Kat smiled

slightly. A lot of women made the mistake of yelling at their boy-friends.

A man doesn't need to be yelled at in order to be trained, she thought.

Her mama had taught her well.

Eight

Dylan didn't want to deal with another mess. It wasn't enough that his father had died suddenly when he'd slammed his Escalade into a concrete barrier on Highway 59. Nope. Butch Grant tended to leave land mines wherever he went. And Dylan had spent his entire life trying to disarm them.

He wasn't surprised when his phone rang early the next morning just as the sun came glinting through the bedroom windows. Dylan opened a blurry eye and reached over to his bedside table.

Perfect, he thought. *What now?*

It was Tim Johnson. Senior partner at Johnson and Bernstein Private Wealth Management, Inc.

"You need to come to my office A-SAP," Tim said in a serious tone.

"What's this about?" Dylan asked.

"I'd rather see you in person."

Dylan sat up in bed. *Perfect*.

"It's not a good time for me, Tim."

"I know about your father, Dylan. That's why I need to see you A-SAP."

Dylan wondered if Tim enjoyed saying the word A-SAP. If this word made him feel important.

"Okay. Give me an hour," Dylan said, resisting the urge to add "A-SAP."

Bad news usually traveled slowly—unless your father was Butch Grant. Then it was like a damned flood.

Kathleen rubbed her eyes and kicked off the sheets. "I'm hot," she murmured. "Who's calling so early?"

"Tim Johnson."

Kathleen rolled over in bed and blinked. "Did you tell him about your dad?"

"He already knew."

"Uh oh. That doesn't sound good."

Dylan leaned over and kissed her hair. "Don't worry about it, babe. Go back to sleep." He got up and padded to the shower. As soon as he'd seen Tim's number pop up on his mobile, he knew it was bad.

His thoughts were confirmed an hour later when he found himself sitting in the River Oaks Trust Building, staring incredulously out the window.

Sitting across from him, behind a massive oak desk—the type of desk preferred by judges, lawyers, and assholes in general—was Tim Johnson.

The money manager was about as white-bread, gumshoe corporate guy as you could imagine. With a conservative banker's haircut stiff and gelled back, a navy suit and tie—nothing to write home about—Tim Johnson of Johnson and Bernstein Private

Wealth Management, Inc., wasn't making any kind of statement. His outfit fit his demeanor—quiet, calculating, snub-nosed, and efficient.

Dylan didn't dislike Tim. The two men just didn't click. Dylan had asked Tim out for beer a few times, but the money manager always declined. His kids had soccer, was usually the excuse.

Now Tim was dropping a bomb. And not just a puny grenade. This was Hiroshima.

"What do you mean, the leases don't belong to us anymore?" Dylan asked. His voice caught in his throat. He was sitting in a stiff leather chair. Dylan gripped the arms of the chair and squeezed with all his strength. *I'm going to throw this god-damned chair out the window,* he thought.

"Your father lost the title to that tract of land in a poker game," Tim said. He leaned across his desk and passed a single page to Dylan. "I received this from Bo Harlan's lawyer yesterday."

Dylan swiped the paper from Tim's outstretched hand. For a moment, he stopped breathing. His hand quivered. At the bottom of the page was his father's signature. In that damned red ink.

There could be no denying what the page clearly stated. Dylan and Wyatt had just lost the last stitch of their inheritance.

"I . . . can't believe . . ." Dylan trailed off.

His mother, the lovely Clarissa Grant, had died of a stroke a few years back, after suffering too many decades of Butch Grant's drinking, gambling, womanizing, and abuse in general. Which proved the general theory that the good die young, but the pricks live forever.

Dylan blamed his mother's death squarely on his father. But one thing Butch Grant had done right—the *only* thing he'd ever done right—was preserve the main mineral lease that had been in the Grant family since they settled in Texas in 1874.

For generations, the well had carried the name of #7, but had been renamed the Clarissa #7 when Dylan's mother had died. After Clarissa's death, it had yielded hefty checks each month for Dylan and Wyatt to split between them.

The sum had once been a whole lot more, but Butch Grant managed to ratchet down his dead wife's family money. He'd lost the other oil wells that had once belonged to the Grant family in his late night beer-stoked poker games, famously nicknamed "Yards and Cards."

Dylan figured that the only reason his father hadn't gambled away the Clarissa #7 was that his wife's name was attached to it. Even Butch Grant wouldn't dare mess with the heavens by gambling away an oil well named after his dead wife.

"I don't understand how this could happen," Dylan sputtered, allowing the paper to drop to the floor. The paper that, signed by his father, would strip the Clarissa from Dylan and Wyatt—the last remaining heirs to the Grant family inheritance.

Tim Johnson leveled Dylan with a steady gaze. In his quiet accountant's tone, he said, "I see it all the time, Mr. Grant."

He was all business, Tim.

Dylan snorted. At a time like this, screaming and carrying on was certainly called for. He leaped from his chair and paced the room. His mouth worked feverishly, attempting to form the words blazing through his head.

"You're telling me Bo Harlan is claiming the Clarissa as his own!" Dylan said, his voice like a fist.

"He says your father lost it to him in a game over fifteen years ago. The deal was your father could keep the rights to all minerals flowing from the well until the day he died, at which point any remaining mineral interests would pass to Bo Harlan."

Tim took off his eyeglasses and began to polish the lenses. First one, then the other. Calmly. As if Dylan wasn't wildly pacing his office. As if Dylan wasn't in dire financial straits.

As if nothing is wrong, at all!

It was time to get Tim's attention. After all, he and Wyatt had been paying the lofty commissions charged by Johnson Bernstein Private Wealth Management, Inc., for many years.

Dylan lurched forward and swept his arm across Tim's desk, sending the files and the paperwork flying onto the floor in a messy heap.

Ka-chunk!

Time stood still for a second.

And then . . .

The unflappable Tim Johnson continued to polish his eyeglasses.

Hearing the commotion, Johnson and Bernstein's luscious little secretary appeared in the crack of the doorway.

"Everything all right in there, Mr. Johnson?" she asked in her baby-doll voice. Dylan saw Jennifer's eyes blinking in the doorway. Her freshly painted cherry red lips so inappropriate for ten A.M.

He strode over to the door and slammed it shut.

Nice move, jerkoff.

Dylan cracked open the door. "I'm sorry, Jennifer." He looked intently into the secretary's wide eyes. "You caught me at a bad time is all."

He broke out into his trademark grin—a grin that Kat referred to as his "Special Sauce."

It worked.

The secretary flashed him a sweet smile, with a hint of sexual undertone that Dylan was used to with women but never acted upon.

The secretary drummed her polished fingernails against the

door frame. "You're probably thirsty, and I forgot to offer you a drink. Would you care for a bottle of Evian or a Coke?" she cooed, fluttering her beautiful dark eyelashes.

"I'm good," Dylan said.

"Well then. I guess my work here is done." This time she winked at Dylan, and the overt sexual offer was more than a hint. Turning on her kitten heels, she sashayed back to her desk, swinging her hips slowly from side to side. She even looked back over her shoulder and gave Dylan a parting smile.

Dylan was in no mood to deal with a flirt. Jennifer was the ultimate gold digger and had already blown Wyatt in the parking lot during her lunch break a few years back. His younger brother had considered it a "fringe benefit" and now referred to Johnson and Bernstein as the greatest money management firm on planet Earth.

Dylan shut the door and swung around toward Tim.

Tim Johnson was eyeing him as if Dylan had sticks of dynamite taped across his chest.

"It's not like I've got sticks of dynamite taped to my chest," Dylan said.

"I can understand why you're upset, Mr. Grant, but trashing the contents of my desk doesn't help matters," Tim said, matter-of-fact. The money manager was sitting stiffly in his leather-backed chair, as if daring Dylan to do something more.

Smooth, Dylan thought. He couldn't do anything to peel the calm veneer off the man. He collapsed back into his own chair, and ignored the pile of stuff on the floor next to Tim's desk.

I'll be damned if I'm going to pick it up!

"Fine. What do you suggest?" Dylan asked, crossing his arms over his chest.

The two men sat facing each other. Square-on.

"You can fight it out in court," Tim said in a somber voice, "But the lawyers don't think you have much of a case. Problem is . . . Bo Harlan did his homework. He's crossed all his t's, dotted all his i's."

Dylan leaned forward in his chair. "Number one," he said, counting out on his fingers, "Bo Harlan robbed my old man blind. I was there during those poker games. I was still a kid, but I was there."

"Who was running the games?" Tim asked. "Bo Harlan or Butch Grant?"

"You know my dad was the ringleader, Tim. But what does it matter? A cheat is a cheat."

"Your father signed away the lease, Dylan. He signed it in front of witnesses. All the men at those games claim that your father lost, and he lost big. He gambled away your family's money year after year."

"Witnesses!" Dylan smacked his hand against his knee and was pleased to see Tim flinch.

"Let's call them what they really were—Bo Harlan's hired guns. I mean, witnesses don't usually carry Smith & Wessons, do they?"

"Are you claiming your father was under duress?"

"You bet."

"Where's the proof?"

Dylan clenched his teeth. *Proof. I'll show you proof when I jam your head up your ass*, he thought. For a moment, he imagined himself leaping across Tim Johnson's desk and grabbing his money manager by the throat. But why kill the messenger? It wasn't the accountant's fault. No matter how smug the senior partner of Johnson and Bernstein Private Wealth Management, Inc., appeared to be.

"Look, Tim," Dylan said, exhaling sharply. "Bo Harlan knew my father was an alcoholic, and that he was out of control. He should've stopped the game."

"Since when is it Bo Harlan's duty to protect your father from himself?"

Dylan flinched. "Tell me something. Why does Bo Harlan need this very last well? The one named after my mom? No matter how drunk my father was, he never would've gambled away—"

A fuzzy vision flashed through Dylan's head. It was a distant memory. Of cigar smoke choking the air, the sound of a bottle smashed against the floor and gunshots ringing through the ceiling. Dylan had remembered being scared shitless. Hiding behind the stinky brown sofa with his hand cupped over Wyatt's mouth, so his younger brother wouldn't cry.

"Hush up, Wyatt! Or we're both gonna get killed!" Dylan had pleaded into his brother's ear. They'd crouched behind the couch for hours while Butch Grant cursed and smashed bottles and shot his gun into the ceiling, causing white spackle to rain down into both Dylan's and Wyatt's eyes.

Wyatt had peed his pants. Dylan had done the same.

"You'll never take the Clarissa while I'm alive!" Butch Grant had slurred.

Dylan had remembered the noise. The terrible noise.

His dad wailing from the alcohol and depression and grief.

That was the night the police showed up. But this time, instead of giving Butch Grant a warning, they'd deposited Dylan and Wyatt at the neighbor's house where the kind widow Ms. Honeycutt fed them hot milk and her famous snickerdoodles.

Dylan wondered if that was the night his father decided to end it for good. The night when the drinking started in earnest. In the past, the whiskey and vodka and beer had been sport.

"I'm sorry, Dylan," Tim said, suddenly, as if he were reading Dylan's mind. Dylan jerked back to reality and scowled across the room.

"The Clarissa #7 is the only thing Wyatt and I have left, Tim! What do you expect us to do?"

"The first thing I'd advise would be to pare down your financial obligations," Tim said, curling his hands under his chin. "You've got to start saving, not spending. And . . ." Tim paused and took a deep breath. "You and Wyatt could consider getting jobs."

"*Jobs!*" Dylan nearly spat the word out. "Dealing with my father was a full-time job, let me tell you!"

"But your father is no longer *the issue.*"

"What the hell do you think I do all day long, Tim? Twiddle my damned thumbs! I'm up to my knees trying to manage this shit!"

"I was referring to your brother," Tim said. "Seems as though Wyatt has been on a bit of a spending spree."

Spending spree?

Dylan was afraid to ask. But the words tumbled out of his mouth. "How much?"

Tim made a big production of leaning over and rustling through the files that Dylan had dumped on the floor. Dylan watched as his money manager pulled a manila folder out of the stack marked "Wyatt Grant." He plopped the folder on his desk and flipped it open, rather flippantly in Dylan's opinion.

"Against my advice, Wyatt took a very sizable loan out against the well—the well that you both no longer own."

"How much?" Dylan pressed.

"Your brother was playing the sports book at some fringe casino in Las Vegas. He's not answering my calls," Tim said, shrugging his thin shoulders.

"How much!"

"Half a million."

Dylan cracked a smile for the first time in a week. *Some things never change*, he thought. *Wyatt will be Wyatt.*

"Half a million bucks," Dylan said. "Is *that all*?"

This did the trick.

For a split second, Tim Johnson raised his eyebrows and looked ruffled, which pleased Dylan to no end. He'd finally flapped Mr. Unflappable.

"There's nothing more I can do," Tim Johnson said, slapping the file shut.

Dylan stood abruptly from his chair.

"Thank you, Tim. You've done more than enough." Dylan strode to the door, swung it open, and walked out.

Nine

Kat had done this a thousand times before, but it never got any easier. She held the toddler tightly in her arms. He squirmed and tried to slip from her grasp as little boys tend to do, wiggling his little body like a worm and then making it go slack. Wiggle, then slack. Wiggle, then slack. She gripped him tighter to keep him from moving.

"No more hurt! No more boo-boo!" he squealed as the doctor tried to surreptitiously slide a needle into the top of his flailing hand.

"Shhhhh, sweet little one. It's okay," Kat murmured, caressing the child's feather-soft hair.

Kathleen cracked open her favorite children's book, *Tales of the Unicorn Land*, and began to read aloud:

> *What is the Unicorn Land?*
> *It is a beautiful large*
> *Forest with large trees*

And bushes.
It has a huge pond called
The Smiling Pond.
And now let me introduce
Some of the creatures
That live in the
Unicorn Land.
Uli the Unicorn who lives in
A pocket of fog.
Then there is
Benny Bear
Tammy Turtle
And Wilberforce, the cross-eyed Snake.
And don't forget
Chico, the Flying Squirrel . . .

As Kat read in her calm voice, the boy stared up at her, his eyes searching her face. A single tear tumbled down his plump cheek.

"No more hurt," he murmured. The anesthesiologist pricked his skin, missed the vein, and had to try again.

The boy let out a painful yelp and kicked his plump little legs, hitting Kathleen in her kneecap.

She flinched, but kept her grip tight.

"Shhhh, we're going to fix you right up, Diego," she cooed. Her heart surged for this boy. His name was Diego Ramirez. And his hair was soft and dark, the color of cocoa beans. Kathleen caressed his hair until the boy stopped kicking, the anesthesia took effect, and he fell into a deep, unconscious sleep.

"It's time," the doctor announced. He lifted the boy's hospital gown and applied heart monitor patches across his small chest.

Kathleen whispered, "Be well, sweet child," as Diego was wheeled toward the operating room.

Dr. Levin, the chief surgeon, had informed Kathleen that Diego's brain tumor could be removed by a complex surgery involving a team of neurosurgeons and the help of a sophisticated MRT machine.

The King Foundation was paying for the operation because Diego's Spanish parents didn't have health insurance. Eighty thousand dollars.

It's worth every penny, Kathleen thought.

She washed her hands in the hospital room sink, and proceeded to walk briskly down the cool hallway, her flat shoes clicking against the freshly mopped floor. This wing of the hospital—this new pediatric wing with its soft powder blue walls—had been built with the money from Kathleen's annual foundation dinners.

Some women reveled in designer handbags, shoes, and jewelry. Well-heeled women enjoyed their purebred dogs, racehorses, and yachts.

This hospital was like Kathleen's Birkin bag.

She'd monitored every aspect of the construction—from the types of screws used in the door latches to the mattresses used in the beds—extra thick, for comfort. Instead of the usual sterile gray hospital walls, Kathleen had spent months painting sunny murals of white puffy clouds and sheep and ponies frolicking through fields of wildflowers.

Under Kathleen's constant supervision, the Pediatric Cancer Center looked less like a hospital and more like a place children could enjoy. There were books and toys and colorful mobiles hanging from the ceilings. In the waiting rooms, there were comfortable couches and chairs for parents, coffee machines, and fresh morning pastries brought in from a bakery down the street.

Stepping inside the chapel door, Kathleen paused to let her eyes adjust to the dim lighting. The hospital chapel was non-denominational. There were no crucifixes, no Hebrew Stars of David, no stained glass depicting scenes from the Bible. Just a warm, cozy, candlelit chapel to which anyone with any religious background could come for comfort.

Kathleen spotted Mr. and Mrs. Ramirez kneeling on the floor. She steeled herself for what would come next. The parents of near-dead children often appeared like the walking dead themselves.

Kathleen surveyed the parents through the flickering candle-light; she noticed that Mrs. Ramirez was choking back sobs, her shoulders hopping up and down uncontrollably.

At the sound of the door, Diego's father pivoted around.

"*Es él muerto?*" in a hesitant voice, asking Kathleen if his son was dead.

"No, Señor Ramirez. *Es un muchacho muy valiente*," Kathleen replied. *He is a very brave boy.*

"*Muchas gracias, señora*," he said, bowing his head toward Kathleen. "*Muchas gracias.*"

Mrs. Ramirez swiveled around, revealing a face streaked with tears.

Kathleen knelt down next to her on the floor. She made the sign of the cross as she'd been taught in Catholic school. Then she reached out and grabbed Mrs. Ramirez's trembling hand.

It was the hand of a woman who was nearly lifeless herself from grief. A hand that didn't squeeze back when Kathleen squeezed, but instead felt cold, brittle, weak.

Kathleen squeezed her eyes shut, and said her own prayer. First for Diego.

And next for herself.

But not for herself, exactly. For the King family lineage.

Please, Lord. Don't let it be true, Kathleen prayed.

When she finished, she stood quietly and slipped out the chapel door.

Ten

I need a cheeseburger, Dylan thought.

And not just your average, run-of-the-mill, fast-food grease burger. He was jonesing for a Becks Prime with lots of ketchup, pickles, and crispy fries. And an ice-cold milkshake.

That's the ticket.

Dylan swung his brother's gleaming million-dollar car—which now even he recognized as absurd seeing as how he and Wyatt were flat broke—into the drive-through window.

As usual, he got the stare from the guy at the takeout window. The are-you-fucking-kidding-me stare.

Dylan reached for his wallet and realized he hadn't gone to the ATM.

Damn. He was clean out of cash.

He reached over and popped open the glove box.

"How much is it gonna be?" he called out to the window guy, who was still gawking at the car.

"Seven-fifty."

Dylan located six dollars in meter money, and a few more quarters underneath the seat.

"Hold the milkshake," Dylan said.

The window guy handed Dylan a yellow bag and a frosty milk-shake. "Don't sweat it, buddy. I can see you need the charity."

"Funny," Dylan said, letting a smile break across his lips for the first time since he'd heard the news about his father.

The smell made Dylan's mouth water, so he whipped into a nearby parking space, plunged his hand into the tantalizing greasy bag, and shoved a handful of salty fries in his mouth.

He slurped his shake and dug into his perfect cheeseburger. A pickle slipped out and fell onto the overpriced leather, leaving a small round stain. Dylan grinned and flicked the pickle out the window.

As much as he wanted to see Kat right now, he needed to eat his burger in peace, and think.

Think about what, genius?

Dylan considered how much he'd spent from his savings account and from the 401(k) he'd set up in his old job at Enron. At least he'd paid off his law school loans before the firm went belly-up and he lost all the money he'd worked so hard to earn in Enron company stock. He'd been in his cubicle at the energy broker-age department when Kenneth Lay's shit hit the fan. Dylan had wanted to kill the fucker, but apparently he hadn't needed to.

He thrust his hand inside the bag and munched another hand-ful of fries.

The Grant family had been in jams before. Wasn't easy when times were tough. Especially in the eighties when the Texas oil business had ground to a screeching halt. Dylan had been a boy, but he remembered his mother and grandmother selling all the furniture, the house, the pickup trucks, and even their Sunday dresses.

"Times like these reveal the strength within us," his grandma told him.

Dylan took a deep juicy bite into his cheeseburger and repeated this mantra. *"Times like these reveal the strength within us."*

He needed a plan. It was that simple.

Until then, Dylan would have to cut down on expenses.

I'll start with the condo.

His twentieth-floor pad at the Royal Arms was costing him a cool five grand a month. Not to mention that Kathleen had been living off him since her grandfather had died. Cullen Davis King would probably roll in his grave if he knew that his only grand-daughter had given away her trust fund to build the Pediatric Cancer Center. But Dylan knew this was Kat's "calling." She'd explained to him that her purpose in life—the reason she'd been spared among her entire clan—had come to her like a dream in the night. Her obsession with curing sick children couldn't be sated with anything less than a full commitment. And Dylan wasn't one to argue with a life calling.

Kat will be crushed to find out about the condo. But we'll both have to make do, Dylan thought.

Next would come the car. A year ago, Wyatt had entered into some slick side deal with Gary the Snake—sole owner of Gary Crumpacker's Luxury Automobiles off Interstate 10.

The deal went something like this. Wyatt gives Gary the Snake a bunch of cash up front to drive a "pussy magnet." Gary the Snake—a.k.a. Con Artist Extraordinaire—keeps title to the car and gets monthly cash payments from Wyatt and hookups to some of the girls Wyatt hangs out with. Wyatt showers Gary with trips to Vegas, hookers, and filet mignons the size of footballs. Gary the Snake still keeps title to the car.

Dylan finished his cheeseburger, licked the tip of his thumb, and crushed the bag underneath the seat. He'd deliver the car back to Gary Crumpacker with a nice new odor.

Just as Dylan turned the key and heard the familiar purr of

the engine, a yellow Hummer slammed into the parking space beside him.

C. Todd Hartwell slid his window down. He was wearing a visor, Oakley sunglasses, and balancing a Red Bull in his hand. "Hey Grant! I called you about that shallow well deal I was putting together. You too good to call me back, hoss?"

Dylan bristled. He knew the oil promoter was always prowling around Kat, trying to get her to sleep with him. He'd even gone so far as to write Kat his version of a love sonnet on a yellow Post-It note that had been delivered to the apartment by one of the Abduls. The note read:

> *Hey Kathleen! Here's some mail I found down in the mail room. Judging from the address, I think you dropped it by accident.*
>
> *P.S. Those jeans you were wearing today were super hot. You remind me of Farrah Fawcett in* Cannonball Run.
>
> > *Kickin' it old school,*
> > *XOXOXO*
> > *C. Todd Hartwell*

Dylan and Kathleen had enjoyed some screaming laughter over that one, but later, after he'd had time to reflect, Dylan didn't think the letter was quite so funny.

Dylan heard a car door slam and watched C. Todd Hartwell stride toward him. The oilman walked like a guy who owned the fucking world. His sun visor like a crown on his head. The can of Red Bull in his hand like a scepter.

C. Todd Hartwell was always just one step away from the law. Oil promoters were guys who found the deals and then "sold them" to pools of investors. Typically they were overblown marketing chumps. The type of guys who would make even the most complicated drilling deals with the worst odds sound like a sure thing.

Like most oil promoters, C. Todd Hartwell was a master pretender. He liked to raise money from investors for deals that he personally had no stake in. Then he'd disappear for weeks at a time to avoid subpoenas from frustrated investors wanting to sue.

One day he'd be on top of the world, claiming that he'd hit the Big One. The Big Money Gusher. Other days he'd be dirt poor and drowning himself in Wild Turkey.

The oilman claimed he was fourth generation Texan, but Dylan knew it had to be somewhere around second generation, at best.

"Sweet car." Hartwell whistled through his teeth, crossing his arms over his broad chest and taking in the full extent of the Bugatti's gleaming black and chrome exterior.

Dylan opened his door and stepped out, but he left the engine idling.

C. Todd punched him hard in the biceps. "What's Up Man!"

Dylan had no choice but to punch C. Todd as hard as he could in C. Todd's upper biceps.

C. Todd winced dramatically and rubbed the top of his muscle. *"Sweet Jesus, Grant!* You didn't have to put the stinger on it!"

He clapped Dylan on the shoulder and grinned. Dylan noticed the big diamond Rolex draped loosely over C. Todd's wrist.

I wonder who he stole it from? Dylan thought.

"Let me tell you about the deal of the century," the oilman started in. He leaned close to Dylan's face, as if he'd watched a sales video entitled *Making Eye Contact with Your Mark.*

Dylan could smell a faint odor—*whiskey?*—on C. Todd's breath.

Hartwell lowered his voice as if he were letting Dylan in on a secret. "I'm talking big money here, man. *Big. Money.*"

"Did you brush your teeth today?" Dylan asked.

Hartwell jerked back. "Why? Am I stinking it up?" The oilman proceeded to perform the stink test. He cupped his hand over his mouth theatrically, and smelled his own breath.

"I'm fresh as a schoolgirl's tits," he announced. And then he raised his arms and smelled under each of his armpits for dramatic effect.

"You've been drinking," Dylan said.

"Aw, hell, Grant. Just a little swing juice is all. I'm hitting the links in fifteen minutes. Why don't you come along for eighteen holes?"

Just what I need. To spend the afternoon golfing with you, Dylan thought.

Dylan dug the toe of his boot into the pavement. "I don't have time for golf today."

"Suit yourself." C. Todd shrugged. "But I thought you'd be interested in a little rumor . . ."

Dylan's ears perked up. C. Todd Hartwell might be a master pretender when it came to selling sham oil and gas deals to over-eager investors, but he had a bloodhound's nose for rumors. And in the oil business, a rumor was almost as good as a sure bet.

The best tactic for Dylan at this point was to act completely bored. He chuckled and clapped C. Todd Hartwell on the shoulder. Jumping back inside the Bugatti's fine cherry leather driver's seat, Dylan shifted the car into gear and rolled down his window.

"Have a good round," he said, saluting C. Todd and slamming the Bugatti into reverse.

The oilman took the bait. He rushed over to Dylan's window and leaned in. "Wanna hear something crazy? I'm dating this superfine chick over at Titan Energy, and she's got access to all the 3-D seismic data."

Dylan breathed through his nose.

Titan Energy. Bo Harlan's company.

"So?" Dylan snorted. He was doing his best to seem nonchalant.

"Bo Harlan just found the biggest field *ever* in North East Texas."

"How big?"

"Fifty million coming out of the ground."

"Nice," Dylan mused.

"So what do you say, Grant? You in or you out?"

Dylan suppressed a smile.

He didn't want to be seen in public with C. Todd Hartwell. But the oilman *did* live in his building.

"How about nine A.M. on Friday?" Dylan said. "The coffee room downstairs."

"Done deal," C. Todd said. He stepped away from the Bugatti and gave the car one last long whistle through his teeth.

Dylan shifted the car into drive. He glanced in his rearview just in time to watch C. Todd crush the can of Red Bull in his palm and lob it unsuccessfully toward a trash can, where it bounced off the rim and fell to the pavement.

C. Todd glanced over toward the Bugatti to see if Dylan had indeed witnessed the failed slam dunk. It was now up to Dylan to do what any other red-blooded American male would do. He circled around the Becks Prime parking lot and shouted out the window, "Nice job, Jordan!"

Eleven

Kat was nursing an iced green tea latte and picking gingerly at her grilled chicken Caesar salad—hold the Caesar dressing, please. She was doing one of her weekly ladies-who-lunch shindigs where she summoned the energy to make nice with a Gucci.

Across the table sat not just any Gucci, but the most powerful and famous Gucci in town. The notorious Shelby Lynn Pierce.

Shelby Lynn was likewise picking at her spinach salad, pushing aside the blue cheese crumbles with her fork as if they were poisonous.

"I can't believe they dump a whole tub of cheese on this," Shelby Lynn drawled. "Remind me never to eat here again."

Nice diamonds, Kat thought.

Shelby Lynn was rolling the ten-carat fancy, vivid, yellow diamond ring around her wedding finger. The stone was so big and perfect it almost looked like a fake. Shelby's nose, hair, and breasts were fakes, but you could be sure her diamonds were as pure as the driven snow.

Like most Texas women, Shelby Lynn Pierce had two dirty little secrets of her own. The first was that Shelby Lynn had been "biblical" with the only man Kat had ever loved.

Dylan Grant and Shelby Lynn had enjoyed a brief fling on a vodka-soaked weekend back in college that probably neither of them remembered all that well anyway. Dylan didn't know that Kat knew. And Shelby Lynn didn't know that Kat knew. But Kat knew everything that happened around her, which was often a burden, if Kat were to tell the truth. It had happened so many years ago, Kat had decided to forgive the indiscretion. Dylan's heart beat in alignment with her own, and about this, there was no question.

The other dirty little secret was that Shelby Lynn's husband, Tate, had been spotted in an elevator of the Lancaster Hotel with a stripper from Treasures, who was of the Asian persuasion. Apparently everybody knew this, except Shelby Lynn. Because if Shelby Lynn knew her husband had dipped his finger in the soy sauce, she would've certainly stormed out of the restaurant.

Shelby Lynn crinkled her perfect little nose and set her fork down. "Kathleen, you can't drench arugula like this!" she tittered. "It makes the leaves wilt."

It's a salad. Not a crisis, Kat thought. She'd talk lettuce with Shelby Lynn Pierce for hours, as long as this most powerful of Guccis bought a table at the Annual Foundation Dinner. The children's hospital needed new lab equipment, and Kat badly wanted to fund another clinical research unit.

"Sweetie, I thought we'd do something different this year," Shelby Lynn drawled. She was tugging the diamond stud in her ear, which was as big as a Volkswagen.

Kat sucked in her breath. Shelby Lynn was always the last person to write out a hundred-thousand-dollar check for her table. And the Gucci always felt the need to "participate" in planning the Annual Foundation Dinner with Kat, as if Shelby Lynn herself was in charge.

Each year, Shelby presented Kat with a "cute little idea." Usually along the lines of a theme party. And each year, Kat would pretend to mull it over, pretend like it was the greatest idea in the history of ideas, pretend, period.

Last year Shelby had suggested bringing Angelina Jolie and having a theme party called "Houston's Cambodian Carnivale."

"We can turn the ballroom into a jungle," she'd said. "And have someone build a miniature Angkor Wat. And have little baby elephants that everyone can take turns riding on!"

"What kind of food would we serve?" Kat had asked.

"French," Shelby Lynn replied, without hesitation. French food was always Shelby Lynn's first answer, although she didn't eat cheese, meat, or heavy cream.

Kat pushed her salad away and summoned the waiter. He appeared and silently cleared the plates. Shelby Lynn leaned forward, accidentally flashing Kat some exposed cleavage compliments of Dr. Franklin Prose, plastic surgeon to die for according to those in the know.

"What's the single greatest invention of the century?" Shelby Lynn asked, tapping her perfectly manicured fingers against the table. She tossed her blond hair over her shoulder like a model from a shampoo commercial and fixed Kat with a purposeful stare.

Kat was hoping the question was rhetorical, but Shelby Lynn continued to stare at her with those wide blue moony eyes and waited for Kat to guess the answer.

"Microsoft?"

Shelby Lynn wrinkled her nose. "No, silly buns. Not computers."

"I don't know, Shelby." Kat shrugged. "How about the airplane?"

"The miracle of flight is only a miracle if you fly private, hon."

Shelby Lynn covered her mouth and giggled at her own little joke. The Pierce family flew private even if they were headed to their ranch, which was just a hiccup outside Houston.

"No, sweetie. I think the most influential invention of the century is *electricity*," Shelby Lynn said, taking a dainty sip from the straw poking out of her Diet Coke.

Kat smacked her palm against her forehead theatrically. "I forgot about the light bulb."

"Our theme could be 'Bright Lights, Big City,'" Shelby Lynn said, waving her hand across the air like a banner.

"Interesting," Kat replied.

"Really?" Shelby Lynn sounded hopeful.

"Yes," Kat said magnanimously.

"I thought we could adorn the ballroom with thousands of itty-bitty little white lights, and have a bunch of cute little waiters dress like Thomas Edison, you know, with those adorable little round spectacles that were so popular back then."

Kat took a deep breath. "It's unique. I don't think anyone's done it before."

"Nope," Shelby Lynn said. "Not even in New York."

New York black tie fund-raisers were the gold standard to which even the wealthiest of Texans compared themselves, even though they acted like they didn't.

"Shelby, I truly adore your idea," Kat said, lacing her fingers underneath her chin, "and as usual, I welcome all your efforts to help raise money for the King Foundation, but at the end of the day, I think Pa Pa would've wanted me to keep it simple."

This was Kat's secret weapon. Uttering her granddad's name—

the venerable Cullen Davis King—was akin to saying what the Lord himself would've wished for the annual dinner.

Shelby Lynn sucked her straw, practically slamming the rest of her Diet Coke. The Gucci knew there was no point arguing with the wishes of the recently deceased Lord Almighty himself. She chewed the bottom of her lip tentatively.

"Shelby Lynn, I would love for you to decide which type of food we should serve," Kat said, with all the earnestness in the world.

Shelby Lynn didn't hesitate.

"French. I think we should go with French this year," she said, her eyes lighting up at the thought of all that delicious food she wouldn't be eating.

"French it is," Kat said, smiling.

Shelby Lynn flashed a genuine smile, plopped her oversized Hermès crocodile clutch up on the table, and pulled out her checkbook.

"Who should I make this out to?"

"The King Foundation Annual Fund." Kat watched Shelby scribble out a one followed by five zeros.

Shelby handed Kat the check. "Here you go, sweet pea. Don't spend it all in one place."

"I guess this means I'm buying lunch," Kat quipped. She watched in pleasure as Shelby Lynn Pierce threw back her beautiful blond head and laughed at the ceiling.

Twelve

Time to get down to business, Dylan thought. *Enough fiddle fucking around.*

He bumped down the slow lane of I–10 in the rusted Toyota pickup that Gary the Snake had talked him into. The truck smelled like a roadside bar after closing time—a mixture of stale beer, old cigarettes, and the cover-up scent of that puke-lemon industrial-grade cleaner.

Dylan had traded in Wyatt's Bugatti, testing the limits of the fine Italian motor on the highway, before informing Gary Crumpacker that no more money, hookers, or trips to Vegas would be forthcoming from the younger Mr. Grant.

"What other cars do you have for me?" Dylan asked, as the Snake escorted him around the lot and tried to sell him a sleek new supercharged Mercedes S-class.

Dylan had put his hand up and said, "Let me tell you something, Gary. I wouldn't buy a Mercedes in *brown*. Do I look like a soccer mom to you? And second, I'm looking for something to bump around town in. I'm talking low-end wheels, bottom of the barrel, here."

Gary the Snake had then tried to sell Dylan a fully loaded Chevy Tahoe complete with custom rims and calf leather seats.

Dylan had stared Gary the Snake straight into his needlepoint black eyes and announced that he had three thousand dollars in his pocket and not a penny more.

That was when Gary took him to the back of the car lot, in a dusty area marked off with a rope and a sign that read, "Service Entrance Only," and presented Dylan with the Toyota truck.

"Sweet ride," Dylan joked, as he jumped up into the driver's seat of the smelly cab.

"Look, I'm not trying to sell you this piece of junk," Gary said, shaking his head. "But for three grand, this is about all I can show you."

"It's perfect. I'll take it." Dylan flipped Gary a roll of hundred-dollar bills tied with a rubber band, and peeled out of the dealership, calling out the window for Gary to send him the title in the mail and make it snappy.

As Dylan plowed down the highway, he was suddenly gripped with an unfamiliar feeling. Panic? He wasn't sure. All he knew was that he was panting like a dog in a desert, and he couldn't figure out why.

The physical symptoms that manifested themselves were akin to what Dylan felt when he thought about Butch Grant for too long. He broke out into a rolling sweat, and his heart began thumping wildly.

Maybe I'm having a heart attack?

Dylan flipped on the A.C. and frowned at the smelly lukewarm air shooting out of the vents. *Damned A.C. is broken*, he thought, cursing Gary the Snake under his breath. He had half a mind to turn the pickup around and go beat the crap out of

Gary for all the advantage the Snake had taken of people over the years. Dylan figured he'd be doing folks a public service by showing Gary why he'd been nicknamed "the Terminator" back in high school.

But Dylan didn't have time for street justice, today. He had to tell Kat what was what. And he had to devise a plan to fix the damage that the dead Butch Grant had inflicted on him and Wyatt.

Dylan raced into the front circle driveway of the Royal Arms. He stepped out of the truck and tossed the keys to Achmed.

"How do you like my new ride, man?" Dylan asked.

Achmed caught the keys in midair and smiled broadly at the joke. Dylan had left the building a few hours earlier in a rare Italian Bugatti, and returned in a rusted-out Japanese truck.

"Very fine automobile," the valet said, in his deep, singsong voice.

Dylan liked how Achmed enunciated his words and referred to cars as "automobiles." His accent sounded very Queen's English, as if he'd grown up in Britain.

Achmed hopped up into the truck, and expertly squeezed it between two Porsches that were blocking the drive.

"How'd you learn to drive like that?" Dylan called out.

Achmed leaned out of the Toyota's driver's side window.

"I was very good driver in my country! A professional driver for top VIP peoples. And sometimes I had to drive around the bombs very fast."

"The bombs?"

"People want to kill the VIP peoples in the car."

"No shit?"

Achmed grinned. "No sheet," he announced, in his proper Queen's English.

Dylan admired Achmed's expert maneuvering as he slid the car into a tight parking space.

Dylan walked toward the sliding doors of the Royal Arms.

He could already make out Poor Eddie's bald head inclined toward the glass—watching the entire Toyota truck drama unfold as if it were a *Saturday Night Live* sketch.

Not today, my man, Dylan thought as the concierge punched the electronic entrance button, causing the sliding glass doors in front of Dylan to whoosh open.

"Mr. Grant!" Eddie exclaimed, as if Dylan were Cary Grant or Hugh Grant, or someone famous like that.

Dylan wanted Eddie to know about the car.

"Check out my new ride." Dylan pointed toward the Toyota.

Eddie rubbed his liver-spotted hand over his bald head and smiled blandly.

"I assume this is a gift for Ms. Kathleen?" Eddie said, going along with the joke.

"You think she'll like it?" Dylan asked.

"I think she'd prefer a diamond ring, Mr. Grant," Eddie replied with a temerity that Dylan found shocking.

Dylan stopped in his tracks. *Has Kat been talking about engagement rings?*

Impossible, he thought. Kat would never share something so intimate with anyone outside her inner circle.

Dylan pointed to the green and white striped Whipley's box tucked behind the FedEx packages on Eddie's desk. "I think you need to lay off the doughnuts."

Eddie shuffled his feet and stared down at the floor.

"Can't be good for your cholesterol," Dylan added.

"I pass Whipley's every morning on the way here. Ahh, the chocolate custard, Mr. Grant. They catch me coming and going." He sighed.

Dylan watched the building concierge motion for him to come closer. Eddie's face broke out into one of his about-to-share-a-rumor smiles. He leaned toward Dylan and lowered his voice to a stage whisper.

"You know, Mr. Grant, the Whipley heir just moved into the building. Penthouse floor," Eddie said, winking slyly as if this was groundbreaking news.

"A doughnut heir in the penthouse, hey Eddie?"

"Land of opportunity," Eddie quipped.

"Yes it is."

Dylan clapped Eddie on the shoulder and walked toward the elevator. With the morning he'd just had, he needed an ounce of peace.

He needed calm.

He needed Kat.

He just wanted to hold her firm little body in his arms, tell her how much he loved her, and stare into her warm, all-encompassing eyes. Kat was his everything. And Dylan felt as long as he had this woman, this beacon of light in his life, it wouldn't matter where he lived, what he drove, or how much money he was able to bring in for the family.

He and Kat could live just like those people in the movies. In a cozy apartment. Maybe even in New York City. They'd participate in all that "urban angst" Kat was always talking about.

"Real artists suffer from urban angst," she'd say.

Perhaps Dylan could get a job waiting tables at a steakhouse. Who knew?

He rode the elevator in silence, thanking his lucky stars that in a few moments he'd be with the woman he'd always loved.

And then, everything will feel all right.

Dylan stepped off the elevator and strode down the hall with a renewed vigor. He'd deliver the news to Kat about his impending financial crisis, and then they would just deal with it. Together.

As Dylan stepped inside the apartment, he realized that he'd forgotten one *huge* detail. A *huge* detail that was now sitting on *his* living room sofa, size twelve feet propped up on *his* coffee table.

"Look who decided to surprise us," Kat said, motioning toward the couch.

"Hi, brother! Don't get too excited, now! You look like you just got raped by a chicken!" Dylan's brother, Wyatt, leaped from the couch and bounded toward him. He grabbed Dylan in a bear hug, picked him up off the ground, and physically shook him up and down like he was dumping out a lawn bag.

"Hi, Wyatt! Long time no see," Dylan said, clapping Wyatt around his shoulders. "Let me take a look at you." Dylan stepped back and regarded his younger brother. Wyatt was still Wyatt. He was taller than Dylan, with a wide barrel of a chest and thick, muscular shoulders. He had the physique of a professional athlete, and with his tousled hair, chiseled chin, and perfect dimples, most people assumed Wyatt was somebody famous. Like a Hollywood actor.

In Las Vegas, where Wyatt lived, he often wore dark sunglasses and a baseball cap pulled low over his brow to help perpetuate this myth.

In short, Wyatt was gorgeous.

"You're still ugly," Dylan declared, with a smile.

Wyatt threw his head back and laughed. "And you're still the luckiest sonofabitch who ever lived," he said, motioning toward Kat. "Tell me, Kathleen, why haven't you dumped this guy?" Wyatt roared.

Kat stood in the kitchen and poured boiling water into her nifty little French press. Dylan noticed that Kat was being rather dainty, holding the kettle with her pinky in the air.

"He cast a spell on me," Kat said fondly, handing Wyatt a steaming cup of her famous Guatemalan brew.

"Awww. Ain't that sweet," Wyatt joked.

"You take milk in it, right?" Kat asked, in her most darling little voice. *She's always like this around Wyatt*, Dylan thought.

When Wyatt was in town, Kat the "starving artist" became Kat Betty Crocker.

"Kathleen, you don't have to make a fuss," Wyatt said, as he waited for Kat to pour a little milk into the top of his cup. "Oh, and I'll take sugar cubes if you've got 'em."

"Of course I have sugar cubes!" Kat exclaimed, pressing her hand primly to her chest. Dylan watched as the Lady of the Manor opened up each cabinet in a desperate search for a box of sugar cubes that surely did not exist. He was surprised when Kat pulled down a box and said, "Here we are." She plopped a cube into Wyatt's cup and handed him a little stirring spoon and cocktail napkin.

"Where's the scones?" Dylan asked dryly.

Kat giggled, skipped straight toward Dylan, and slapped him hard on the rear end. "Isn't this great to have the whole family here?" she said, giving Dylan a nice little welcoming peck on the lips.

Some family, Dylan thought, throwing his arm around Kathleen's shoulder. In a way, Kat was right. *This is our family*, Dylan thought. Even though he and Kat weren't married, or even engaged, she was as close to blood as Dylan had.

Dylan watched his younger brother limp back toward the couch. It always pained him to watch Wyatt walk. Ever since the *accident*, his younger brother had always tried so hard to make his gait seem normal. His exertion was apparent in every step he took. He rounded his left leg just a little to keep up with the right, swinging his arms wide to make people focus on his upper body, not his lower.

Wyatt lunged into the burnt leather sofa, and took a sip of Kat's coffee.

"Better than crack," he proclaimed, causing Kat to blush and break out into a sheepish little grin.

"Wyatt brought presents," Kathleen announced. On the kitchen counter, Dylan saw a gift bag with tissue paper poking out of it. Kathleen stuck her hand inside the bag and plucked out a sea blue cotton T-shirt that read "Malibu Is for Lovers."

"Nice," Dylan said, as Kathleen tugged the T-shirt over her head and modeled it around the living room.

"Don't worry. There's one for you, too," Kat said, holding up another shirt.

The shirt was black with white lettering. It featured one word: "Zeus."

"Hey. I like it," Dylan said.

He couldn't figure out why his brother would give him a Zeus T-shirt, but who knew with these west coast types. There was always the latest buzz. Dylan wasn't one for trends, but to be a good sport, he pulled the shirt over his head anyway.

"It fits," he announced, holding out his arms.

"So, what's the word, brother?" Wyatt asked, beaming proudly at them from the couch.

Dylan wondered how to answer this question. He turned and shot Kat a serious look. And his eyes told her all it needed to tell.

"Oh no. What's wrong?" Kat asked immediately. She could read Dylan better than a spy.

"Why don't you take a seat next to Wyatt," Dylan said, hustling her toward the couch.

Kat plopped down next to Wyatt and crossed her arms over her chest.

"We're all ears," she said.

Dylan stood in front of the couch like a drill sergeant. Legs spread apart, arms at his sides. Zeus T-shirt on.

"I have some major news I need to tell y'all," he began.

"Is this about Dad's death?" Wyatt asked. His younger brother was looking up at him; a deer in headlights.

Dylan stared at the floor. He could feel Kat's eyes boring into him. Waiting for him to deliver the "major news."

Hells bells, he thought.

Thirteen

In Texas, when wounded animals die on the side of the road, the vultures come flapping in. It was the same for humans.

With Butch Grant's death, the vultures had swirled in. Dylan and Wyatt hadn't even buried their father, and already Bo Harlan had staked a title claim against the last remaining oil well in the Grant family, and with it he had taken the rights to all the future oil wells to be drilled on their family land.

The final straw was the poker game. To win an oil well in a poker game was one thing. But to win an oil well in a poker game against a drunk—against a man known for being weak and out of control—against a man who'd lost everything except the last remaining oil well named after his wife, well . . .

That's just wrong, Kat thought. She watched Dylan pace in front of the couch. He'd worked up a sweat talking about Bo Harlan.

Bo Harlan, also known as "Wild Bo" for the streak of shock white hair running through his dark locks, was one of those men for whom the world was one big game. There were winners and losers, and Wild Bo considered himself a winner. Everyone else, by default, was a loser.

As Dylan described the poker game, and the piece of paper signed in Butch Grant's telltale red ink handwriting, Kat felt a certain power surge up inside her.

I'll have none of this, she thought.

Kathleen Connor King had something that Bo Harlan didn't have, despite his wealth and fame and reputation as being the meanest, baddest, most wildly successful wildcatter that Houston had ever seen—and that was her name. She was a King, but Bo Harlan would be a Harlan until the end. No matter how much wealth he'd acquired, the Harlan name didn't mean diddly-squat. And in the elite circles of Houston, Texas, a name still meant something.

More than something, Kat thought.

She made a vow to herself. She'd be damned if Wild Bo got away with this. But until she devised her plan, she would have to play a role. The role that Dylan and Wyatt expected. The role of poor little needs-to-be-taken-care-of Kathleen.

It would be fine. Her mother had been quite the actress.

Fourteen

"Dylan Charles Grant!" Kat shrilled. "Are you telling me we've got to move outside the Loop!"

Dylan cringed. Kat wasn't taking this well.

"Why don't you just kill me and get it over with!"

Not well at all, in fact.

"C'mon, hon," Dylan pleaded. He glanced at Wyatt, who just shook his head and stared down at his size twelve, hand-stitched Lucchese boots.

Wyatt won't be any kind of help, you can be sure of that, Dylan thought.

Not when Kat had her nose *up in it* all the way.

"It's just temporary," Dylan said. "Until we get back on our feet. Otherwise we're going to blow through our savings."

"I'd rather be in jail!" Kat boomed. For such a small girl, she had quite an impressive mouth.

Dylan knew that in certain ways Kat was right. As the world's only starving philanthropist, it was crucial for her to stay inside the Loop.

In Houston, Texas, you either lived inside the Loop, or you didn't. People who didn't often pretended that they did, as in: "We live in Memorial City—it's very close to the Loop."

Very close, indeed. But no cigar. As any Realtor worth her respective salt would tell you, it was location, location, location. The Loop was Loop 610—a sweeping circle of highway that surrounded central Houston like a moat. The Guccis typically lived within the moat, preferably in River Oaks, but some streets around Rice University, also known as Southhampton, were also considered très chic.

The Guccis also lived right off the Loop—technically outside—but just on the other side of the Galleria—in old Tanglewood, the gated community of Stablewood, Memorial, or near the Houstonian Country Club and Spa.

Dylan knew that Kathleen never drove outside the Loop for any reason whatsoever, unless she was going on a road trip. Like to Austin or San Antonio. Otherwise, there was never any reason to leave.

The fact that her grandfather, or "Pa Pa" as Kat called him, had been one of the wealthiest and most powerful oil men in the state was of little consolation now that Kat had given her money away.

After her grandfather's death, Kat had gone through a "dark period." She auctioned off the corpus of the old man's estate and donated nearly everything she owned to the foundation, thinking that everything was fine and dandy with her future tied inextricably to Dylan's rising star.

Dylan didn't want to inform Kat that it took money—*a lot of money*—to be a bleeding heart.

She still has the ranch, Dylan thought. *At least she kept that.*

The Tangled Spur was a dusty ten-thousand-acre tract that she'd kept for purely sentimental reasons. The land had some

grazing rights, and Kat was paid a small royalty income each
month by the farmers who kept their cattle there, but this was
just enough to pay the property taxes and provide Kat with a
little spending money.

Kat loved the Tangled Spur. A ranch that had carried the King
family crest for more than a century, but still. No one had ever
found buried treasure there—which in Texas terms, meant oil
and gas.

Dylan began to pace back and forth in front of the couch. He
knew that Kat would starve before she sold the ranch for land
value alone.

"I guess you're angling for me to sell Tangled Spur," Kat spoke
up suddenly, as if reading Dylan's mind. "Isn't that right? Well,
before you speak another word, let me make myself clear. I will
eat dirt, Dylan Grant, before I sell my family's land."

Dylan frowned, noticing how Kat had emphasized the "eat
dirt, Dylan Grant."

Now it's getting personal.

"C'mon, Kathleen," Wyatt sputtered. Dylan's younger brother
slapped his palms against his knees, huffed with exertion, and
stood from the couch.

"No one's asking you to sell Tangled Spur," Wyatt announced
with tremendous gravitas, as if he had a handle on the situation.

He limped over toward Dylan.

"Don't you worry, Kathleen," Wyatt said, puffing out his chest.
"Dylan and I will come up with a plan to resurrect ourselves,
here."

"You just don't get it." Dylan sighed, shaking Wyatt's hand off
his shoulder. "There's no more money. No more leases. No more
checks. We're broke, Wyatt."

Dylan squared off toward his brother, his fists planted firmly
at his hips like a squad commander.

I'm so tired of this, he thought.

He was sick of picking up his brother's mess. Sick of taking care of Wyatt as if he were Dylan's own son. Sick of it, period.

"Actually, we're worse than broke, Wyatt. Broke would mean we were at *zero*. But because someone in this room decided that he was Rain Man, we're now in debt up to our eyeballs with—*I forget*—which casino was it again?"

Wyatt glared at Dylan and scuffed his boot along the wood floor. Dylan could tell from the crestfallen look on his brother's face that the bomb was about to drop.

"The Golden Cowgirl," Wyatt said, under his breath.

Just perfect, Dylan thought.

"I've never heard of that casino," Kat piped up.

It couldn't be a reputable casino, Dylan thought. Like the Bellagio or the MGM Grand or even the Wynn Las Vegas, where perhaps Dylan could get a lawyer to reason with 'em about Wyatt's debt. It had to be a fringe casino. A place that enlisted a bunch of goons who'd watched too many *Godfather* movies and probably thought they were the freakin' old school consigliere themselves.

"I don't think this guy Felix will hurt me," Wyatt said, shuffling toward the kitchen. "He knows I'm good for it."

Dylan chortled. He laughed so loudly that his entire body shook and his eyes got moist with tears.

"How on earth are you good for it, son?" Dylan asked his brother.

"The car." Wyatt shrugged.

"You mean the car Gary Fudge-packer loaned you?"

"Loaned me! Hell, I must've paid three times over that ride!"

"I assume you have the title then?"

Dylan hated himself for doing this.

It was easy being smarter than Wyatt. He'd been smarter than

Wyatt his whole damned life. Which was often a burden because Wyatt thought he was about the smartest cat on the planet. Dylan remembered reading something by Confucius—a quote in a fortune cookie that described his younger brother to a T: *Real knowledge is to know the extent of one's ignorance.*

That was Wyatt's problem. He didn't know the extent of his damned ignorance.

Dylan didn't want to bust his brother's balls about the bad deal he'd made for a loaner car that he never owned outright. So he let it drop.

"There's *no more car*," Dylan announced, watching Wyatt's eyes widen in dismay. "I traded it in this morning for an early model—hell! We'll just call it 'vintage' truck."

"Ooh," Kat said, rubbing her small palms together. The idea of a vintage truck had piqued her interest.

Wyatt wasn't so keen. "Do you mean vintage? Or do you mean shit on wheels?" he asked, hobbling over toward the kitchen.

"Well, if we all pile in the front seat, and load up the bed with watermelons, we could set up the Grant family roadside fruit stand." Dylan smirked.

"Oh brother," Kat said.

"I need a drink," Wyatt said.

Kat followed Wyatt into the kitchen, reached up to the liquor cabinet, and wrestled out a large bottle of Patrón she'd been hiding for emergencies.

"Tequila?" she asked.

"You bet," Wyatt said.

Kat liberated three shot glasses from the dishwasher, poured the tequila neat, and served the shots to Wyatt, Dylan, and herself.

"To Dylan and Wyatt Grant, my two favorite men on earth," Kat said, raising her shot glass high in the air.

"To making a comeback," Wyatt said, clicking his glass against Kat's.

You guys are both nuts, Dylan thought. He slammed the shot, felt the burn in the back of his throat, and had to admit, it felt damned good.

Just then, Dylan's cell phone rang in his pocket. He slipped it out of his jeans and checked the caller ID.

"Hello?"

"Mr. Grant," said the voice in a hushed whisper. "This is Ned Greely over at Colonial Funeral Home. The urn is ready for you to pick up."

"Fantastic."

Dylan grabbed the tequila off the bar and took a swig straight from the bottle.

Fifteen

Kat wandered through the hospital, wishing she'd worn a sweater. Her flimsy T-shirt didn't do much to fight the cold air blasting down from the air-conditioning vents.

I will not be an alcoholic. I am stronger than Ketel One, Kat thought. She reached the hospital elevator and stabbed the button.

She needed to be away from Dylan. She needed time to think.

I need to check on my babies, she thought.

The elevator doors swooshed open, and Kat stepped inside. The goose bumps on her arms were now large and pronounced, as if she'd broken out in hives.

Pretty.

Kat pushed the button for the sixth-floor critical care unit. The children who weren't going home anytime soon were on the higher floors of the hospital.

Closer to heaven, Kat thought. Whenever she set foot inside the children's wing, she felt a certain wholeness to her existence, a content feeling that had been lacking ever since her parents and sister died.

These children, although not her flesh and blood, provided her with something she desperately needed.

A reason to "keep on keepin' on," as her Pa Pa would've said in his booming voice.

Kat wound her way through the critical care unit and paused outside Diego's room. She peeked in at the toddler and saw that he was sleeping soundly after the surgery. His heart monitor was beeping steadily and his blood pressure looked good. Dr. Levin had already called her with the news. The brain surgery had been a success, and Diego would be home in time for his birthday.

Kat smiled and blew Diego a kiss. She walked briskly toward another room and stepped inside.

Maria was sitting up in bed, playing with her Barbie dolls. Kat watched the child mash the faces of the two Barbie dolls together in a forced smooch.

"Who are your friends?" Kat asked, in a soft voice.

Maria glanced up and flashed Kat an all-knowing smile, the type of smile that only little girls of a certain age had a flair for.

"This is Kelly. And this is Billy," Maria announced, holding out the Barbie dolls for Kat to come say hello.

Kat looked down at the Barbie dolls and introduced herself. "Why hello there, Miss Kelly. Have you been kissing Mr. Billy?"

Maria kicked her little legs and screeched with laughter. "You saw it! You saw the kiss!"

"I did." Kat took a seat next to Maria's bed. She put her hand on the child's shaved bald head and checked the scar on her right occipital.

Kat had never been to nursing school, but she'd read the *Journal of Nursing* from cover to cover and spent enough time in the hospital to know about as much as anyone. She was self-taught in the tradition of midwives and other women who'd apprenticed in hospitals.

Healing well, she thought, seeing how the black stitches stood in steep contrast with Maria's white shaved head. There were a few red welts from the needles, a large blue bruise, and a few apple-colored splotches on Maria's skin. It wouldn't be long until the doctor snipped the stitches out, and Maria's hair would start growing back.

Bald, sick children suffering from cancer, Kathleen thought. Sometimes she wondered why. Why sickness afflicted the meek.

"I want Cathy Caterpillar!" Maria shrieked, and threw her head back against the pillow in fits of laughter.

"Cathy Caterpillar . . . coming right up!" Kat said, plugging her finger into Maria's little belly and watching the girl howl with laughter. She reached over to the bed tray and pulled the *Tales of the Unicorn Land* book into her lap.

In a soft voice, Kat began to read.

Beauty and the Butterfly

Cathy Caterpillar
Was sitting on
A big yellow sunflower near the pond.
It was a warm
Sunshiny day.
She should have been
Happy but she was crying.
Just then, Uli Unicorn
Came by and asked her
Why she was crying.
Cathy told Uli

She was sad because
She was so brown and ugly
And drab.
Uli said, "Have patience and you will be
Happy."
Cathy had no idea
What Uli was talking about.
About three months passed and
Cathy Caterpillar began to
Feel strange.
She went to the Smiling Pond
And looked at herself in the
Water.
She couldn't believe her
Eyes. She had turned
Into a beautiful butterfly!

Kat felt Maria's body go slack. The little girl had fallen into a dreamy sleep, her small tummy rising in pitches and falls. Kat felt her own eyes begin to droop close. Last night, she'd suffered from severe insomnia, which she imagined was a result of too much coffee, and the stress of Dylan and Wyatt.

While the two Grant brothers slept soundly, she'd spent the entire night painting a neon green giraffe eating leaves from a bright orange tree. She planned to present the canvas as a gift to Diego when he left the hospital.

As Kathleen began to drift off, she felt a hand touch her shoulder.

"Ms. King?"

It was Dr. Levin. Making his rounds. The chief surgeon and hospital administrator stood over her shoulder, looking down at her with an unmistakable paternal flicker in his eye.

"I heard you wanted to see me," he said. Kathleen roused herself from Maria's bedside.

"Yes, I wanted to inquire about . . ." Kat paused, and searched for the right word. Finally, it came to her.

"A job," she said, primly, tucking her chin against her chest and staring up at Dr. Levin.

Dr. Levin patted the small paunch of his belly the way he always did when he was thinking. With the amused glint in his eye, and his hand pressed against the round of his belly, Kat had an image of a laughing Buddha statue she'd seen at an art gallery once.

"A job?" he asked quietly.

Kat tried hard not to blush. This was rule number one of being "Those with Family Names."

Rule number one: Never look down at one's shoes. Always make eye contact. Appear calm, stately, and in control.

Kat had taken measured refinement to another level, as her demeanor in public was the talk of the town among the Gucci set. The Guccis who envied her, and who aspired to be born to the King family name, often were quoted praising Kat's "poise" in the glossy society magazines. In Houston's glossy press, Kat was often referred to as Texas "royalty."

It was common for the captions under Kat's photos to read, *Kathleen Connor King spotted at the Black Tie and Boots Gala in a majestic gown of unknown origin. Ms. King sipped from a single champagne flute all evening and seemed to channel Grace Kelly with her stunning frock and stately updo.*

Unbeknownst to the world of society, Kat had found the "gown of unknown origin," in a costume shop on the gritty east side of San Antonio, while shopping for used canvases. Her "stately updo" was a Kat specialty—a last-minute throw-your-hair-up-in-a-loose-bun-and-stick-a-dainty-seed-pearl-clip-in-it. Hairclip, four dollars and ninety-nine cents, Chinese import Web site.

Kat inhaled nervously and brushed a strand of hair from her face.

Dr. Levin had begun to regale her with a list of volunteer duties around the hospital.

He doesn't get it, she noticed. He assumed that Little Miss Philanthropist who paid for everything the hospital had, including his own salary, wanted more volunteer work—like counseling troubled parents, or making sure the break room was stocked with coffee and creamers and sugar packets.

Kathleen held up her hand and shook her head. "I'm looking for a paid position," she said bluntly.

Dr. Levin was the only person in Houston, and possibly the entire world, whom she could share this with. He was strictly business. And didn't have a gossip bone in his whole body.

But, Kat noticed, he blinked at her several times.

"You mean . . . a salaried job, Ms. King?" He swallowed. "With benefits?"

Kat shrugged.

Sure, she thought. *Why not?*

"You're chairman of the board of this hospital, you could have my job if you wanted it." Dr. Levin chuckled.

"No, Dr. Levin. I don't want your job because you have the hardest job in the world," Kat said. She'd known Dr. Levin since she was a mere child, and noticed how old he'd started to look. With tufts of gray hair spurting from behind his ears. Her grandpa had once told her, in his rough and swagger voice, that Dr. Levin was the type of Hebrew surgeon who held God in his steady hands every day. And that "only special people" knew what it was like to hold God in their hands.

"Of course, Ms. King. A paying job it is," Dr. Levin announced. "Come with me."

He led her through the powder blue hospital hallway and ushered her inside his cramped, paper-stuffed office.

"Sit, sit," He motioned for Kat to take a seat. "So, let's see what the budget has in store for us." He swooped behind his desk, opened a file drawer, and took out a thick manila folder.

"We just hired two more nursing staff this week to fill the weekend gap," he explained, pulling on a pair of reading glasses, and breezing through the folder.

"Looks like we could cut the Children of Hope program, and that would give us room to start you around . . . let's say . . . forty-five thousand dollars?" Dr. Levin said the number hesitantly, as if he wasn't sure if Kat wanted more, or why a woman from the wealthiest oil family in the history of Houston would want a salary in the first place. But he wasn't the type to question.

The Children of Hope program had been one of Kat's ideas. In it, children who were released from the hospital after their surgeries were paired with nurses who came to the home to help parents with the day-to-day primary care role. The nurses would drop by the child's house to deliver medicine, check blood levels, and make sure the child was recovering. The program had received many accolades in the press, and Kathleen had been awarded a Philanthropy of Peace medal from the Women's League of Texas, which she kept in her precious belongings drawer at home.

No, the Children of Hope program is here to stay, Kat thought.

"Any other ideas?" she asked, fidgeting in her chair.

"A few of us could do without an end-of-the-year bonus," Dr. Levin said, flapping his hand at her. "Look Kathleen. I'm an old man. I already have a swimming pool in my backyard. What else do I need?"

Kat's eyes roamed over the photos of Dr. Levin's family smiling at her from the silver frames on his desk.

I'm not taking a penny of your salary, Kat thought.

"I wouldn't feel comfortable with that," she said.

Across the room, Dr. Levin eyed her over the top of his reading glasses.

"Ms. King, in order to put you on the payroll, we have to make a few tweaks here and there. But remember, this is *your* foundation. *You* bring in the money. So just tell me what you want."

Kathleen stood from her chair and stretched her legs. She rolled her ankle in a circle and felt a small pop.

"For starters, I would like to get periodic updates on Diego Ramirez," she said.

Dr. Levin patted the front pocket of his white lab coat. He pulled out a pen and scribbled himself a note.

"You've become close with this patient?" he asked, raising a bushy eyebrow.

Kathleen nodded. "I guess I'm wondering if my presence here matters," she said. She was lying now. But this was the only way out. To lie. She couldn't press on about the money. She couldn't say, *Dr. Levin. Your benefactor is broke.* No. Things had to proceed in a nice, smooth line. The way they always had.

The doctor took the bait. "Ms. King, you are the reason we exist. You are the reason for"—he waved his hand across the room—"for all of this." He paused, took his reading glasses off, set them on his desk. "Whether you're reading bedside stories, or spending time with these parents, you're doing an invaluable service." He folded his hands together and gave her a meaningful look. "I assure you, Ms. King, your presence matters."

Kat beamed. "That's all I needed to know."

Dr. Levin stood from his desk and gave Kat a quick handshake, just before she bounded out the door.

Sixteen

"We're SOL," Wyatt said, taking a slug from his beer. He wiped the froth off with the back of his hand.

Wyatt was known for his "movie star eyes." And now Dylan's brother was using them to dramatic effect. Raising two perfect brows and staring at Dylan with his huge blue sparklers.

Dylan knew he didn't have Wyatt's good looks. In contrast to Wyatt's blond hair and blue eyes, Dylan's features were dark. The running joke was that Dylan's mother had slept with the postman, and all that jazz. Of course, Dylan and Wyatt were both the unfortunate sons of the recently deceased Butch Grant.

Ah, the shame of it, Dylan thought.

He sat next to Wyatt, nursed his Heineken, and pondered. He estimated that there were five big problems facing him. *I should write this down,* he thought. Grabbing a cocktail napkin off the bar, Dylan motioned for the bartender goddess in her tight jeans and shimmering low-cut top.

She breezed over and flashed Wyatt one of those take-me-home-or-leave-me-forever smiles.

"Another round, boys?" she asked, staring at Dylan's brother as if he were Brad Pitt.

"I need a pen," Dylan said sharply.

"I would love another beer, darlin'," Wyatt grinned.

The bartender goddess wiped her hands against her jeans, served Wyatt a draft beer on tap, and flicked a pen across the bar toward Dylan.

Dylan felt his brother's eyes peering over his shoulder as he scribbled out a list on the napkin.

THINGS TO DO:

1. Pay off Wyatt's gambling debt.
2. Kill Bo Harlan.
3. Steal Titan Energy's seismic data and drill our own well.
4. Liquidate savings account, move to cheaper apartment.
5. Ask Kat to get married before she wises up.

Wyatt nudged Dylan in the ribs and took a slug from his beer. "You can't ask Kat to marry you while you're plumb broke, you dumb shit."

Dylan whirled around on his bar stool. "Why not? Kat is the last person to give a damn about the cash."

"Which is why she gave away *her entire trust fund*. But think of *her* feelings, man. You've been dating her since the playground and high school and college and all these years, and she's been dying to get married and all of a sudden, you decide it's up and time to tie the knot."

Dylan stared at his brother. "Your point?"

"What lit the fire under your butt?"

"I love her," Dylan said.

"Jesus, you're like a bad movie." Wyatt shook his head.

Dylan glanced over at the urn sitting on the bar stool next to him. No one had noticed it, of course. Dylan had toted the urn inside the bar like it was no big deal. As if he was carrying a briefcase.

It's a fitting tribute, really. To have a last drink with dear ol' Dad, Dylan thought. Butch Grant had spent his entire life in a bar, so why not enjoy one last round?

"Should we raise a toast to Butch?" Wyatt asked, and for a split second, Dylan saw an angry glint flash across his brother's eyes.

"Sure."

Wyatt raised his beer in the air. "Rest in peace, you sonofabitch."

Dylan chuckled and rapped on the urn with his knuckles. "I couldn't have said it better myself."

Seventeen

The reinforcements had arrived in the form of Crazy Aunt Lucinda. Everyone called her "the Duchess." Not because Aunt Lucinda was titled or wealthy or any of those things, but because she held her nose upturned like royalty. As if she were constantly sniffing something amiss in the air.

So here sat the Duchess. On Dylan's sprawling leather couch, no less. Admiring the view from the windows with her nose upturned in the air as if she'd just smelled a fart.

"Mighty expensive view, sugar," Aunt Lucinda said, crinkling her eyes in Kat's direction.

Kathleen tiptoed across the floor and handed the Duchess a cup of Earl Grey. She loved Aunt Lucinda, whom she called her aunt even though Lucinda wasn't her own flesh and blood. She'd been Kat's nanny growing up.

"Dylan chose this apartment when he was working at Enron."

"Must be some rent," the Duchess mused. She took a sip from

her tea and stared out the window toward the downtown sky-scrapers. "Who does he think he is? Mister Donald Trump?"

"What am I going to do, Lucinda?" Kat folded her arms across her chest. "And don't be shy when you tell me."

"Have you told him yet?"

Lucinda was eyeing Kat the way she sometimes did. As if Kat were the one at fault.

Kat took a sip of tea. *Hopefully the cinnamon chai will help calm my nerves.*

"I haven't had a chance to tell him. My doctor's appointment was the same day he went to the funeral home."

"When do you plan on telling him? Never?"

Kathleen shrugged. "He hasn't buried his father yet. I think the news can wait, don't you?"

"He's not a child, sugar. How do you expect to move forward if you're not being honest in your relationship? If you're *trickling* out information on *your* own terms?"

Kathleen bit her lip. It was just like Lucinda to call a spade a spade. Even if the old woman was a bit crazy.

I can't have children, Kat thought. The reality hit her like a hammer.

"What am I going to tell him, Lucinda? That I'm barren. That the King family name *dies* with me!"

"Come here," Lucinda said. She set her teacup on Dylan's coffee table and reached her arms out for Kat.

"I didn't mean to judge. Come give your aunt some love."

Kat rushed forward and hugged Lucinda tight. It was the first time the two women had hugged since Pa Pa's funeral. Kat thought back to Lucinda's black toile dress. The type of fancy dress that older black women wore to funerals. Filled with lace parts running high up the neck. A wide-brimmed black hat pulled low over the Duchess's eyes.

Lucinda Jones Washington had borne the loss—so personally. Her grief-stricken face etched like fine black marble.

Kat had always suspected her grandpa and Lucinda had been intimate, but it took the funeral to nail it home. Now, Kat was sure, sure.

Cullen Davis King had found happiness with the one woman in his life who gave a damn. The woman who, when he fell sick, changed his bedsheets, fed him piping hot chicken soup, and cared for him more than anyone.

Before she'd given away her entire inheritance to the King Foundation, Kat had made sure Aunt Lucinda was set for life.

The Duchess received a check each month and lived in Cullen King's old white-columned house in River Oaks, which she would live in until the day she died. Kat figured the house belonged more to Aunt Lucinda, a woman who'd spent half a century living there and caring for things, than anyone else.

She sat on the couch and let Aunt Lucinda pat her on the back, the way her nanny used to do when Kat was little. Patting gently as if Kat needed burping.

"There, there," Aunt Lucinda said, "all better now?"

The Duchess closed her strong hands over Kat's shoulders and held Kat out for her to examine. Her mocha eyes, as deep as canyons, lit up at the sight of Kat's features.

"You're beautiful, sugar, just like your mama was. Dylan would be a fool," she said, shaking her head and tsk-tsking with her lips.

"I need to tell him the truth," Kat said. "So he can choose whether he still wants to marry me."

"Speaking of marriage, what's the word?" Lucinda shot back. "It's time that boy got on the stick."

No kidding, Kat thought.

"I don't know. I guess we fell into something comfortable."

"It's been comfortable for *years*. I mean, look at you, child.

Here you are. Socked up inside this apartment all day long. He's got everything he wants."

Kat giggled and covered her mouth. "Maybe I should pretend I'm pregnant."

Aunt Lucinda pounded the sofa with her fist.

"Girl, you got the devil in you!" she hooted.

"Look. Let's be realistic here, Lucinda. Dylan wants to have children. It's not fair to him. He deserves to be with a woman who can give him a real family."

She furrowed her brow. Thinking of her barrenness had put her into a funk. She hadn't been sleeping well. Even her eyes looked dark underneath. Reaching her hand into her empty teacup, Kat pulled out the tea bag and set it on top of her eye.

"You crazy, child," Aunt Lucinda said. "Tea bags, cucumbers, these fancy-schmancy spas, nothing works like good ol'-fashion Vaseline. I use it every night. A little dab under each eye. You should try."

Kat pressed the tea bag firmly against her eye and felt a stream of warm tea trickle down her cheek. She dropped the tea bag into the cup and wiped her hand across her face.

"The tea bag fountain of youth," she said.

"Are you sure you can't get pregnant, sugar? Don't listen to those doctors. They don't know hoo-ee." Lucinda flicked her finger in the air and pointed up at the ceiling. "Have you spoken with the Lord?"

Kathleen sniffled. "I tried. But I think he was having lunch with Joel Osteen."

"Nonsense, child!" Crazy Aunt Lucinda clapped her hands, causing Kat to flinch. She proceeded to poke Kat in the ribs, which Kat recognized as Lucinda's coming-to-Jesus move.

It was Lucinda's way of torturing Kat—poking her in the ribs to nail home her point. Which was usually a Psalm from the Bible. Lucinda read the Bible like cats drank milk.

"*He* transforms the barren woman into a glad mother of children, hallelujah. That's from Psalms," Lucinda announced.

"So, you're saying I should pray more?"

Lucinda arched her eyebrow as if to say, *Duh.*

"You're right." Kat sighed. "But that still doesn't solve the marriage question."

Lucinda shifted on the couch, causing the cushion under Kat to slide out.

"Why don't you ask him to marry you, sugar? Be a modern lady, like your mama was?"

"Get real."

"I'm serious as a stroke, honey. You take that boy someplace romantic. You look him in the eye and you say: *Dylan, I may not be able to bear your child, but if we love each other, we can find a way. I'm ready to get married. How about it?*"

"You want me to say, *I'm ready to get married. How about it?*"

"You can put your own spin on it."

No way in hell, Kat thought. She leaned back against the couch and scratched a small welt on her leg. "That's not traditional. The girl asking the guy."

"Kathleen, you've been living with him since you were in college! At this point, what does it matter?" Crazy Aunt Lucinda was looking at her now. With those wake-up-and-smell-the-coffee eyes.

"You want to marry that boy, don't you?"

Kat nodded vigorously. "More than Brad Pitt."

"Well then."

"What would I do without you?" Kat said simply.

"Oh, sugar. I'm not gonna be around forever," Lucinda said,

rubbing her arms. "The way this old woman's bones have been cracking, I think the Lord is ready for me."

"Nonsense," Kat said. She didn't know how old Lucinda was. No one did. It was a closely guarded secret. Like more closely guarded than who killed JFK.

"I'm getting up there in the years, child."

Kat managed a smile. "How old are you? I always forget."

The Duchess clucked and turned her nose up in the air.

Eighteen

Dylan and Wyatt bumped along I–10 toward Winnie, Texas. Sabine Lake, the site where they'd chosen to scatter Butch Grant's ashes, was located just off Port Arthur, between Galveston and Beaumont.

They rode in silence, with the muted sound of the Toyota's tinny radio blaring bad country music. Once in a while, Wyatt would clap Dylan on the shoulder and cast an odd look across the passenger seat.

They weren't sad, per se.

No.

Butch Grant had done too much damage over the years. His death was simply an event. A loose end that needed tidying up.

It is what it was.

In his final will and testament written in awful red ink, Butch had requested for his ashes to be scattered over Dylan's mother's grave.

Not in a million years, Dylan thought, gunning the accelerator.

Not only would Clarissa Grant have rolled in her grave, she probably would've sat up and slapped Dylan in the face.

So Dylan thought of the next best thing. Sabine Lake. His father's favorite fishing hole. Sabine Lake—the site of the childhood incident that had robbed Wyatt of a decent childhood and installed a permanent limp in his God-given, Adonis-like physique.

He and Wyatt hadn't returned to the lake in more than twenty-five years. It had haunted their childhood dreams, and to this day, Dylan still had nightmares.

As the first signs of water appeared in the distance, Wyatt released an audible shudder.

"You ready for this, brother?" Dylan asked.

Wyatt glared at the urn that Dylan had propped behind them in the cramped backseat of the pickup.

"Dad was one mean sonofabitch, wasn't he?" Wyatt said.

Dylan clenched his teeth. "The man couldn't handle his alcohol, Wyatt. Some people can drink. Others can't."

He clicked the window wipers to clear the windshield from all the splattered bugs. When he glanced back at Wyatt, he saw that his brother had done the unthinkable. Wyatt had rolled up the leg of his jeans to the knee. He was wearing his Lucchese boots, but Dylan could make out the prosthetic flesh-looking silicone of his brother's fake leg.

Wyatt glared at the urn and thumped his fist against his prosthetic leg. "Before we put you to rest, *Butch*, I want you to take a *good long look* at Captain Ahab."

Captain Ahab. The name hung in the air like radiation. Dylan was stunned that Wyatt had uttered it.

Captain Ahab was the name Butch Grant used to taunt his youngest son. When Wyatt was relearning how to walk. Or when

Wyatt made a mistake in school. When Wyatt did anything that young boys are prone to do, period. It was always, without fail, Captain Ahab.

"Stop it, Wyatt!" Dylan commanded. His tone sounded stern, and Dylan immediately regretted it. He didn't want his brother to relive the memories. He just wanted this whole charade over with.

"Captain Ahab, my ass," Wyatt muttered.

"We're here," Dylan said. He eased the truck up to the edge of the lake, and listened to the tires crunching the sandy gravel underneath.

In front of them was the wood plank dock where Wyatt had almost bled to death.

Dylan turned and stared at his younger brother.

"Keep it running," Wyatt ordered.

"You got it." Dylan slammed on the parking brake, but left the keys in the ignition, with the motor idling.

He and Wyatt climbed out.

"Let's get this over with." He wrestled the urn from the backseat. The two brothers walked slowly down the wooden planks, Dylan toting the urn in front of him.

Wyatt spat into the water. He turned toward his brother. "You think we should say a few words or what?"

Dylan noticed that his younger brother's eyes looked clouded over. He stared listlessly at the water.

"I've got nothing to say, do you?" Dylan asked.

"Guess not."

Dylan knelt down onto one knee and tipped his father's remains upside down. The gray ash tumbled into the water, causing a milky cloud. Dylan paused and let the cold, hard fact sink in. His father was dead. And here was the proof. Squatting low on the dock, he stuck his hand into the lukewarm water and swished violently until the ash sank away. He wiped his hand against his jeans, and stood up.

"Guess that's that," he said.

Turning toward Wyatt, he saw that his younger brother had begun to cry.

Nineteen

Kathleen was about to pull an Ingrid Bergman. Her mother, bless her heart, had been a huge fan of Ingrid's films. The top three movies being *Anastasia*, *Murder on the Orient Express*, and *Casablanca*, of course.

Although Kathleen had been technically raised by the Duchess, her own biological mother, in precious moments between ladies' luncheons and society events, had taught her a thing or two.

Kat's lesson plan ran strictly along the lines of how to "act Ingrid." That is, how to get what you wanted from a man. These lessons were taught before puberty. And so, as the Duchess brushed Kat's hair or gave her a bath, her mother would breeze into the room and drop one of her favorite Ingrid-isms.

Remember, dear. It is not whether you really cry. It is whether the audience thinks you are crying.

This was one of her mother's favorite lines. And she would use it often. Right before she kissed Kat on the top of the head and whisked back to her ladies' luncheons and society events.

Kat didn't regret her mother's lack of mothering. She felt as though she'd had the blessing of two mothers. And that was more than most people could ask for.

Kat pedaled her bike furiously down Allen Parkway, and then crossed over to the bayou that snaked into downtown Houston. She was heading for Bo Harlan's office, on the penthouse floor of the now defunct (and considered haunted) Enron Building.

Harlan had snagged the prime commercial office space for a steal after other companies had passed up the opportunity. And now Kat planned to burst into the gleaming penthouse office which had graced the cover of *Houston Modern Luxury* magazine.

Kat pedaled quickly into downtown, past the throngs of people walking to work, and the Mexican taco vendors with their push-carts. The smell of fried tortillas was tantalizing, but Kat didn't want to risk having taco breath.

When she reached Travis Street, she hopped off the bike and walked it the rest of the way. She didn't want to break a sweat. Especially since she was wearing a flowing vintage Halston dress with four-inch heels.

People on the sidewalk were staring.

I probably look ridiculous, Kathleen thought, pushing the bike in a cocktail gown and heels. She'd spritzed herself with perfume, dabbed a sexy sheer lip gloss across her lips, and inserted small cups into her bra to make her cleavage stand out. If anything, her appearance could be described as va-va-voom.

She reached the front entrance of the former Enron Building, locked her bike to a nearby rack, and made sure not to get grease on her dress.

Stepping inside the cold lobby, Kat paused and gazed around. Titan Energy had erected a sign with its logo splashed across. It was a playing card. Bo Harlan's signature card.

The oilman was renowned for winning oil wells in his midnight poker games, by using the wild card—often the joker.

And so the joker, the playing card, was his trademark.

Kat sashayed toward the elevators, waved airily at the security guard who tried to stop her, and made her way to the penthouse floor.

Bo Harlan's face registered more than surprise when Kat pushed her way into his massive corner office. She'd marched right past his voluptuous secretary and breezed into his office, without so much as a phone call or appointment.

"My mother always told me that powerful men *love* to be surprised," Kathleen announced to Bo Harlan's shocked face.

She shot him a devastating smile and took a seat in one of the chairs in front of his desk.

Bo Harlan's secretary rushed through the doorway, looking flustered and out of sorts.

"Mr. Harlan! I'm sorry, sir! She just barged right in!"

Bo Harlan eyed Kathleen the way a lion eyes a gazelle and shooed his secretary away with a flap of his hand. He was a stubby man. His face reminded Kat of a slobbering bulldog.

"Why, Kathleen Connor King! To what do I owe the pleasure?"

Kat watched the oilman's ruddy cheeks blush. When it came to women, Wild Bo wasn't good at maintaining his poker face.

"I bet you love it when a woman catches you off guard, Bo," Kat said. She giggled, covered her mouth, fluttered her eyelashes. The whole nine yards. Then she leaned forward in her seat and watched as Bo took in the view of her small but perky cleavage.

He tugged at his collar and cleared his throat. "It doesn't happen often, Kathleen, that a woman will catch me off guard."

"But when it does, Bo, I bet you get hotter than an egg on asphalt."

A smile streaked across the oilman's lips and his face got flush.

I should do it right now, Kat figured. *This is the perfect time to ask for the money.*

"As you know, Bo, I run the King Family Foundation," Kathleen started her pitch. "And we do this little dinner every year."

"Little dinner!" Bo Harlan sputtered. "That's an understatement if I've ever heard one." The oilman bounced around in his thick leather chair. He was about to get invited to the most prominent society event of the year. Kathleen's dinner was strictly by-invitation-only. It was the hottest ticket in town. And possibly the whole state.

"Well, you're right, Bo. It's a *big* dinner in terms of financial commitment. But I prefer to think of it as a *little* dinner because *so few* people are invited. I keep the guest list private and exclusive."

Wild Bo stared intently at Kathleen, knotting his bushy eyebrows and working his lips feverishly. She sensed that he was nearly on the edge of his seat. To be invited to this dinner would be a huge step up socially for the wildcatter.

She pressed on. "The dinner benefits the Pediatric Cancer Hospital, Bo, which I can't tell you"—Kathleen paused and placed her hand daintily against her chest—"how near and dear to my heart this place is."

Bo Harlan stared at her petite little body, and for a second, Kat saw him stop breathing. He broke into a confident grin.

"Well, Kathleen. I would love to help out. In any way, shape, or form."

"I knew you would, Bo. That's why I'm here," Kat smiled, graciously. "I'm instituting a new program this year called the 'VIP Donors' Table,'" she said. She was now making things up on the spot.

"This will be the main table at the dinner, with only a few

select, handpicked people. Now, I'm warning you, Bo. The price is a bit steep, and I don't want you to go into cardiac arrest." Kat giggled.

"Name it." Bo Harlan was already pulling out his checkbook and flipping it open on his desk.

"Five hundred thousand."

"For the table?"

"For a single ticket."

Bo Harlan licked his lips.

"Who else is doing this?"

"I'm sorry?" Kathleen shot Bo a puzzled look.

"Who are your other VIP donors?"

Kathleen smiled. She couldn't blame the oilman for being shrewd. Of course he wanted to know who he'd be sitting with. *You want to see how far you can stretch that money, don't you?*

"Most of my VIP donors prefer to remain anonymous, Bo."

"C'mon, Kathleen. Throw a dog a bone."

Kathleen winked and lowered her voice to a whisper as if she was about to let the oilman in on a luscious secret. This was Ingrid Bergman Acting Class 101.

"I will tell you this, Bo . . . my *dear* friend, Shelby Lynn Pierce, will be sitting at the main table," Kathleen whispered.

Bo Harlan's poker face disintegrated upon hearing Shelby Lynn Pierce's name mentioned aloud. He looked like he was about to bust a gut at the thought of sitting next to a female Pierce. *I mean, after all. The Pierce family was simply . . . beyond.*

"I . . . we . . . ." he stuttered. "We haven't been formally introduced."

Of course you haven't, Kathleen thought.

Bo Harlan stared down at his checkbook.

"Done," he said finally.

He made a big show of scrawling out the half-million-dollar check and handing it over to her with a flourish.

"Well, aren't you the sweetest thing," Kathleen cooed in her baby-doll voice.

"Hell, Kathleen. I don't make all this money for nothing."

That was easy, Kathleen thought.

She smiled and lifted herself delicately out of the chair. Kathleen swirled up to Bo Harlan's desk, leaned over, and kissed the surprised oilman on his sweaty forehead. Then, without a word, she swooshed out the door.

Bo Harlan's secretary with the fake tan and the fake breasts was staring at her, so Kathleen waved pleasantly. Which elicited a "Have a nice day" from the poor girl.

She stepped into the elevator and pushed the button for the lobby. Her plan was simple. She'd deposit the check in the escrow account, just as she'd always done. That way, Bo Harlan could show a charitable tax deduction. But then Kathleen would start drawing a salary. Nothing major. Just enough to cover the rent, and her and Dylan's living expenses.

Everyone assumed Kathleen was a bleeding heart, but that didn't mean she was stupid. Her mama had always told her that a woman was supposed to have a little nest egg on the side that was no one else's business but her own.

She wasn't about to tell Dylan about her meeting with Bo Harlan, or the fact that she'd gotten Wild Bo himself to write a half-million-dollar check in a matter of seconds, because Dylan would blow through the roof, Kathleen was sure of it.

As Kathleen breezed past the massive "Titan Energy" sign gracing the lobby, she glanced at Bo Harlan's signature playing card logo etched in gold filigree.

Queen beats joker, she thought, with a sneaky smile.

Twenty

Dylan wasn't the paranoid type, but the black sedan that had been tailing him and Wyatt since they'd left Sabine Lake was all wrong.

The area around the lake was populated by hicks and rednecks. And hicks and rednecks didn't drive black sedans with dark tinted windows. First of all, it was too damned hot for that type of car in Texas. And second, that type of car was not a truck.

Therefore, Dylan figured they were being followed.

He turned and glanced at Wyatt. His brother was no longer crying, thank God, but his face had assumed a woeful expression.

Dylan checked the rearview. "Don't look now, but I think we've got company."

"You've been watching too many movies, bro," Wyatt said.

"I'm serious. Check it out. Black car. About a quarter-mile back. Been following us for twenty minutes."

"Oh shit! It's *Felix*!" Wyatt shouted.

"How do you know!"

"Nevada license plate!"

Dylan pounded the steering wheel with his fist. "Jesus, Wyatt! I thought you said they would leave you alone?"

This was not what he needed. Not today. Not some gambling goons from some shithole casino in Vegas hot on their tail.

"Gun it!" Wyatt shouted.

Dylan ignored Wyatt and kept his foot pressed smoothly on the accelerator.

"C'mon! *Speed up!*" Wyatt yelled.

"Calm down, brother," Dylan ordered. "Now, let's think this through before we do anything rash."

He glanced out the windows. He and Wyatt were driving around the most remote area of the lake. They'd already passed all of the pretty houses fronting the water, and were now motoring down a dirt road "shortcut" that led out to the freeway. This was not the place to encounter a bunch of meatheads.

But Wyatt was never big on brainstorming. Before Dylan could stop him, the younger Grant rolled down his window, raised up his right fist, and flashed the black sedan the bird.

"It's go time!" Wyatt said, and his voice was all amped up. Like he was ready to fight.

"Why the hell'd you do that?" Dylan shouted. He watched in the rearview as the sedan sped up and clipped his back bumper.

Dylan gunned the accelerator, but it felt as though the Toyota were weighed down by a thousand elephants. With the increased speed, the truck fishtailed back and forth over the dirt road. The black sedan gained speed and raced up alongside them. Dylan glanced to his left and saw one of the sedan's tinted windows rolling down. That's when Dylan spotted the gun.

"Those fuckers have a gun!" Wyatt shouted.

Dylan stomped his foot on the accelerator but the truck was a piece of junk. It was easy for the sedan to keep the same speed

alongside them. Dylan could see a man wearing metallic sunglasses. Metallic Sunglasses was waving the gun, motioning for
them to pull over. The freeway was still far off in the distance.

We are so fucked.

Metallic Sunglasses had lost patience and was now pointing
the gun, the barrel poking out the window toward Dylan's face.

Dylan felt angry now. Angry as a tornado. He jammed on the
brakes, wrenched the steering wheel to the right, and pulled over
onto the gravel side of the road.

Dylan swung open his driver's side door and jumped out of the
truck. The sedan pulled over about fifty feet ahead. He bucked
out his chest and snorted. He'd be damned if anyone was going
to point a gun in his face on the very day he'd buried his father.

Out of his peripheral vision, Dylan saw that Wyatt had climbed
out of the truck and was doing his best to catch up to him.

Four men wearing dark suits exited the black sedan at once,
which wasn't a good sign in Dylan's opinion. They weren't big
men, but Dylan could tell from their hardened expressions that
they'd been in a lot of fights. He knew these types of guys. The
type that would throw a dirty punch or pull out a knife. Four
men to two. Not quite the Alamo. But still. Formidable.

Metallic Sunglasses was carrying a gun. The other three were
carrying baseball bats.

This isn't going to be pretty.

One of the men looked like the boss of the others. He was
shorter than the other men, dark-skinned, and had the smartest
eyes of the bunch.

Felix, Dylan thought. He pivoted around to Wyatt and pointed
at his younger brother's chest. "Don't say a word! Let me handle
this," he hissed.

"*Felix! You sonofabitch!*" Wyatt barked. "*I told you I'd get
you your money! Now, back the hell off!*"

So this was the tactic the younger Grant had chosen, Dylan thought. The dumbest tactic possible. To incite more anger.

Shut up, Wyatt. SHUT UP!

Dylan realized in a flash that he was more pissed at Wyatt than at the men walking toward him with baseball bats and a gun.

Dylan spun on his heel and pushed Wyatt as hard as he could. Wyatt was caught off guard, and he stumbled on his prosthetic leg.

"*Shut up, Wyatt! I told you to let me handle this!*" Dylan roared, nearly bursting a lung.

Dylan saw the punch coming, but it was too late. Wyatt arched his fist back and connected a strong punch squarely into Dylan's arm. Dylan fought dirty by kicking Wyatt's fake leg out from under him.

Wyatt jerked backward and fell on the gravel, and Dylan leaped on top of him. The two brothers rolled around, punching, kicking, scratching, and generally bruising the crap out of each other, until Wyatt got dirt in his eyes and called for quits.

"Time out, time out!" Wyatt sputtered, waving his arms like a referee.

Dylan was out of breath, and his lip was split and bleeding from Wyatt's famous "upper crunch" elbow thrust.

Wyatt was coughing up dirt and his right eye was swelling up with a nice fat shiner, compliments of Dylan's expert right hook.

"Are you finished?" came a voice from above them.

Dylan looked up and realized his vision was blurred by sweat and dirt. It was Felix. The bookie looked somewhat bemused, but tried to maintain a steady face. This was serious business after all.

"I'm Wyatt's brother," Dylan said, as he wrestled himself to his feet. He brushed himself off. "Dylan Grant," he said, holding out his hand as if he were in a business meeting.

Felix regarded this unusual gesture. A handshake? The bookie took Dylan's outstretched hand and said, "Nice to meet you. I'm the guy your brother took for five hundred G's in Vegas."

Dylan said, "I heard."

Felix was wearing a gold crucifix around his neck. The figure of Christ was done in pave diamonds.

Wyatt had sat up on the gravel and was trying to pick something out of his eye, but he managed to throw in his two cents. "I told you, I'd get you your money, you peasant!" he spat.

Two of the men reacted quickly. They walked toward Wyatt with their baseball bats poised to strike. Felix held up his hand. "Wait."

Dylan mustered a smile. "Look, my brother is in over his head. He can't play the sports book to save his life, and he knows this, but for some reason, he keeps going back as if his luck's going to change." Dylan turned and glared at his brother. "I told you the Hoyas had no shot at the championship."

"They choked in the last five minutes of the game," Wyatt growled.

"I want my money," Felix said, as if he was reading a line in a movie.

"How about I make you a deal?" Dylan offered.

"No deals," Felix said, flashing a solid gold tooth with a single diamond in the center. "Deals are bad for business, my friend. You give one guy a deal, and soon everyone finds out. Your brother owes me five hundred G's. Me and my boys are here to collect."

Dylan wiped blood off his lip. He considered the small sum of money he had left in his savings account. He'd planned on using it to pay the rent and some of his and Kathleen's expenses until he got his feet back under him, but now Wyatt's welfare was at stake. It seemed as though he'd spent his entire life bailing people out. First his father, now Wyatt.

"How about a down payment?" Dylan asked.

A trickle of sweat rolled down Felix's dark cheek. "How much?" the bookie asked.

Dylan jogged back to the truck and grabbed a checkbook from inside the glove compartment. He scrawled out a check for fifty thousand dollars and held it out for Felix to examine.

God, I hope this works, Dylan prayed.

"My company doesn't accept personal checks," Felix said, causing all the men around him to snicker.

"Look, I'll pay you fifty now in interest, and then another twenty-five when I pay you back the principal," Dylan said. "That's an extra seventy-five thousand in your pocket . . . in exchange for your time."

"I don't like to chase my money," Felix sneered, his gold and diamond tooth glinting in the sun.

"Five hundred and seventy-five thousand," Dylan said. "And we can put this baby to rest." Dylan held out the check toward Felix.

Please take it. Please just take the check.

Felix stared at the check as if it were a knife.

Dylan flashed a winning smile. "Do we have a gentlemen's agreement?"

Felix paused. He seemed to consider that Dylan referred to him as a "gentleman."

"Don't make me come back here," he said, crushing his finger into Dylan's chest. "I hate Texas."

Dylan allowed himself to exhale. He pointed down the dirt road. "About five miles north, when you reach the freeway, you'll find the best taco cantina in Texas. Mamacita's. You can't miss it. Her hot sauce will make a believer out of you."

Felix's wet tongue flicked against the gold tooth. He waved the check in the air: "If this bounces . . ." he began.

"It won't," Dylan said quickly.

Felix stared at Dylan, a hard stare.

"Look. I'm not stupid," Dylan said.

"I have a good feeling about you." Felix tapped the check against his hand. He motioned to his men, and they all climbed into the sedan and drove off.

Dylan grabbed Wyatt's outstretched hand and helped his younger brother stand up off the gravel.

"You okay, little brother?"

"You knocked the crap out of my eye," Wyatt grumbled. "But it was better coming from you than from them."

"Not a bad plan, right?"

"Nope."

Dylan and Wyatt trudged back to the truck. Dylan felt tired, suddenly. As if his body couldn't move. It had been a long day— what with burying Butch Grant, getting into an ugly fistfight with Wyatt, and then promising to pay a bookie five hundred and seventy-five thousand dollars in cash that he didn't have.

With great difficulty, Wyatt climbed into the truck and plopped down onto the passenger seat. "How are we gonna get the money?" he asked, as if he'd read Dylan's mind.

Dylan turned the key in the ignition and flicked on the radio.

I have an idea, he thought.

Twenty-one

Kathleen was in one of those moods. The mood for sex. She always lost herself with Dylan. It was so natural between them. But instead of sex, she was being probed in a different way altogether.

Dylan and Wyatt arrived back at the apartment late after midnight looking flush, bloody, and bruised.

Oh my God! Kathleen thought, when they trudged through the door.

"What on earth happened to you two?" She jumped from the couch in shock. Her canvas was laid out on the coffee table. She'd been painting a yellow crocodile in a purple swamp.

Dylan pointed to his busted lip. "You think this is bad, hon. You should see the other guy."

"What other guy?"

Dylan pointed at Wyatt, and they both broke up laughing.

Kathleen crossed her arms over her chest and began to tap her foot. The death march tap. Dylan and Wyatt stopped laughing.

"Did you get in a fight?"

Dylan motioned to his brother. "Bottom line, hon. Paul Newman over here owes this guy Felix five hundred thousand bucks," Dylan said. "And Felix wanted his money today."

Kathleen rushed over to Dylan and threw her arms around his neck. "Dylan Charles Grant! Thank God you're okay!" She shot a disappointed look at Wyatt. "This is your fault, you know. But I love you anyway."

Wyatt scraped his boot along the floor. Kathleen knew that Dylan's younger brother was a softie when it came down to it. Below that big, gorgeous hunk of an exterior.

"So these guys attacked you?" she asked, looking from Wyatt's face to Dylan's. Checking the dried blood under their noses and the bruises on their arms.

Dylan and Wyatt shot each other a quick glance. Kathleen knew that look. It meant they'd decided in advance to tell her a certain "version" of events.

"Yes," they both said in unison.

They're lying to me, she thought.

Kathleen took two steps backward and gave them a hard stare. She began to tap her foot again, but this time she did something even scarier. She gave Dylan and Wyatt the silent treatment. That is, she stopped talking altogether, and turned away from both of them. She knew they wouldn't be able to withstand the shame for long.

"Anybody want a Dr Pepper?" Wyatt asked. He walked over to the fridge, and Kathleen heard a can popping.

"Kathleen, you want a Dr Pepper?"

Kathleen didn't make a peep. This would really scare the crap out of them, she knew. It was only a matter of seconds before Wyatt came to his senses. She heard him sputter.

"All right, Kathleen. You win. Dylan and I had some words and it got out of hand."

Kathleen whirled around. "Figures," she said. "So you did this to *each other*?"

Wyatt held up his can of Dr Pepper. "Seemed like a good idea at the time."

Kathleen stared at Dylan. He was scratching at the bloodied bruise on his arm.

"So why did you lie?"

"Hey now, wild Kat," Dylan said, looking pointedly at her. "I'm not the only one hiding things. Eddie told me you paid the rent today. How'd you get that kind of money?"

Kathleen tossed her hair over her shoulder and wandered toward the bedroom. "Good night, Wyatt," she called out.

"Night, Kat."

Dylan was in hot pursuit, and as soon as they reached the bedroom, Kathleen shut the door behind them.

"You didn't tell me you had money tucked away," Dylan said, searching Kat's eyes.

"My mother once told me that every woman should have her own savings account . . . for rainy days." She gave Dylan a meaningful look. Even with his busted lip and bruises all over, her man was killer handsome.

"Listen here. I can take care of my woman. I don't need my woman paying the rent," Dylan huffed, all high and mighty. He began to pace in front of the bed.

Kathleen stifled a giggle. Her mother had taught her long ago that men needed to feel superior in order to maintain their confidence. It was all about ego.

Never go Dutch, her mama had instructed her. *They'll end up despising you for it.*

And so Kathleen used all her effort. She lifted up her shirt, flashed Dylan her breasts, and said, most bluntly, "Honey, I'd love to talk this money stuff all day long but we've got some fucking to do."

Kathleen jumped on top of the bed and spread her legs apart. She was wearing a short little denim skirt and white lace panties.

"I don't know if I can." Dylan winced as he unzipped his jeans and let them pool around his ankles. Kathleen helped him lift his shirt over his head and saw the black and blue bruises blooming across his ribs.

"You're a mess," she whispered.

"Tell me about it." Dylan tumbled down on to the bed next to her with his boxer shorts and socks on, and closed his eyes.

Kathleen pulled out a small bottle of baby oil from the bedside table and rubbed some in her palm. She snuck her hand inside his boxer shorts and began stroking up and down until she felt him become aroused. She shimmied off her white panties and flung them on the floor. Then she climbed on top of Dylan and glided him inside her.

"Oh, honey," he moaned, as Kathleen began sliding her hips around in a slow circle. Dylan gripped her waist and began to thrust himself in and out, hard and fast. They both moved together, with Kathleen bouncing faster on top of him. She grabbed the top of the bed frame for support, and threw her head back.

"Oh yeah. Just like that," Dylan moaned. Kat thrust herself down on top of him until his face contorted in pleasure and he stifled a cry.

"Oh, honey. I'm going to finish," he choked. Kat plunged down on top of him.

Afterward, Kat rested her body inside the crook of Dylan's warm embrace. She watched her big wounded bear's eyes droop close and he began to snore soundly.

I want to marry you, she thought.

Twenty-two

The next morning, Dylan woke with a renewed vigor. He knew that he'd failed to pleasure Kathleen last night. So he wanted to make it up to her.

He raced over to the bed and fumbled with the condom in his hand. He bit the edge of the square foil packaging, and ripped it open.

"Ladies and gentlemen, we have liftoff," he announced, staring at Kat's naked body lying across his king-sized Tempur-Pedic mattress. She was too much sometimes, Dylan thought. Lying on her back with her legs spread apart, revealing her private business through red crotchless panties trimmed in black lace. Kat had an array of fun panties at her disposal, and she wasn't shy in the least.

Kathleen scowled at the sight of the condom. Dylan glanced down and began to unroll it quickly before his mind got the best of him.

"We don't need those anymore," Kat said, shooting him a sad, puppy dog look. As if she were a woman bereaved, instead of a woman about to get good and laid.

Dylan stopped unrolling the condom and let it dangle. "C'mon, Kat. This isn't the best time to be thinking of children. Not with our cash flow predicament."

Kat propped her elbow up on the bed and stared at him. A hard stare.

"I have something to say . . ." she started.

Dylan shook his head.

Oh God, not this.

He snapped the condom off, threw it on the floor, and sat down next to her. Plunging his head into his hands, he let the unthinkable escape his lips, "You're already pregnant."

"Well, don't sound *too happy*," Kat shot back.

They never fought. Dylan considered how he never argued with this woman. This woman who filled his core with everything he'd ever lacked. No matter what had happened in their respective pasts, and a lot had happened, he and Kat had always been, like, teammates.

Dylan didn't have it in him to fight with her now.

"I'm thrilled, sweetheart," he said softly. He leaned over and kissed Kat on the forehead, inhaling the sweet scent of lavender in her freshly washed hair.

"You smell good," he said absently. A pit was beginning to form in his stomach as the news sank in.

"I'm not pregnant, dodo head," Kat said, bolstering her hand against her naked hip.

Dylan searched her eyes, noticing how her entire face had taken on an ashen expression. She wasn't smiling. Kat always smiled.

Something's wrong.

He took Kat's delicate hand in his. "Tell me," he said.

"I'm an empty vessel," Kat said.

Empty vessel?

Dylan knew Kat was artistic and everything. But sometimes he wished for plain English.

"Come again?"

"Empty. Like Hannah in the Bible."

Okay, this was pushing it. Was Dylan supposed to know who this Hannah person was? He scratched his chest and lay down naked next to Kat, so he could stare up at the ceiling.

"I'm not familiar—"

"Hannah couldn't have children."

Kat took a deep breath and sighed one of those weight-of-the-world sighs. "I can't have children, Dylan."

Dylan lay still on the bed. He never saw the rain cloud coming. But apparently the shit storm had arrived. Why, oh why, had everything gone south?

"You . . . can't . . . have . . . children," he repeated, in a low voice. He heard sniffling next to him, turned, and saw that Kat was trying to hold back the tears. This woman, for whom children meant the world, was barren?

What kind of cruel joke is this?

Kat wouldn't cry, Dylan knew. She'd been raised since birth to think crying was something of a sin in itself. An admission of weakness. A last resort.

A true Texas blue blood would let hell freeze over before shedding a single tear.

"How?" Dylan asked.

"My ovaries," Kat shrugged. "That cyst I had last year caused serious scar damage."

The sniffling had stopped. She'd regained the legendary King family facial expression—blasé.

She scooted toward him and rested her head on the crook of his shoulder. She felt warm and fragile all of a sudden, cuddling up to him like that.

"You're relieved from duty, Dylan. You don't have to marry me," she said, in a rather blasé, emotionless tone.

Dylan sat up abruptly and grabbed Kat by her elbows.

"Jesus, Kathleen! Are you breaking up with me? Yes, I'm broke. And yes, you know *for a fact* you can have any man around. But I'll take care of you better than anyone else, I swear. Give me time."

A glimmer of a smile streaked past Kat's lips. "You're pretty cute when you're all riled up," she said.

Kat began to stroke Dylan down below until he relaxed. She knew her way around him, that was for sure. He couldn't imagine lying in bed with anyone else. The thought disgusted him, actually.

Dylan took a deep breath and felt himself become aroused as Kat worked her usual magic. Rubbing him just the right way.

She was a daring little thing, all right.

"I'm not breaking up with you," she whispered. "But I can't have children, and I thought you'd like to know."

"I don't believe this," Dylan said. "When did you find out?"

"Tuesday."

Dylan nodded. The day he'd gone to the funeral home. *Figures*, he thought.

You've had a quite a week, champ.

In the past seven days, Dylan had found out that his father had been killed in a car accident; that he and his brother were broke and in debt; and that the woman he'd loved since the fourth grade couldn't bear children.

Dylan took a deep breath.

He only had one thought: *Make her laugh.*

"Don't worry about it, babe," he breathed into Kat's ear. "We can get one of those surrogate ladies, and I'll close my eyes and have sex with her," he teased.

Kat pinched him hard on his bare bottom. "I was thinking we'd adopt one of those African babies like Madonna did."

"*Argghh,*" Dylan moaned, as Kat's hands began to move faster and faster. "I'd rather have sex with the surrogate woman."

"That can be arranged, my dear."

Kat jumped off the bed, raced into the closet, and returned a moment later wearing a dark wig that she'd worn on Halloween one year, and Dylan's cowboy hat perched on top of her head.

"Ta-da," she said, posing in lace panties and a cowboy hat.

He watched in pleasure as she straddled him, crotchless panties and all, and began to rock back and forth, like a bucking cowgirl, on top of him. Last night had been good, but this was bound to be better. This time, Dylan concentrated on giving her pleasure as she thrust her hips back and forth. She felt so good and warm and wet sliding all over on top of him. He gritted his teeth and waited until she threw her head back and moaned loudly.

"Kathleen," Dylan whispered.

"Shhh." She pressed her finger to his lips. "You don't have to say it."

I love you, hon.

Twenty-three

Dylan zipped into the elevator wearing his morning costume. Jeans, flip-flops, and his new Zeus T-shirt, which had inexplicably become his favorite. He'd considered wearing a suit, but figured he didn't want to look too fancy for his coffee meeting with C. Todd Hartwell.

It was best to be rumpled, just out of bed, steaming cup of coffee in his hand. Dylan checked his watch. He was only fifteen minutes late.

Better to be twenty, he thought. But he'd already made it this far.

He rode to the ground floor of the Royal Arms and strode toward the conference room. Kat had made him a wickedly strong cup of Guatemalan brew, and for the first time this morning, Dylan regarded the mug.

Damn it, Kat! On this morning, of all mornings, she'd handed him a mug that read: "Best Boyfriend Award!"

She'd given him the mug as a stocking stuffer last Christmas. Dylan scowled and walked briskly toward the concierge desk, where he spotted Eddie gobbling a Whipley's chocolate glazed, and thinking no one was watching him.

"Morning, Mr. Grant!" Eddie sputtered, wiping specks of glazed sugar from his lips.

Dylan set the coffee mug on Eddie's desk. "Keep this for me."

Eddie eyed the mug's slogan. "Ah, Mr. Grant. She cares for you more than oxygen." The concierge sighed under his breath.

Enough is enough, Dylan thought. He decided not to allow these personal remarks to slide.

"What are you trying to say, Eddie?"

Eddie wiped his hand against his uniform pants. "Oh, Mr. Grant. I just like Ms. Kathleen so much."

So do I, Eddie. Dylan broke into a smile and thumped his fist against the concierge desk. "Don't you worry about Kathleen, Eddie. I'm going to do it right. I'm just waiting for my moment."

Eddie smiled broadly, revealing chocolate crumb–stained teeth.

Dylan pointed at the Whipley's doughnut box tucked behind Eddie's desk. "I thought you were going to lay off those things. Can't be good for your cholesterol."

"*Mr.* Whipley moved in last week, so I get them *for free.*" Eddie gleamed, as if he'd just won the lottery.

Dylan flinched. Eddie had never called anyone besides Dylan "Mr."

Only for Dylan had Eddie reserved the revered status of "Mr. Grant." But now Eddie was calling the doughnut guy "*Mr.* Whipley." Probably because the doughnut heir had moved into the penthouse.

Dylan wanted to ask Eddie what the Whipley heir looked like—was he short and stubby like a Napoleon-type fellow, or tall and striking and someone to worry about?

It would have to wait.

Dylan saluted Eddie and flopped down the hall toward the conference room. He clicked open the door, stepped inside, and was immediately overwhelmed by a smell. It was the scent of cheap cologne doused over skin as if the person were trying to put out a fire.

Well, well. What do we have here?

Dylan raised his eyebrows. Smiling up at him from the conference table was 1) C. Todd Hartwell; 2) Louisiana Steve—the Infectious Disease—wearing ten thousand gallons of Drakkar Noir; 3) and his own brother, Wyatt.

Jesus. Is the circus in town?

"Look who's decided to join us," C. Todd Hartwell said. He motioned for Dylan to take a seat next to Wyatt.

"No lie, dawg. You pull a stunt like that for a meeting with the brothers and you'd get a cap in yo' ass," Steve snickered, as if he were a black guy from Compton, and not a short little white dude from New Orleans.

Dylan noticed Wyatt was sitting at the head of the table, Big Swinging Dick that he was.

"Larry, Moe, Curly," Dylan shot back. He had a fleeting image of himself bolting from the conference room. Just turning on his heel and running out the door as fast as he could. But instead, Dylan plopped down into a chair next to his younger brother.

He was amused, if anything.

"Morning, brother," Wyatt said, clapping Dylan on his knee.

"I thought you were still asleep," Dylan said. He wondered what the Younger was up to.

Wyatt wants in on this deal, he thought.

"We've got one more joining us," C. Todd said, checking his watch.

Just then, a tall, elegant man dressed in a crisp suit and tie that made Dylan's mouth go dry stepped into the room.

"I'm Jonathan Whipley," the man announced, in a tone that sounded like Yale or Harvard or one of those other East Coast schools.

Everyone stood from the table to shake the glazed doughnut heir's outstretched hand, as if the king himself had arrived.

Dylan stood, too. He surveyed the man of the moment. Jonathan Whipley held himself with a certain grace. Dylan had seen this grace only twice before. In Cullen Davis King, and in Kathleen Connor King. It was something you either had or didn't have. And Dylan knew he didn't have it.

Nope. Not the son of Butch Grant.

He threw on his most engaging smile and said, "Pleasure to meet you, John."

The king paused and shot Dylan a crisp look. "I go by *Jonathan*," he said, eyeing Dylan's T-shirt.

Dylan blinked.

"Now that we're all here and we're all looking pretty, I'd like to get started," C. Todd Hartwell announced. He took a slug from a can of Red Bull.

Before Dylan knew what was happening, C. Todd Hartwell was passing maps around the table.

Dylan unfurled the map and stared. He'd heard the C. Todd Hartwell had a nose for finding out where the big minerals were located, but until this moment, he hadn't realized how good the oil promoter actually was. The map Dylan held in his hand had cost roughly three million dollars to produce. That's how much a seismic shoot at this depth would be. Dylan knew that C. Todd Hartwell didn't have that kind of cash. So this meant that the data was hot.

C. Todd Hartwell had stolen it or copied it or somehow gotten his grubby hands all over it.

Dylan noticed that the survey name and abstract number had

been blacked out. This meant that no one besides C. Todd knew where the minerals were located.

Smart, Dylan thought. C. Todd was clever, indeed.

In Houston, Texas, the race to drill was all that mattered. And, in the oil and gas business, there was never any trust. It wasn't that men weren't good on their word—it was just that there was too much money at stake—too many rolling factors to deal with—and too much competition. Greed would turn even a God-fearing pastor into a liar, and Dylan had seen it happen. With his own pastor, Father Bookings, who was now serving ten years in Huntsville State Prison for using church donations to fund his own oil and gas scam. Which was why Dylan never attended church anymore, and reserved his own charitable donations for Kathleen's hospital.

Dylan glanced around the room and quickly did the math. C. Todd Hartwell would be captaining the deal. The guy with the information was always the lead dog in the pack. In reality, C. Todd was part slick salesman and part thief. Rumor had it that he was good at wining and dining girls at big oil companies with access to the right files and to the office copy machine.

Steve the Infectious Disease would be the operator. Dylan was surprised to learn that Mr. Louisiana had started out as a roughneck, and then gotten experience at drill sites all over south Louisiana and the Gulf Coast.

Jonathan Whipley was an investor and would write a big check. And this left Dylan and Wyatt.

Why did C. Todd invite us to the meeting? Dylan wondered.

The oil promoter obviously believed that he and Wyatt had the backbone and the stomach for risky oil deals.

Houston was the biggest small town on the planet when it came to gossip. Dylan wondered if C. Todd had somehow found out about Wyatt's gambling losses. After all, it was the oil promoter's business to know everyone's business. And C. Todd probably figured that a guy who lost half a million in Vegas surely wouldn't blink at the idea of a risky oil investment.

Dylan leaned back in his chair and let his mind wander. He considered how he and Wyatt were both broke. The image didn't fit the reality. He also thought of Kat. Of Kat paying the rent. She had money tucked away somewhere, and he wondered if it was a lot. It had been a heckuva lot more before she'd decided to give it all away to her hospital.

Don't think about that. She's perfect. Even if she can't have children.

Dylan felt his throat tighten.

C. Todd began his presentation—he was circling the table like a hawk, and as he passed by, Dylan got a clear scent of Wild Turkey.

"So you fellas can see from this map that there is a huge untapped field out there that hasn't been drilled. I mean, no one is bothering to touch it—not Exxon, not Shell, none of the big guys. They're too interested in the offshore deals, so they don't want to waste their time on making this hole. But it's no small deal—I mean, we've got five guys in this room. And, if we're splitting it up five ways—and we turn it on, and it gushes like a dog in heat—then we're talking big money."

"What do you assume the production will be?" Jonathan Whipley asked. His tone was formal, as if he'd been private schooled all his life. Dylan wondered how a doughnut heir knew anything about oil wells. Maybe this wasn't Jonathan Whipley's first rodeo. Maybe he'd invested in some other oil deals before.

Or maybe he's faking it, Dylan thought.

"Good question," C. Todd replied, which made Dylan want to gag.

"Let's say we produce a quarter million barrels a day, then at today's prices, I figure we'll score checks of around a hundred thousand apiece each month."

C. Todd Hartwell crossed his arms over his burly chest, and Dylan noticed that his shirt had yellow sweat stains under the armpits.

"That's bad ass," Wyatt piped up, in traditional not-knowing-when-to-keep-his-mouth-shut Wyatt style. "Where do I sign?" Wyatt glanced theatrically around the table for a pen. The other guys cracked smiles.

Dylan peered at the seismic map again. *Something's wrong here,* he thought. He traced over each quadrant with the tip of his finger.

C. Todd, you sneaky sonofabitch.

"This data is incomplete," he blurted, which quieted the room.

"How do you mean, dawg?" Steve asked, scratching his cheek. Mr. Louisiana was sporting green suede pants and a leopard fedora perched sideways on his head.

"This is fringe data. See"—Dylan held up the map—"this part shows the edges of where the minerals are located. It's like a treasure map that's been ripped into two pieces. The other half—the important half—is missing. What we're looking at is the edges. We could drill all along the edges and never hit the big field."

C. Todd Hartwell stared at the floor like a man who'd just been busted.

Steve took off his sunglasses and threw them across the table.

"The other half of the map is locked up in Bo Harlan's office," C. Todd said, shrugging his shoulders. "But I plan to get it by this weekend."

Jonathan Whipley spun around in his chair. "Don't tell me you're stealing this data from another company."

"Who said anything about stealing?" C. Todd said, cracking his knuckles. "The information was mine to begin with. Bo Harlan took the map from me a few months ago in one of his poker games, so I'm going to liberate it back from him."

Dylan tried not to laugh. Here was a prime example of a thief pointing fingers at another thief. It was almost too much fun.

"How do you plan to get it?" Steve asked. He was drumming his fingers on the conference table now, and staring at C. Todd as if he were about to kill him. Dylan realized that Steve was actually kind of scary. The way people from Louisiana tended to be. Dylan figured they'd all been crossbred from pirates and Indians and slaves, which was why Cajuns were so artistic and weird and violent.

C. Todd dropped down into one of the chairs and sighed. It was obvious to Dylan that he'd been drinking the night before since the oil promoter was sporting the classic hung-dog hangover look. His cheeks looked flush with rosacea, and his eyes were dark and baggy underneath. When the oilman leaned forward across the table, Dylan could smell last night's Wild Turkey.

"My girlfriend works at Titan Energy," C. Todd admitted. "She's the secretary for the big boss man himself, and since she's so hot, Bo Harlan gave her a key to his office."

"Bo Harlan's office is probably covered in maps. How does *your girlfriend* know what she's looking for?" Dylan asked, which was the next logical question.

"She doesn't. So I've got a little sting operation planned for this weekend."

"Romantic," Dylan said.

"Problem is," C. Todd said, "I need help. And I hear from your brother that you guys aren't too pleased with Wild Bo, either."

Dylan shot Wyatt a disapproving look. It was one thing to discuss family matters with a money manager. It was quite another to discuss them with the biggest mouth in the city.

Jonathan Whipley jumped from his seat and managed to knock

his chair over. The sophisticated doughnut heir, with all his private school breeding and Harvard mouth, was looking flustered.

This pleased Dylan to no end.

"Count me out," Jonathan said. "I'm not going to be involved with anything illegal. Especially breaking and entering."

"This is the oil and gas business, man. Not the doughnut business. Everyone's hands are dirty. Goes with the territory," C. Todd announced. He produced a roll of breath mints and popped one in his mouth.

Jonathan Whipley stroked his tie. "I'm going to pretend I didn't hear this." He strode toward the conference room door. "Call me when you have more details and I'll decide whether I'm still interested."

C. Todd said, "Sounds like a plan."

As soon as Jonathan was out of earshot, C. Todd grinned. "Twenty bucks says he used to be an Eagle Scout."

"How do you plan on breaking into Bo Harlan's office?" Dylan asked.

C. Todd plopped his feet up on the conference table. He was wearing flip-flops, and his toes looked gnarly.

"My girl—she's got one of those electronic key cards to the entire building, and a key to Bo's private office. Problem is, he's a paranoid sonofabitch so he's got an alarm on his office door."

Nice, Dylan thought. So this is where Wyatt came in on the deal.

The younger Mr. Grant had spent two years living with a master burglar in Vegas. He'd learned a few tricks of the trade himself, like how to bypass car alarms, office alarms, and house alarms. Although Wyatt never used these burglary skills, Dylan considered it one of his younger brother's greatest talents.

Wyatt stared wide-eyed at the oil promoter. "How'd you know I could bypass alarms?"

The oil promoter chugged the rest of his Red Bull and burped loudly. "It's my job to know everything about everybody. But don't take it personal, man."

Wyatt stood from his chair and lumbered toward the doorway. "I'm hungry," he grumbled. "Let's go eat."

Twenty-four

The best steakhouse in town for chasing skirt was Smith & Wollensky, which was why it was nicknamed "Smother and Molest-Me." With its cheerful green and white sign beckoning patrons, Smith and Wollensky attracted a colorful and well-heeled lunch crowd. Usually there were a bunch of E&P guys, along with the women who loved them, and a sprinkling of plaintiffs' lawyers to keep everyone on their toes. The women running around the steakhouse during lunch were typically the type of girls who dress for a nightclub during the day. Lots of bustier tops, high heels, exposed cleavage, and hair extensions.

Dylan wasn't interested in these women, but the other guys wanted a meal with a view. *I guess I'll have to suffer*, he thought. Since the four men were planning a theft, it would've been smarter to choose a more out-of-the-spotlight locale. But the steak and potatoes were calling their names. And Wyatt said he was jonesing for béarnaise sauce.

Dylan, Wyatt, C. Todd, and Steve scored a cocktail table inside the bar, so they could watch the action. The lunch scene was in full gear by the time each guy ordered his steak, potatoes, and beer. And by scene, this meant the bustier-clad women frittering from table to table chatting with men they knew.

Dylan cut into his rare steak and watched the juices run out onto his plate.

"What kind of alarm system are we talking about?" Wyatt asked, grabbing the bottle of ketchup and smacking it until it dripped out over his French fries.

C. Todd's face assumed a grim expression. He'd obviously done his homework. "Passive infrared," he announced.

Wyatt sat back in his chair. "This should be interesting."

"What's the problem, dawg?" Steve asked. He was staring at a group of girls sitting at the table next to them, but managed to turn his attention back to Wyatt.

"Passive infrared alarms are used in museums, banks, and places where people want high security. It's not easy to penetrate because it detects thermal heat, like changes in body temperature," Wyatt said.

Dylan put his fork down. "Leave it to Bo Harlan to install a museum alarm system on his office door."

"So what should we do? Some smash and grab job?" Steve asked, his mouth full of steak.

C. Todd crushed a French fry with his fork. "Building security is too tight over at Titan. They'd have the police on us before we got off the elevator."

Dylan nodded. "It's better if Bo Harlan doesn't know anyone was poking around his office. Let him think that everything's fine."

"Shhh! Speak of the devil!" C. Todd hissed. Just then, Wild Bo himself strode past the table with a gorgeous woman trailing him. She was a redhead and she was wearing what looked like an outfit for a high-priced prostitute. Upon passing the table, she shot C. Todd a sly, sexy little look.

Hi baby, she mouthed.

C. Todd winked and mouthed the words, *See you later?*

She nodded and swooshed past them.

"That's one fine piece of *booty*," Steve said, in appreciation.

"Hey, that's my girlfriend you're talking about." C. Todd grinned.

Dylan watched Bo Harlan wade over to the largest banquet table in the bar, also known as the "power table." The oilman had ignored them, of course. Snubbed them as he'd walked by. Bo Harlan was short, squat, sweaty at all times, and had a shock of white hair running through his dark locks—*a powerful-looking little fucker*, Dylan thought.

The oilman surveyed the room and pretended not to see Dylan. He accepted one of the tall menus from the waiter who had appeared and was swirling around him.

Dylan was livid. Bo Harlan had seen him. And the oilman knew very well who Butch Grant's son was. It was just too much.

I think it's time I said hello, Dylan thought.

He leaped up from his barstool.

C. Todd held out his arm and tried to stop him. "Hey now! Let's not do anything stupid."

Dylan wrestled himself from C. Todd's grip and marched toward Bo Harlan's table. He was going to tell the oilman just where he could stick it. For stealing the last oil well in the Grant family, a well that had been named Clarissa after his mother—an oil well that Butch Grant, no matter how drunk or far down in a poker game—would never gamble away.

Even though he and Wyatt had been stripped of every last stitch of their inheritance, it wasn't about the money. That oil well was hallowed ground as far as Dylan was concerned. He'd rather plug the whole thing up before letting Bo Harlan touch one penny of his family's entitlement.

Before Dylan could reach the table, the room quieted. What had once been the click, clatter, and eruption of a boisterous lunch crowd suddenly became hushed. That's when Dylan spotted her. Walking through the throngs of people in the bar—it was as if the Red Sea had parted.

Kathleen Connor King had just graced Smith & Wollensky with her presence. And that presence was felt by everyone in the room. Dylan watched as the love of his life walked straight toward Bo Harlan's table. He was so stunned, he couldn't move. It was as if his entire body had gone paralyzed.

Kathleen hadn't spotted him among the bar crowd, so Dylan waited and watched.

Bo Harlan set his menu down and jumped to his feet. "Kathleen!" he boomed in a loud voice so everyone in the restaurant would know that it was he—Bo Harlan—whom the queen was here to see.

Kathleen flashed Harlan a dazzling smile that made Dylan nearly faint. She took a seat next to the oilman, and her movements were so fluid, so beautiful that now all eyes were on her. Bo Harlan's little redheaded secretary might as well have been a potted plant for as much attention as she was receiving. No, it was Kathleen who ruled the roost.

She was dressed exquisitely in what Dylan knew to be a ninety-nine-dollar dress. He knew because he'd bought it for her at a thrift store outside Luckenbach. It was hanging on a rack behind a bunch of T-shirts that read "I Got Lucky in Luckenbach," but leave it to Kathleen to find a gem among garbage. The dress looked like Roberto Cavalli and was made entirely of black Icelandic pony fur.

It was one hot little number, and Kathleen wore it like no one else could. Most women would look trashy in a dress like that, but not the granddaughter of Cullen Davis King. Kathleen made the dress look regal. As if she'd just stepped off the runway in Milan or Paris or New York.

What are you doing, Kathleen?

Dylan trudged back to his table. He felt Wyatt, C. Todd Hartwell, and Steve staring at him.

"What is Kat doing with Bo Freakin' Harlan?" Wyatt asked, posing the most obvious of questions.

"I'm sure it has something to do with the foundation dinner," Dylan said. He was thinking on his feet. Trying to save face.

Bo Harlan was eyeing Kathleen like a bird dog eyes a dove, which made Dylan angrier than hell, but he couldn't say much. After all, Kat was a sight to behold.

Maybe Wyatt had been right. Maybe Kathleen was heading for greener pastures. A woman like her needed to be kept in the way she'd been accustomed to. And Dylan was now flat broke.

The fact that he'd waited so long to ask her to marry him suddenly seemed foolish. *What the hell have I been thinking!*

"Let's keep our eye on the prize, fellas," C. Todd Hartwell said. He was trying to sway the conversation back to business. For him, business and whiskey came first. The women would follow.

Wyatt pushed his plate away. "I need a space heater and a Mylar suit," he announced. "Plus we need a getaway driver—someone who's good and fast—just in case we run into the police."

"Like that dude in *The Transporter.* I loved that movie," Steve said, licking steak sauce off his thumb.

"Exactly," Wyatt said.

Dylan was trying not to stare across the room at Kathleen. The love of his life had just leaned toward Bo Harlan and placed her delicate hand on his broad shoulder. The oilman was laughing at something she'd said, which made Dylan's hair stand on end.

"I know our getaway driver," Dylan said, absently. "His name is Achmed. And he's one of our valets."

Twenty-five

Kathleen was smiling through her teeth. She'd spotted Dylan, Wyatt, and C. Todd as soon as she'd walked in. They were sitting with the guy from Louisiana who lived in the building and who was always dressed a bit funky. Kathleen knew from Eddie, the building concierge, that Mr. Louisiana had left New Orleans after Hurricane Katrina and was rumored to be connected with a "rough element." Eddie had also informed her about Dylan's meeting this morning in the conference room with Jonathan Whipley.

Kathleen's mother had taught her to treat service staff like her own family, which was why Crazy Aunt Lucinda was now living in the King family home, and why Kathleen had taken Eddie to see Dr. Levin a few weeks ago. The fact that Eddie complained about a range of physical ailments concerned Kathleen, and so she'd had the foundation pay for Eddie to have every sort of test performed. The results were not surprising to Kathleen, but they were to Eddie. He was one hundred percent healthy. At most, he suffered from a mild case of bloating and high cholesterol from all the junk food.

Kathleen had given Eddie a good talking-to and sent him to a nutritionist to work up a diet that he could stick with. She knew he was still sneaking doughnuts in the mornings, but he'd gotten a heckuva lot better. He was eating salads for lunch, and walking a mile each evening when he got home from work.

In exchange, Eddie had taken it upon himself to "report" to Kathleen all activities occurring in and around the Royal Arms.

She'd known in advance that Dylan and Wyatt would be at Smith & Wollensky, because Eddie had overheard them talking about steaks and seen them all pile into C. Todd Hartwell's yellow Hummer.

Kathleen could feel Dylan's eyes boring a hole into the back of her head, but she was listening intently to Bo Harlan.

Certain women in Texas were known for having the warmest smiles and the coldest hearts. But Kathleen's smile was genuine. She listened for an hour as the oilman went on about his divorce, how much he loved his kids, etc., etc . . . how hard it was to find a woman who wanted to date him for him—and not for his checkbook.

Kathleen found herself liking Wild Bo. *Sure, he's a bit rough on the edges*, she thought. But despite what he'd done to Dylan and Wyatt, there was something sweet about Wild Bo.

Earlier that morning, when Bo Harlan's secretary had called requesting the lunch meeting, Kathleen had politely declined.

This was protocol. To make powerful men like Bo Harlan work for it—just as her mama had taught her.

Kathleen hadn't been surprised when a few seconds later, the phone rang again, and it was Wild Bo himself. He'd said, "Kathleen, I'm taking you out to Smith & Woll today and I won't take no for an answer." She'd just sighed into the phone and said she'd be there at noon.

Bo Harlan had just written a half-million-dollar check, and that kind of cash didn't come without strings. She was used to "doing the follow-up lunch." To find out what her big donors wanted from her.

Kathleen suspected why Bo Harlan had called her to lunch. The oilman was secretly interested in dating Shelby Lynn Pierce, even though Shelby Lynn was still technically married.

Everyone in Houston knew the marriage was on the rocks, especially after word had gotten out that Shelby Lynn's husband had been spotted in the elevator at the Lancaster Hotel with an Asian stripper. It was all people could talk about, even though no one was actually saying a word.

Bo Harlan was digging into his steak like a zoo animal at feeding time. He was in the middle of giving Kathleen his résumé. He'd grown up in a working-class family. He'd worked his way up in the oil industry, first working out in the fields, and then for a large energy company until finally breaking out on to his own. He'd made a lot of money and a lot of enemies, but—"Heck, Kathleen, this is the oil business, who hasn't?" Bo Harlan seemed to view himself as a maverick among men. A guy who'd gotten a bad rap because other men envied him, not because he was a thief nor a liar, nor any of these things. He was a damned good poker player. "And other men—well, Kathleen, they just can't handle losing."

Kathleen poked gingerly at her steak. She would've preferred the salmon, but Bo Harlan had insisted on ordering for both of them, and she didn't want to rob him of his chance to feel like the man in charge. *The food isn't important*, she thought. She could stop by the Smoothie Shack after lunch to tide herself over.

When Bo was finished delivering his biography of himself, Kathleen touched him on the shoulder and said, "Men like you are always in the crosshairs."

This seemed to please him to no end. The oilman's face reddened with delight, and his cheeks flushed pink. He cracked a smile and said, "Kathleen, you're wise beyond your years."

As they ate, Bo Harlan's secretary sat across from them in the booth and sipped quietly on a Diet Coke. She was well trained, that was for sure. And she didn't make a peep. It was just like Bo Harlan to show up at lunch with his "assistant" being present, so he could look super busy at all times.

"Would you like some dessert, my dear?" Bo asked Kathleen. She'd barely touched her steak, but had cut it in a few pieces to make it look as though she'd eaten.

Kathleen fluttered her eyelashes.

We could be here for another hour, she thought. The oilman obviously intended to drag things out.

"I'd love some," she cooed.

Bo Harlan made a big show of getting the waiter's attention, and then ordered one of everything off the dessert menu. Kathleen leaned over and told him she would love a cappuccino.

"And a *cappuccino!*" Bo roared, startling the waiter, who nearly capsized his tray of drinks for another table.

Kathleen giggled and covered her mouth. "You're too much fun."

Bo Harlan wiped his napkin against his lips and plopped it on the table. Then, remembering the company he was with, he grabbed the napkin and set it back on his lap.

"I met your grandfather once," he said.

Oh dear, Kathleen thought. *Here it comes.*

"A long time ago. Heck. I was just a kid. Couldn't have been more than twenty-two, twenty-three years old."

Kathleen raised her eyebrow. *Not this again.*

She'd heard different versions of the same story hundreds of times. The story about how her grandfather had given a speech that inspired hundreds of impressionable young men to seek a better life for themselves, and to find their own destiny, out in the mineral fields of Texas.

Martin Luther King had a dream.

John F. Kennedy had "*Ich bin ein Berliner.*"

Ronald Reagan wanted to "tear down that wall."

Cullen Davis King spoke of "churning and burning." Ah, the joys of tapping thousands of feet under the earth to discover new mineral fields.

"It was a speech he gave at the Petroleum Club," Bo Harlan began. Kathleen glanced at the ruddy-faced oilman and saw that his eyes were tearing up.

"And I'll never forget what he said that day."

"Tell me," Kathleen prompted. She knew the speech by heart because her mother had written it. She'd read it to Kat over and over while Aunt Lucinda brushed her hair, bathed her, and got her ready for school.

"He said the most important thing in a young man's life was to establish a credit, a reputation, and a character."

Kathleen nodded. "I know this speech well," she said.

"I bet you do."

Kathleen took a small sip from her cappuccino. She touched her fork to the cheesecake on the table and took a small nibble.

"Those words were actually first spoken by John D. Rocke-feller," Kat said, adding, "My grandfather was a fan."

Bo Harlan rocked in his chair. "From one oligarch to another." As if on cue, he stuck his fork into the chocolate cake and gobbled about half of the slice in one huge bite.

Kathleen wondered when Bo Harlan was planning to make his move. So she decided to hurry things along.

"Thank you for lunch, Bo. I've had a lovely time."

"I'm glad you could find the time," Bo Harlan said. "I know that the Houston charity circuit must keep you awfully busy. I mean, I see your photos in every magazine around. Can't be easy being a philanthropist on the move. So, tell me again. Who's going to be sitting at my table? I forget."

"I haven't quite worked out the final table arrangements, but I did want to introduce you to *my dear friend*, Shelby Lynn."

"I'd love to meet her," Bo said, adding quickly, "and her husband, of course."

Bingo, Kat thought.

"Oh goodness. Tate never comes to these things. Shelby comes by herself, poor thing. Which is such a shame because we have a nice band there and Shelby loves to dance, but she never does—unless it's with the girls."

"That's too bad . . . that she doesn't have anyone to dance with," Bo Harlan stuttered.

"I'll tell you, she is such a treasure. She helps me plan the entire event from soup to nuts. Did you know that she's a fantastic decorator? I mean, that woman has an eye, I tell you."

"Really?" Bo drawled out the word so it sounded like *Reeiiilee?*

Kathleen knew that she needed to tread carefully. Since Shelby Lynn was still officially married, Kathleen couldn't set her up on a date. All she could do was dangle a fish in front of Bo Harlan, but it was up to him to take the bait. She couldn't spell it out for him any clearer. Luckily, the oilman was clever.

"You know, that reminds me," he said. "I've been meaning to hire a decorator for my office. Last month, they did a spread in *Houston Modern Luxury* magazine but I don't like how it turned out. I asked them to come back for a reshoot next week."

Kathleen pressed her hand to her chest. "Oh my gosh, Shelby would be perfect for the job! But it doesn't sound like we have much time."

"Could you ask her if she's interested?"

"Consider it done." Kathleen stood, kissed Bo Harlan on the forehead, and cascaded out the door. She was glad that Dylan had left the restaurant. She could deal with him when she got home. Until then, she was on a mission.

Twenty-six

"Did you see that movie, *The Thomas Crown Affair?*" Wyatt asked.

"Love Steve McQueen," Steve grunted.

"Not the original, I'm talking about the remake. With Pierce Brosnan and that hot chick. They used a heater to steal the painting," Wyatt said. "Just like we're about to do."

Dylan glanced around. He and the three stooges were in Home Depot. Their mission: acquire a large space heater.

"How does it work, dawg?" Steve asked. He was wearing white sunglasses inside Home Depot. Mr. Super Fly.

"We need to raise the temperature around the alarm so it doesn't detect the change in my body temperature when I go to disarm it."

"How do you know this stuff?" Steve asked.

Wyatt shot Steve his movie star smile. "My former roommate was a bank robber. He was famous for pulling off some of the hardest bank jobs that the cops have ever seen—well, he needed a place to stay for a while, so I put him up. We sort of became buddies, and went to casinos a few times, and he showed me the tricks of the trade. Just for fun. Then he up and disappeared." Wyatt began counting out on his fingers. "I figure he's either dead, in jail, or sittin' on his millions in Mexico."

Dylan pointed to a huge box on the bottom shelf.

"Is this the one?" he asked.

"It's gotta be at least three hundred and fifty thousand BTUs," Wyatt said.

Dylan checked the box. "Yep. Here we go. On the count of three . . ." Dylan, C. Todd, and Steve lifted the heater box and struggled to make it to the cash register.

"You wanna give us a hand with this, dawg?" Steve asked Wyatt.

Wyatt trailed behind the three of them, and Dylan grimaced. Most people didn't know about Wyatt's fake leg, but since the four men had bonded over steaks and potatoes, Wyatt decided to pull up the leg of his jeans and show them the prosthetic. Right inside Home Depot.

"Shit, dawg! I'm sorry. What happened? You get nailed by a shark or something?"

"Yeah, something like that," Wyatt said.

Dylan watched his brother limp slowly through the store aisles, and his mind flashed back to the fishing trip. They were only kids at the time.

"We're gonna go blastin' and castin', boys!" Butch Grant *shouted, chugging down whiskey and chasing it with beer. Blasting and casting was a well-known Texas pastime that involved shooting birds while simultaneously fishing from a small motorboat and drinking Miller Lite or Bud straight from the can.*

*Butch had rounded the boys into a small leaky boat,
set out for the middle of Sabine Lake, and once in the
deep water, tossed his sons overboard. Then Butch Grant
had told them to swim. Fast! He'd slurred. He'd cast a
fishing rod out, letting it sail over the boys' heads, and
then took aim with his shotgun and started shooting fish.
Wyatt's leg got in the way of a speckled trout.*

*Dylan remembered his brother screaming, the blood
rising up in the water just like in the* Jaws *movie, both
of them treading to stay afloat. He remembered how his
father yelled that Wyatt was just a "lil' whiney girl who
needed to stop cryin'." And then Butch Grant had done
the unthinkable. He'd set off in the motorboat, leaving Dylan and Wyatt to make it to shore on their own.
Wyatt, losing blood. Dylan, his arm around his younger
brother's neck, dragging him onto the pebbly shore, the
rocks as jagged as broken bottles beneath their feet.*

Maybe he wasn't quite Hitler, Dylan thought. But still. Butch
Grant was better off dead.

When they reached the cash register, Dylan felt his body retreat
into a cold sweat. He had no way of paying for the space heater.
C. Todd Hartwell had already sprung for lunch, and in guy terms,
this meant that the next round was on someone else.

Dylan looked at Wyatt, who shrugged helplessly.

The cashier rang up the total and it wasn't cheap.

Steve reached for his wallet. "Wanna split this, dawg?" he
asked Dylan, which made things more embarrassing. Just last
week, Steve had seen Dylan drive up to the Royal Arms in a
million-dollar car. And now what? Dylan couldn't spring for half
of a damned appliance?

"I'll spring for the Mylar suit," Dylan said, thinking on his feet. "Wyatt and I will order it off the Internet and I'll put a rush on delivery."

"I need one with a hood," Wyatt piped up.

Steve reluctantly pulled out a few Benjamins from his alligator money clip, and flung them toward the cashier.

"Keep the change, doll," he told her.

Hauling the heater into the parking lot, Dylan and Steve worked furiously to cram the large box inside C. Todd's Hummer. It barely fit but they finally squeezed in around it.

"We look like idiots," Dylan remarked.

"You're the one wearing a Zeus T-shirt," C. Todd Hartwell said smugly.

"Yeah," Dylan retorted. "Because I'm the Greek god of fuck-ups."

When they arrived back to the Royal Arms, Dylan made everyone swear a pact. "We've got to promise we're not gonna go shooting our mouths off."

Dylan cast an eye toward C. Todd Hartwell. "Can we trust your girl?"

"She's gonna give me the key after she locks up on Friday. I told her I'd take her to Cabo," the oilman said, rolling his eyes.

"Good. Then it's settled." Dylan flagged down Achmed. "Gentlemen, let me introduce you to our getaway driver."

Achmed ran to the Hummer. When he arrived in front of Dylan, he was breathless.

"Hello, Mr. Grant. What may I do for you?"

Dylan decided not to beat around the bush. "The four of us are going to steal some shit from this guy's office."

Achmed scuffed his black shoe along the pavement. "Why are you telling me?"

"We need a getaway driver, and I thought you'd be interested."

"One thousand dollars. Flat," Achmed said.

Funny, Dylan mused, *how everyone was a capitalist.*

"Saturday," Dylan said. All the men stuck out their hands and shook on it.

Twenty-seven

Kathleen adhered to the mantra of "Those with Family Names."

These rules were hard and steadfast and were taught nearly at birth by *mothers* of "Those with Family Names":

Rule number one: Never apologize.

(As in, "Sorry I'm late." Or, "Sorry, I forgot to call you back.")

Rule number two: Never explain.

(Explaining is unnecessary for Those with Family Names. As in, "The reason I couldn't join you at the luncheon is that I was having my eyelashes filled." Or, "I'm dressed like this because I just got back from the gym.")

Rule number three: Never lower your chin.

(As in, Never look at the floor. Never stare at your feet. Never show humility. For example, if you have an awful blemish on your forehead the size of Oklahoma and happen to be caught wearing tatty jogging clothes and no makeup in line at Starbucks, you must, under every circumstance, maintain the strength of character from within—so that by the time the Gucci finishes sizing you up, she wishes she had a blemish on her forehead, tatty jogging clothes, and no makeup on. In fact, this Gucci—in her little Marni pants and Chloé top—should feel drastically overdressed to be in line at Starbucks at this hour. This Gucci should lower her head in shame, and rush back to her Range Rover, head low to the ground.)

The problem was . . . this Gucci happened to be Shelby Lynn Pierce. And while being a King beat being a Pierce on any day of the week, Kathleen would show her girlfriend due respect.

Upon leaving Smith & Wollensky, she'd called Shelby Lynn and asked her to meet for an afternoon tea. It would be difficult broaching the subject that everyone was talking about but pretending not to—that is, the subject of Tate's blatant infidelity.

But Kathleen wanted to know for sure whether Shelby was "back on the market." This was information she needed. And she didn't want to disappoint Bo Harlan by giving him false hope.

Kathleen had considered that Shelby and the oilman might make a good match. It was just something she felt. An intuition about their respective personalities.

Kathleen's main reason for inviting Shelby Lynn for tea was to ask if she wanted to decorate Bo Harlan's office for a photo shoot with *Houston Modern Luxury* magazine.

This request was a no-brainer. Shelby Lynn would drop everything for the job. And not because she needed the money. The Houston socialite was from one of the most prominent families in the city, with the Pierce Building downtown, the Pierce wing on the new contemporary arts museum, and the Pierce Library at the university.

What Shelby Lynn Pierce desperately wanted was *recognition*—recognition for her talent as a decorator, a "theme-tress," if you will. Her taste was big, expensive, and over-the-top, but it fit her personality to a T. Shelby Lynn was all about flair. Which was why Kathleen was startled when she saw this most famous of Pierces appear inside the Starbucks wearing the Marni pants, the Chloé top, and . . . a diamond tiara.

Kathleen stood from her seat and tried not to let her jaw drop. "Shelby, how darling you look," she said. Shelby fluttered up to the table and gave her two dramatic cheeky air kisses.

"I'm starting a new line of tiaras," Shelby said, easing into her chair and dropping her oversized Chanel bag onto the floor. "And I'm using real diamonds, of course."

She took the tiara off her head and handed it across the table to Kathleen. "Try it," she commanded.

Kathleen giggled and said, "Don't mind if I do." She placed the tiara on her head and said, "It's mine now, Cinderella, and I'm not taking it off."

Shelby smiled and tugged at her large diamond chandelier earring. "Keep it for a while, girlfriend. It suits you."

Although Starbucks wasn't known for having table service, Shelby Lynn motioned to the guy behind the counter to bring her a tea, as well. He nodded and left a line of customers to deliver Shelby her tea nice and hot.

"Mmmm. Tazo chai with honey. Just like I like it, Tom," Shelby said, smiling up at the barista.

He blushed and said, "Thank you, Shelby Lynn."

Kathleen tried not to smile. Shelby Lynn was good. She could have someone serve her tea and then thank her for the privilege.

She and Bo Harlan would make a good pair, indeed. It wasn't that they were mean or bad people in the least, it's just that it was difficult for a super hyped-up Type A personality to find his or her equal in this world.

Shelby Lynn took a sip from her tea and said, "Tate and I had sex."

That ends that, Kathleen thought.

"When?" she asked.

"Last year," Shelby Lynn drawled, and then laughed. "I just read this research study on Google. Did you know that twenty million married couples in the United States have sex less than ten times a year?"

"So they're more like roommates?"

Shelby Lynn slapped her palm against the table. "Exactly."

Kathleen eyed her friend. "What's wrong, honey?"

"You know as well as I do—as well as the entire world." Shelby shrugged. "Everyone knows about Tate and his little affair at the Lancaster."

"Is it serious?" Kathleen asked. She'd long since believed Tate was a scoundrel.

Shelby Lynn pursed her lips. "He moved into a suite at the Hotel ZaZa last month. The last I heard, he was getting on a flight with her to Miami."

Kathleen shook her head. This just wasn't right. It was one thing to have a quiet affair, but quite another to leave the mother of your two children while you jetsetted off to south Florida.

Shelby Lynn summoned the guy behind the counter, and he nearly toppled over himself trying to get to the table. She held up two perfectly manicured fingers. "I'll have two slices of lemon pound cake for me. Kathleen, you want anything?"

Kathleen knew it would be verboten not to indulge, especially since Shelby Lynn was about to do the unthinkable by eating not one, but two! slices of cake.

"I'll have the blondie," she said.

"Coming right up," the barista guy said, as if he were working at a five-star restaurant. A moment later he reappeared with the snacks.

Shelby Lynn smiled up at him and said, "You are the sweetest thing, Tom," to which he once again replied, "Thank you, Shelby Lynn."

Kathleen picked a piece of coconut off the top of her blondie and flicked it into her mouth.

She watched as Shelby Lynn—who never ate anything—gobbled up both slices of pound cake in a matter of seconds.

"I think I'm going to be sick," Shelby said, after it was over.

Kathleen lowered her voice. She reached her hand out and touched Shelby gently on her wrist. "Shelby, you can't stay at home and mope. You are a young, beautiful, *vibrant* woman with a great head on your shoulders. It's time you did something for yourself for a change."

Shelby Lynn burped and covered her mouth. She was wearing a huge antique ruby on her wedding finger, instead of her diamond band.

Kathleen took a deep breath. "Shelby, I would love if you helped me plan the foundation dinner this year."

Shelby sat back in her chair and tried to hide her emotion. For a woman of her stature, blasé was the way. But Shelby broke out into a gleaming super-white smile.

"I have so many great ideas!" she tittered. "I mean, the whole harem girl and camel theme is over. And people have killed the biker ball disco. I was thinking we could do something more along the lines of 'New Discoveries.'"

"I like that," Kathleen said.

For the next few minutes the two women discussed the dinner, and then Kathleen brought up Bo Harlan's office-redecorating project.

"Wild Bo. Ick." Shelby Lynn wrinkled her nose at the sound of his name, and let out a small burp.

"He's not bad. In fact, I had lunch with him today," Kathleen admitted. She knew that if Shelby Lynn hadn't heard about Kathleen's appearance at Smith & Wollensky by now, the society princess would certainly hear it from the grapevine by the time dinner rolled around.

"You did not!"

Kathleen held up her hand. "As God is my witness."

"What's he like?"

"Short, clumsy, and one heck of a talker. But you know something, Shelby, I sort of like him. I mean, I know he's a shrewd businessman who's screwed everybody under the sun, including Dylan's father, but you know how those boys play when they get in the mud." Kathleen bit her lip. "I don't know. Maybe he's got a bad reputation because he wins all the time."

Shelby Lynn thought for a moment. "Okay, Kathleen. Tell him I'll do it." She wagged her finger in Kat's direction. "He's got to pay me, of course, just like he'd pay any other professional decorator."

"Of course he'll pay you, silly." Kathleen knew Bo Harlan would pay Shelby twice the going rate, if not more.

"How about this weekend?" Shelby asked.

Kathleen smiled. "Sounds perfect."

Shelby Lynn took a sip from her tea, bent sideways over the table, and threw up into her Chanel purse.

Twenty-eight

Kathleen arrived back at the apartment and found Dylan sitting on the bed in his boxer shorts. Her heart melted at the sight of him, looking boyish and vulnerable and sexy all at once. Without his shirt, Dylan's chest was perfect. Not too hairy, and cut with fine, lean muscles that rippled down his abdomen.

He looked up at her and said, "Why are you wearing a crown?"

Kathleen rushed into the bathroom and checked herself in the mirror. She'd completely forgotten about Shelby Lynn's tiara. In fact, she'd left Shelby Lynn more than three hours ago and run several errands around town. She'd picked up the dry cleaning, bought milk, and zipped into the post office . . . in a tiara.

"Oh Lord," Kathleen said, plucking the tiara off her head and setting it on the bathroom counter. She spritzed herself with a small dab of perfume and brushed her teeth.

She walked back into the bedroom and kissed Dylan on the top of his head. He moved away from her and scowled.

"I saw you at lunch today," he announced, as if it were some surprise.

"I saw you, too, honey," Kathleen said sweetly.

For a moment, Dylan's face measured a range of emotions. He seemed flustered at first, shocked, and finally, angry. Kathleen could tell he was mad because Dylan always stared down at his feet when he was angry, and never looked her directly in the eye. It was if he couldn't stand the sight of her.

"Bo Harlan! Bo Harlan of all people! Here I am telling you about what he's done to my family, how he stole the Clarissa from my dad, and the next thing I know, I see my woman having lunch with him! He's the reason we're broke, you know!"

Kathleen took a deep breath. The rules didn't seem to apply when it came to her man. The rules of never explain, never apologize, and never show humility. But she wasn't going to go down without a fight. Dylan had to start learning how to trust her judgment. She was no wallflower. And if that was what he wanted in a woman, he could find someone else.

"Don't get your knickers in a twist," Kathleen said firmly.

Dylan jumped off the bed. In his boxer shorts, he looked so fine, Kathleen really wanted to leap on top of him. So she attempted just that. She lunged toward him, threw her arms around Dylan's neck, and tried to kiss him, but he pushed her away.

He was holding on to her wrists so tightly, it startled Kathleen.

"Let go of me!" she squealed.

Dylan clapped his hand over her mouth and whispered in her ear. "Be quiet or you'll wake Wyatt up, and that's the last thing I need!"

Kathleen nodded her head and Dylan let go of her wrists. She'd never seen him this riled up before. He was pacing in front of the bed. Stomping, more like it.

"Bo Harlan is *not that bad*," Kathleen said. She knew it was the wrong thing to say. She knew it as soon as the words tumbled from her mouth. But she couldn't help herself. It was the truth. And she always spoke the truth.

"Not that bad? *Not that bad, Kathleen!*" It was now Dylan who'd raised his voice. His entire body was shaking as he circled in front of the bed like an alligator on a leash.

Kathleen thought he looked so adorable that she had to stop herself from giggling. She'd only make him angrier if she laughed.

"He's really pulled the wool over your eyes, hasn't he, Kathleen? I mean, you're a smart woman. Don't you see what he's trying to do? He's using you!"

"Of course he is, honey."

Dylan stopped in his tracks. "I can't believe you go and meet him in public! In front of me, and all the world to see? Do you realize how many people are going to be talking about you, Kathleen? Behind your back?"

"Bo Harlan just wrote a half-million-dollar check for the foundation," Kat said. She realized, suddenly, that she was tired. It had been a long day.

"And you invited him?"

Kat pulled her dress up over her head, stripped off her panties, and kicked off her shoes.

"Don't try it," Dylan warned. "I'm not in the mood."

"I'm tired." Kathleen sighed and walked over to the nightstand. "I'm getting ready for bed." She pulled one of her T-shirts from the drawer and put it on. Dylan's antics were trying her patience. She needed to end this.

Dylan continued his frantic pacing.

Kat climbed into the bed, flipped on the reading light, and picked up a novel she'd been reading.

"So it's like that," Dylan said.

Kathleen placed the book in her lap and looked at him. "You need to trust me," she said. "I'm not some idiot, you know."

"I . . . I . . . Kathleen . . . I didn't mean . . ."

It was almost too cute, really.

Kathleen took off her T-shirt, and threw it on the floor. She began rubbing her breasts and making funny kissy faces at him.

"Is this how you're gonna behave every time I try to have a serious conversation?" Dylan asked. He crossed his arms over his chest, but Kathleen could tell that the lust was starting to set in.

Men, she thought. *So easy.*

"Honey, I love you, and I agree that Bo Harlan has a bit of the devil in him, but so did your dad—and honestly, no one knows the real story. *Not even you.*"

Dylan stared at the floor. When he finally spoke, his voice was barely audible.

"Listen to what I'm telling you, Kat. When Wyatt and I were kids, Bo Harlan and my dad played poker. Well, there was this one time. Dad was drunk, as usual, and things got out of hand. Bo had brought some guys with him, and they had guns."

"Did it ever occur to you that Bo Harlan was afraid of *your dad*?"

It was a fair question. Dylan's father had been a mean drunk. An out-of-control, abusive loser in Kathleen's opinion. Which was why Wyatt was missing the bottom part of his leg below the kneecap. It was a wonder that child protective services hadn't rescued them as kids, but Dylan and Wyatt had been so scared, they'd lied out of their teeth and said the fishing incident had been an "accident."

Dylan shook his head. "I can blame Dad for a lot of things, Kathleen, but that doesn't make what Bo Harlan did right."

"I know, sweetie," Kathleen whispered. She patted the bed next to her. "Come to me."

Dylan hung his head. His eyes seemed tired, too. Kathleen knew that the recent financial pressures had been stressful for him. He collapsed onto the bed, rolled toward her, threw his arm around her, and squeezed her tight.

Kathleen loved it when they were like this. Fitting so perfectly together in each other's arms.

She felt Dylan's hot breath against her ear.

"I'm worried about us," he said. "Worried about our future."

Kathleen turned and faced him. She looked into his eyes and stroked his cheek with her hand. She couldn't tell Dylan about the salary she was taking from the hospital—and how Bo Harlan's money was funding them for a little while until they landed on their feet. She couldn't tell him this because it would make him feel bad. Even though he'd been taking good care of her for years, Dylan's Achilles' heel was his pride.

Kat considered all that this man had done for her. It was Dylan who'd been by her side at her mother's and her father's and her grandpapa's funeral. Dylan who'd helped with all the arrangements. Dylan who supported her mission to fund the hospital. And Dylan who showed her the type of compassion and love that other woman could only dream about.

Kat stroked her hands through Dylan's hair, and watched as his eyes closed.

"It's time for someone to *help you* for a change," she murmured. But he was already fast asleep.

Twenty-nine

Dylan awoke before Kathleen, which surely set some kind of Guinness record. He knew what he needed to do. There was no time for delay.

Skipping his usual shower and shave routine, Dylan walked straight to his closet and threw on a pair of jeans, boots, and his cowboy hat. He tiptoed past the bed, slid open his sock drawer, and rummaged around until his fingers found what he was searching for. The Ziploc baggie was inside one of the socks. He pulled it out and stuck it in his pocket.

Dylan rushed downstairs and jumped in the truck. He washed it, filled it up with gas, and drove to the supermarket to get some flowers.

Kat was a daisy girl. She wasn't big into roses, but Dylan chose a red rose anyway because it meant love. He grabbed a bundle of daisies, too, just to make her smile.

Then he jumped back in the truck and drove to the bakery she loved and bought two croissants, some banana nut bread, blueberry muffins, jams, juices, the whole shebang, and had the counter guy pack it up like a picnic. While he was waiting, he downed a cup of strong coffee and asked for another, which he drank right after that.

He was wired now, and he could barely wait to wake her up.

Dylan raced back to the Royal Arms, and instructed the valets to keep the truck running.

As he strode past the concierge desk, he pointed at Eddie. "Today's the day, my man," Dylan said, and winked.

Eddie broke into a broad grin. "You mean it?"

"Yep," Dylan said. "But mum's the word."

"Ms. Kathleen will be so happy, Mr. Grant." Eddie sighed.

When Dylan stepped back into the apartment, Kat was awake and making coffee. She was wearing her nightshirt and a pair of burnt orange sweatpants that read, "Go Longhorns!" across the rear.

"You're up early," Kat announced. "Coffee?"

"We're going on a road trip," Dylan said. "So I need you to get ready."

"Oooh!" Kathleen clapped her small hands. "Should we invite Wyatt?"

Dylan shook his head. Wyatt would love having a day to himself loafing on the couch watching football, or doing whatever it was that Wyatt did to entertain himself.

"I want it to be just the two of us." Dylan patted the Ziploc bag in his pocket to make sure it was still there. "C'mon, Kat, let's giddy up and go."

"What should I wear?"

"You need your snake boots," Dylan said, even though he knew this would spoil the surprise.

Kathleen squealed. She could barely contain her excitement. She jumped up and down on the kitchen tile and then ran to the bedroom. Within what seemed like thirty seconds, she was ready.

Dressed in jeans, snake boots up to her knee, a white cotton T-shirt, and on her head . . . the diamond tiara.

"Nice look, hon." Dylan chuckled.

Kathleen giggled and covered her mouth. "I thought we could take some funny pictures."

Camera! He'd forgotten all about that. "Thanks for reminding me," he said. Dylan grabbed the digital and ushered Kat out the door.

"Right this way, Queen Elizabeth."

She gave him a playful slap on the arm. "Stop it."

They reached the elevator, and Kat turned to him and smiled. "I know where we're going."

"Wasn't hard to figure out."

"We haven't been to the ranch in ages," she said. "What made you all of a sudden want to drive to Tangled Spur?"

"You'll see. It's a surprise."

Kathleen crossed her arms over her chest. "If there's a for sale sign on the property, you're a dead man."

Dylan threw his head back and laughed. He grabbed Kat around the waist and squeezed her butt cheeks. "Too much sass and not enough *ass*," he said.

"Don't you worry about that," Kat said, shooting him The Look.

Dylan would've dropped trou and taken her in the elevator right then, but by that time, the elevator doors whooshed open and they'd reached the lobby.

And besides, the sex could wait.

Thirty

Kat wondered what all the fuss was about. When Dylan opened the door of the truck, she saw the flowers draped across the passenger seat. The white daisies weren't wrapped in your standard green tissue paper, but instead were loosely spread all over the place. In the center lay a single red rose.

"Dylan!" Kat kissed him on the lips. She wondered what the protocol was for loose flowers spread inside a truck. Was she supposed to sit on them during the ride? Or pick them up one by one and lay them on the dashboard?

Dylan grabbed the flowers up in one big bundle, held them under Kat's nose as a bouquet, and commanded her, "Smell."

"Lovely," she said, confirming the smell. Dylan smiled and then threw the flowers over the seat into the back of the pickup.

There go my daisies, Kat thought. She knew the flowers would not be able to withstand a two-hour journey in the Texas heat. But it wasn't her business to start taking over. This was Dylan's show.

"Climb in," Dylan said.

Kat noticed that her boyfriend was looking quite smug this morning. More so than usual.

She climbed into the truck and switched on the radio. Immediately a song came on. If any song could be considered "their song," this was it. Dylan had obviously gone and bought the CD to surprise her.

It was Don Williams. It was the song Kat and Dylan sang to each other sometimes when either of them was feeling blue that day. It was "Lord, I Hope This Day Is Good."

Kat clicked her seat belt, sat back in the truck, and realized that Dylan was about to break up with her.

After all these years, he'd suddenly decided it was time to sow his wild oats somewhere else. Kat wondered if her lunch with Bo Harlan had somehow lit a fire under Dylan's butt, and got him thinking about life without her. Certainly seeing her with another man had put Dylan ill at ease.

Dylan jumped into the driver's seat. Kat remained silent as he pulled the truck away from the Royal Arms and steered out toward the highway.

They had such a long history together that Kat could barely believe what was about to happen. She imagined the events that were about to unfold.

Dylan would drive her out to her grandfather's ranch—which was now technically her ranch. The Tangled Spur was the perfect place for him to drop a bomb of such mega-proportions.

He would start by telling her how much he loved her, and would always love her. Then, he'd shower her with compliments about what a great person she was and blah, blah, blah.

Then he'd say, *Kathleen, I brought you out here because I need to tell you something. I can't be in this relationship anymore. It's not fair to me that you're barren. I've always imagined myself having a wife and kids. But I hope we can remain close friends.*

Kathleen stared out at the scenery whizzing by. The Don Williams song ended, and Kat reached for the radio and switched it off.

When the doctor told her about the cyst on her ovary, Kathleen had known in an instant that her and Dylan's relationship might come to an abrupt end. It wasn't that he didn't love her, it was just that Dylan had always spoken about being a father—a better father than his own father had been. It was as if he had something to prove.

"You hungry, hon?" Dylan asked. He reached behind her, pulled out a sack with the Kraft Bakery logo, and plopped it in her lap. Her favorite breakfast in the whole wide world. This was so Dylan. To end things on such a kind note by making her feel special, by making her know just how much he cared.

"Dig in, Kit Kat," Dylan said.

A pain erupted through Kat's stomach. *Great*, she thought. *My last meal.*

Kat flipped down the visor and stared at herself in the mirror. The fact that she was wearing a tiara made the pain worse. But, alas, she would accept her fate with a smile, as she'd learned to do.

Never let them know you're disappointed, her mama had always said. Kat pulled a croissant out of the bag, popped open one of the plastic containers holding the strawberry jam, and dug in. She ate like an animal, like she was famished and had never eaten before. For some reason, she felt extra-hungry this morning and a bit nauseous as well. It was probably the stress.

Dylan glanced over at her. "You okay?" he asked.

Kat smiled at him—a big, beaming, beautiful fake smile. She'd pull her best Ingrid Bergman yet.

Thirty-one

Dylan wondered why Kathleen had been oddly quiet during the entire ride to the ranch. *Women*, he thought. With women, you never could tell.

After a few solid hours of driving, they'd reached the Tangled Spur. He pulled the truck up to the gate, jumped out, and opened the padlock. Then he ran back to close the gate behind them so that none of the deer would run loose into the road. Kathleen's ranch had a dusty gravel road that wound through the hill country and down toward the stream. Her ranch was one of the few around that had water rights. That was, a prized stream that ran over the limestone rocks and ended in a series of beautiful dipping pools.

The ranch house had long since burned down, but there was an old trailer that some of the hunters passing through sometimes used.

Dylan knew the exact spot where he wanted to propose. On top of the Wishing Rock, smack-dab in the middle of the stream.

When Kathleen was a young girl, Cullen Davis King had trav-

eled to the ranch with her in tow. There he'd sit her down and tell
her stories about a famous rock. A rock that, if Kathleen believed
it to be true, would grant all her wishes. The Wishing Rock was
a beautiful marbleized-looking stone that had become soft and
smooth from years of stream water flowing over it. The only way
to reach the rock was to wade out into the middle of the water
and climb on top of it.

Over the years, the colors of the rock had become even
brighter, with hues of green, blue, and orange from all the minerals the water carried.

Whenever Kathleen was upset she'd pay a visit to the Wishing
Rock to wish for things to get better. Dylan had driven her to the
Wishing Rock many times, including the day after her grandfather's funeral, and the time when one of the children at the
pediatric hospital was in critical condition, and Dr. Levin had
solemnly informed Kathleen that there was nothing left for them
to do.

Dylan parked the truck near the stream and got out. A group
of deer had stopped in their tracks, and now Dylan and the
buck were in a staring contest. Dylan said, *"Scat!"* and the deer
hopped off into the brush and disappeared.

Dylan saw that Kathleen was just sitting in the truck, staring
straight ahead—catatonic. She'd been acting strangely all morning. Being quiet almost the entire ride. And when he'd tried to
turn on the Don Williams CD, she kept flipping it off until he
gave up.

Dylan walked around to the passenger side and opened her
door for her.

"Step on out, princess," Dylan said, taking Kathleen's hand
and helping her out of the truck.

Kathleen smiled beatifically. "What a lovely day," she said, and
Dylan agreed. The sky was as blue and sturdy as Texas sky could

be, and there was a slight cool breeze that kept the mosquitoes away.

Dylan said, "C'mon, let's go to the Wishing Rock." He watched Kathleen's face turn ashen, and he wondered suddenly if she knew what was about to happen. Kathleen was always one up on him.

The antique Kashmir sapphire encrusted with sparkling diamonds was burning a hole inside Dylan's pants pocket. It had been his mother Clarissa's ring. Not the engagement ring his father had given her. No, that diamond had been pawned off a long time ago by dear old Dad.

This ring had been handed down to Clarissa Grant from her own mother, who'd gotten it from hers, and so on. Dylan wasn't quite sure how far back the ring went, but an appraiser had once estimated its date to be in the mid-1800s.

Clarissa Grant had handed it to Dylan for safekeeping on her deathbed. "Don't show your father," she'd instructed him, because Clarissa knew this ring wouldn't last in the hands of Butch Grant.

The ring was the sole heirloom that Dylan had from his mother. She'd left a pair of cuff links and an antique man's pocket watch for Wyatt. But the ring—her most prized possession—went to her firstborn son.

Dylan had never shown the ring to anyone, including Kathleen. He considered it one of the few good memories, one of the last moments he'd shared with his mother, and part of his history.

Dylan watched Kat wade knee-deep into the stream and make her way toward the Wishing Rock. He knew his mother would approve.

Thirty-two

Kat had been substituting sex for the real issue. Dylan was absolutely right. Whenever he had a problem with her, she stripped off her blouse, or flashed her butt, or did something to get his mind off the fact that she was never going to be able to provide him with the family he deserved.

It wasn't fair to him, she realized, to try this ploy once again. Kat had considered getting out to the Wishing Rock and then stripping off her jeans, snake boots, and shirt. She knew that it would be difficult for Dylan to break up with her if she were standing on the Wishing Rock naked. But she also knew that she was putting off the inevitable.

Kathleen got halfway out to the stream in waist-deep water, and wondered if she should pull a Virginia Woolf and drown herself. She'd seen the movie with Nicole Kidman, and, while tragic, Kat felt there was a certain amount of grace for a woman to walk into a river and just drown herself like that. It was almost biblical.

Kat ran her hands across the cool water, causing little ripples.

She took in a deep breath and decided to get her hair wet. So she dunked her head backward.

The diamond tiara fell loose and Kat scrambled to grab it before it sank. Damned thing. She'd forgotten about it again.

Kat scowled. Why was she wearing the stupid thing, anyway? Was it whimsical? Or just plain ridiculous?

She'd wanted to give Dylan a laugh. But now, who cared?

Kathleen turned and saw Dylan step into the water. He'd taken off his snake boots and rolled up his jeans to the knee, which was dangerous, but that was Dylan for you. If he got bit by a rattler or a moccasin, he'd probably figure out a way to suck the damned poison himself. Plus they had a snake kit in the trailer just in case.

Kat stared at the tiara in her hand and then tucked it back on top of her head, because there was no place else. The damned thing was too big to fit into her jeans pocket.

She felt like hurtling it across the water and letting it sink, but Shelby Lynn would never forgive her.

Kat's jeans and boots were soaking wet as she dragged herself out of the stream and boosted herself up onto the cool, smooth Wishing Rock. For a moment, she just lay there with her eyes closed, listening to the sound of the water trickling by.

Dylan would be here any minute. To . . . break up with her.

Kathleen's eyes popped open. Over her dead body! Over her dead body, indeed! What the hell had she been thinking!

There was no time to lose, so Kathleen hurriedly took off her T-shirt and bra, kicked off her boots, and stripped her jeans down.

Dylan was staring at some hawk circling up in the sky above, and so it gave Kat a moment to stand up—in full commando—with her hands against her hips.

Wearing the tiara like a helmet, she stood there firm. And naked.

Dylan's gaze fell upon her and he stopped in the middle of the water and stared.

"What on earth are you doing, Kathleen?" he asked, looking stunned. This was the first time Kat had been naked on the ranch. She knew she must look a sight. Standing in the middle of the stream on the Wishing Rock, with her hands planted firmly on her hips, wearing a diamond tiara.

And then Dylan said something that made Kat's heart fall into her stomach.

"Get dressed, please."

His voice was quiet. Eerily quiet. And Kat felt as if she'd been sucker punched. She grabbed her T-shirt, balled it up, and threw it at his head.

"Hey! What's the matter with you, Kathleen?"

"You're making a mistake, Dylan Charles Grant!" she shouted. Kat was angry now. She shimmied her jeans back on and her boots, and kicked the water so that it splashed up high into Dylan's face.

"Jeez, wild Kat! Settle down now," Dylan commanded her. He boosted himself up onto the Wishing Rock and handed her the now soaking wet T-shirt.

"Let me help you put this on," he said. Kat struggled as he tried to pull the T-shirt down over her head.

"Jesus, woman. What's gotten into you?"

Kat wouldn't cry. Not in a million years. Not ever. She shook her head violently to keep the tears from spilling.

"You're making a mistake," she hiccupped.

"I don't think so." Dylan cupped her chin in his hand and stared deeply into her eyes. Kat nearly fainted on the spot. She made a quick wish on the Wishing Rock and saw a flash of white light that she suspected could only be divine intervention.

Before she knew what was happening, Dylan was dropping

down onto one knee. He'd pulled something out of his pocket. Something shiny. Something that glinted in the sun and flashed into her eyes.

It was . . . a ring.

"Kathleen Connor King," Dylan said in a formal tone.

Oh my Lord, Kathleen thought. *He's proposing!*

"I know that times have been a bit rough, lately. But it's in times like these that our relationship shows its true colors," Dylan said. He stared up at her and his eyes became moist.

"Kathleen . . . will you do me the great honor of becoming my wife?"

Kathleen felt his hand touch hers. He kissed the top of her palm, as if she were a real live princess.

"B-b-but," she stuttered. "What about the babies?"

"We'll find a way. Just like other people do," Dylan said quietly.

Kathleen looked down into his solid eyes, and she knew her answer.

"Yes," she said. "A million times, yes!"

Dylan broke into a smile. He rolled the ring gently onto her engagement finger. It was too big for her, but Kathleen couldn't believe her eyes when she saw it.

The sapphire was cut in a way that revealed its deep natural blue color, with two half-moon-shaped diamonds on either side. Quite simply, it was stunning.

"Dylan!" she breathed. "Where on earth?"

"My mother," he said. "And before that, my grandmother. And before that . . ." He shrugged. "Let's just say it's been in the family a long time."

Kathleen couldn't help herself. She threw her arms around Dylan's neck and showered his face with kisses. It might have been sappy, but this was the most blissful day of her life.

Dylan was laughing. "You got so angry when I told you to get dressed. But I didn't want us to remember this moment with you being naked and all," he said.

Kathleen giggled. She couldn't stop staring at her hand. She loved that it was a sapphire. She loved that Dylan had given her a family heirloom. And she loved that he'd chosen this place, of all the places in the world, to ask for her hand in marriage.

The Wishing Rock had done its duty. Things couldn't be more perfect.

Thirty-three

They'd decided to take a little hike around the ranch. Since Kat's clothes were soaking wet, Dylan had hung them up on a tree. Kat was hiking in her snake boots, panties, and bra. On her finger was an antique sapphire, and on her head, a diamond tiara.

There goes my woman, Dylan thought, watching Kat expertly maneuver around some tough terrain. She was a tomboy in some respects, having grown up with such a tough grandfather. Kat's mother had died early on.

Dylan had met Kat's mother only once, and the memory was a foggy one. He remembered her being glamorous, the most glamorous woman in the entire room. Like a butterfly, she'd swept in and fluttered around everyone, casting a warm glow wherever she went. He remembered her looking down at him—he was just a kid—and then bending down to wipe some smudge off his face.

"Handsome boy," she'd murmured, which had caused Dylan to blush. This was his only memory of Kat's mother. As he watched his new fiancée climb over rocks and trudge through the sharp grasses that made up this unforgiving ranch terrain, he wondered if she didn't have more of her grandfather in her than anyone. Cullen Davis King was considered Texas nobility if there ever was such a thing, but he wasn't afraid to get his hands dirty. One of the most famous photos taken of Kathleen's grandfather showed him out in an oil field, his clothes and face streaked with black, working right alongside the rig men.

If anything, Kat had this type of . . . gravitas.

Dylan picked up a rock that was smooth and flat and perfect for skimming, and flicked it across the stream. The rock bounced twice and sank. He bent down to pick up another rock, and froze in his tracks.

A patch of crude bubbled up from a patchy hole in the ground. Dylan bent down and stuck his fingers in the hole. Then he smelled what could only be described as the sweetest smell on earth.

I'll be damned . . .

He knew exactly what oil in its natural state looked like.

The Tangled Spur had always been considered dry. For years Cullen Davis King had drilled for oil on other people's land, and rumor had it that his own land was cursed to be forever dry. Which was why he'd sought it elsewhere.

Kathleen had always assumed her land was dry, because the neighbors didn't have wells drilled on their property, either. The law in Texas was the law of capture. That was, you could build a well on your own land as long as it was four hundred and sixty-seven feet from the property line of your neighbor's property. Then you could drain your neighbor's minerals, because under Texas law, you could capture anything underneath the ground as long as the drill site was on your own property. If your neighbor got mad, his only remedy was to drill his own hole and try to drain the minerals faster.

Dylan whistled for Kat. "Hey, hon! Come take a look," he called out.

Kat came scrabbling back toward him. "What is it, my dear

fiancé?" she asked. She had now started calling him her "dear fiancé," and it seemed as though the name would stick.

Dylan pointed to the hole.

Kat pinched her nose. "Eew. What's that smell?"

"How did your grandfather determine that this land was dry?" Dylan asked.

Kat's eyes grew wide, and her lips started to tremble.

"What are you saying?" she asked.

"See this rock. Look at the grease slick." Dylan pointed to the ground. "Now, I don't know what's down there. It could just be some surface stuff and nothing to get too excited about, but heck, we could be standing on a damned ocean!"

Kat crossed her arms over her chest. "No. It can't be. Pa Pa would've known," she said. "He wouldn't have let something that huge go by the wayside."

Dylan dropped the rock and kicked it. She was right. Tangled Spur had been Cullen Davis's ranch for as long as anyone could remember. And Kat's grandfather had spent so much time on this land, he surely would've noticed a patch of bubbling crude.

Dylan figured that Kat's grandfather had seen the patch and ignored it. The land possibly had a bit of surface oil, but nothing worth drilling deep for.

A deep rig, one that could drill down thousands of feet, cost well into the millions to run—and that money could be lost in an instant if the rig encountered a dry hole.

If Cullen Davis King, a man who was known for taking extraordinary risks, hadn't bothered, then there was probably nothing there.

Dylan shrugged. "Well, it's nice to know the Tangled Spur isn't as dry as we thought," he said.

He and Kat hiked back to the pickup truck. He watched as she put her clothes back on and climbed into the passenger seat.

"I think I'm over the tiara," she said, taking it off her head and slipping it inside the glove box.

Dylan dug the heel of his boot into the dirt. "I bet I could pay off Wyatt's entire gambling debt with that thing."

"Yeah, but the wrath of Shelby Lynn Pierce is much worse than those casino sharks," Kat said. "Plus I told her I'd return it over the weekend."

Dylan thought about the weekend. Saturday was just three days away. He considered telling Kat about the heist, about the map he was planning to steal from Bo Harlan's office, but decided against it.

It had been a beautiful day. He didn't want to spoil the memory of their engagement with petty details of a breaking and entering.

"I'm hungry," Kat said.

"I hear you," Dylan replied. He walked around to the driver's side and jumped into the truck.

As he pulled toward the gate, he considered the hole he'd found. He was comfortable with forgetting about it. But that nagging feeling of *what if* kept tugging at him. *What if* Cullen Davis had died before telling anyone about an ocean of oil underneath his property? *What if* he'd known but had kept it a secret?

Dylan reached the gate. He shielded his eyes from the searing Texas sun and took one last glance around. A group of deer were clustered underneath some trees, but that was about it.

What he really wanted to do was drive the perimeter of the entire ranch, just to see if Cullen Davis had staked a well. It would be simple to spot. A single stake hammered into the ground at the site where an oil well should be drilled.

"Your fiancée needs a taco," Kat called out.

Dylan locked the gate and jogged back toward the pickup.

"Coming right up, my fiancée," he said.

Thirty-four

Fridays were balloon day. Kathleen moved confidently from room to room at the hospital delivering balloons to all her children. For the kids who were well enough to sit up in bed, she tied balloons around their tiny wrists. For the others, she left the balloons on their windowsills. Read them books. And checked their charts with the nurses.

When Kat reached Diego's room, she gasped. The boy had undergone a complex brain surgery that Dr. Levin had called "successful."

She was expecting Diego to be in recovery. Sitting up in his bed, with his head shaved and bald, watching cartoons or playing with some of the toys Kat had left on his nightstand.

Diego looked comatose beneath a tangle of wires. He was breathing through a respirator, and hooked up to a monitor that beeped constantly to show his vital signs.

One of the nurses buzzed into the room, tapped at a hanging IV bag, and wrote down Diego's vitals in his chart.

"What . . . happened?" Kathleen choked.

"His lung collapsed," the nurse said. "And he came down with a serious infection to boot."

Kat's hand shot to her mouth and she nearly gagged. She knew that it wasn't possible to save every child. Pediatric cancer was a formidable adversary. But she'd made a promise to Diego's parents. A promise she intended to keep.

"Where's Dr. Levin?" she demanded.

The nurse checked her watch. "In his office, I believe. He doesn't do rounds for another hour."

Kat nodded and approached Diego's bedside. He had a tube taped over his mouth that ran down into his throat, and his chest was rising and falling in steady rhythm with the respirator. She reached down and caressed his warm hand.

"You are a strong boy," she whispered. "Do you hear me, Diego? You are a strong, *strong* boy. And you will get through this!"

Kathleen closed her eyes and said a quiet prayer.

"Ms. King?" a voice said, from behind her.

Kathleen whirled around. It was Dr. Levin. His eyes seemed sad, and his white lab coat was covered with what looked like an old coffee stain.

"One of the nurses paged me," he explained.

"I was just on my way to your office," Kat said.

Dr. Levin walked over to Diego and checked his monitor. Then he flipped open a metal chart and read over the results. "This is a tough one." He sighed.

"Don't tell me that," Kathleen said. "I want to hear good news with this one."

Dr. Levin leveled a hard stare at her. "I'm afraid I don't have good news. I tried to call you but it went straight to voice mail."

Kathleen bit the bottom of her lip. "I was out at the ranch and my cell phone doesn't get reception."

Dr. Levin motioned for her to follow him. "Come with me." He ambled down the hallway toward his office.

Kat followed him. Her body had gone into shiver mode, and she couldn't stop her limbs from quaking as she walked.

Inside his office, Dr. Levin took off his lab coat and changed into a fresh one he had hanging behind the door.

"Damned hot chocolate," he said, pointing out the stain. He flicked a finger in the air and said, "I can't see without my eyeglasses. Don't ever get old."

Kathleen attempted a smile. Leave it to Dr. Levin to try and provide some levity. "Have a seat," he said. He dragged a stack of files off one of the chairs and motioned for her to sit.

"Where are Diego's parents?" she asked.

"The mother and father both work two jobs," Dr. Levin said. "They come at night. Sometimes they sleep in the chapel on the pews."

Kathleen swallowed. "Have you told them?"

Dr. Levin plopped down into his chair. He rested his hands across his broad belly, with his fingers interlaced. He furrowed his brow, and Kathleen noticed the deep wrinkles fanned out across his forehead. She didn't know how old Dr. Levin was, but his age was starting to take a toll.

"We're making Diego as comfortable as possible," he said in a low tone. "But I think it's time we tell the parents that his prognosis doesn't look promising."

"There's nothing left we can do?"

"Kathleen, we do the best we can. And you've made that possible."

Kathleen waved her hand as if to say: *Don't bother thanking me.*

"I'll tell his parents," she said.

Dr. Levin patted his stomach. "You're the only person at this hospital who speaks Spanish better than me."

"You don't speak Spanish."

"Exactly."

Kathleen shook her head. "Don't try to be a comedian," she said. "This is not the time."

Dr. Levin nodded. "You don't have to do it. We have the grief counselor."

"I want to."

Kathleen thanked Dr. Levin. She walked as if in a trance toward the chapel. It was five o'clock. Diego's parents should be arriving any time now. And it was up to her to inform them that their son was dying.

Thirty-five

"No, no," Diego's mother was crying uncontrollably. She dropped to her knees, clasped her hands together, and shook her fists toward the heavens.

Diego's father sat solemnly in a pew. His face was ashen, the face of a man in extreme anguish. But he didn't shed tears. It was as if his body was too tired to produce them.

Kathleen rested her hand on his shoulder. She noticed how weak he felt underneath his shirt.

She'd started off by telling them the hospital had done everything they could. They'd attempted an operation that few hospitals even attempt, with equipment that few hospitals even have. But Diego's brain tumor was spreading. His lung had collapsed. And an infection was ravaging his body and making everything worse.

It was only a matter of time, she'd said.

Diego's father raised his head and looked into her eyes.

"¿*Cuándo?*" he asked, which meant *When?* When would his son die? When would he have to endure the pain of this reality?

I don't know. Kathleen shook her head. *"No lo sé,"* she replied.

"No, no, no!" Diego's mother cried out. She shook her fists up toward the ceiling, as if fighting off an invisible demon.

Kat was at a loss. She didn't know what else to do. So she dropped down onto her knees next to Diego's mother, grabbed the woman's hands in her own, and began to pray.

Thirty-six

Saturday was the day of the big heist. Dylan, Wyatt, C. Todd Hartwell, and Steve had taken a vote. They'd conduct the "operation" around dusk, when the sun was just beginning to set. This was the least likely time for anyone to be in the building, and yet it would still be light enough outside, so they wouldn't have to use flashlights. Flashlights might look suspicious coming from the windows of the Titan offices.

"Just dress normally," Dylan had said. "We don't want to look like a bunch of men in black."

The plan was simple. C. Todd Hartwell would unlock the building with the key he'd "borrowed" from Bo Harlan's sexy little secretary. Dylan and Steve would unload the heater and bring it up the service elevator, while Wyatt changed out of his normal clothes and into the Mylar suit.

The four men would "rendezvous" outside Bo Harlan's office.

There, they would jack up the heater to raise the temperature to around one hundred degrees. And Wyatt would slowly approach and dismantle the alarm.

Once inside Harlan's personal office, C. Todd Hartwell and Dylan would find the seismic map and make copies, while Steve and Wyatt dumped the heater and the Mylar suit. The four burglars would exit the building one at a time so as not to arouse suspicion, and get into the yellow Hummer driven by Achmed which would be circling the block.

Dylan woke up on Saturday morning and felt a rush of adrenaline. He didn't feel guilty in the least for the crime he was about to commit. Bo Harlan had it coming.

If anything, he felt bad about lying to Kat. He'd already told her that he'd be at the tavern with Wyatt, shooting darts.

Dylan reached his arm out across the bed and realized that Kat had already gotten up. Hmm. This was strange. Usually Kat woke Dylan up on Saturday mornings, drew the shades up high, and ordered him to "Rise and shine, sweet cheeks."

Dylan noticed that she'd been in a funk last night when she got home from the hospital. She hadn't bothered to eat any of the chicken Wyatt ordered from Hunan Palace, and she'd snuck off to bed early while Dylan and his brother watched *Raiders of the Lost Ark*.

"Kath-leeen," Dylan called out. There was no response. He rolled out of bed, pulled on a pair of sweatpants, and ambled to the kitchen.

Kat was nowhere to be found, but then he saw her. Sitting out on the balcony with her feet up on the railing. A cup of steaming coffee in her hands.

She was smoking a cigarette, too, which startled Dylan.

He poured himself a cup of coffee from Kat's French press, slid open the balcony door, and stepped out into the sun.

"Good morning, my fiancée," Dylan said.

She looked up at him, and Dylan saw that her face was streaked with tears. The woman who never cried. Alone. On the balcony. In her pajamas with the monkeys all over them. It was almost too much for him to bear.

Dylan set his coffee cup on the patio table and rushed over to Kat's side. "What's wrong, sweetheart?" Seeing her like this, his heart swelled in his chest and he felt as if he'd been punched.

Kat shook her head and wiped the tears from her eyes.

"I'm losing a child," she said.

Dylan didn't understand. "You're . . . pregnant?" He placed his hand on top of Kat's head, and patted her hair.

"His name is Diego Ramirez. Yesterday I told his parents that he wasn't going to make it."

Dylan sucked in his breath. "Oh, hon. I'm sorry." He knew that Kat's hospital work was difficult. She'd lost children before, but this time she was taking it more personally than the others. He suspected it was because of Kat's personal health situation, the fact that she was unable to bear children of her own.

"What can I do?" Dylan asked. "Tell me."

Kat shrugged her small shoulders. "Nothing. Dr. Levin said there was nothing left."

"Does the family need money?"

"Why, you got some?" Kat snapped.

Dylan felt like he'd been slapped. He drew his hand away, but then realized that Kat didn't mean anything by it. She was in pain.

"You know what I mean," Dylan said. "Do they need something to tide them over?"

"They need a healthy son."

Dylan stared out at the Houston skyline. Storm clouds were moving in from Galveston and the air smelled like rain.

He began to rub Kat's shoulders. "You believe in miracles, don't you?"

Kat stabbed out her cigarette. "Don't you mean fairy tales?"

Dylan stared out into the distance. "I think it's time for a miracle."

Thirty-seven

Dylan, Wyatt, Steve, and C. Todd huddled behind the Enron Building. The rain was pounding down, fast and furious, covering the cement sidewalk in a slick sheet of water.

Dylan had instructed Achmed to circle the building every ten minutes. They'd driven C. Todd's wasp yellow Hummer, which stood out among the other vehicles on the road. Dylan figured that most felons would drive a low-key sedan, and that the cops wouldn't suspect a bunch of guys cruising around in a Hummer. The fact that the getaway car was yellow was actually a positive, he figured.

Dylan surveyed his posse. Wyatt was wearing his usual jeans and polo shirt with the collar upturned at the neck. In his hand, he carried a small gym bag that held the Mylar suit.

C. Todd Hartwell was wearing shorts, flip-flops, and a visor—just your everyday Saturday outfit. In his hand was his requisite can of Red Bull.

Steve was wearing snakeskin loafers, red velvet pants, and a loud Hawaiian shirt. On his head was a hat cocked sideways that

Dylan recognized as being the type of hat preferred by pimps and drug dealers.

"I said to dress normal." Dylan scowled.

"This is normal," Steve hissed.

"Dude, it looks like P. Diddy threw up all on you," Wyatt said.

"Drop it, Wyatt. He's wearing what he's wearing," C. Todd huffed. The oilman chugged his Red Bull.

Wyatt clapped his hands. "Okay, gentlemen. Let's go find us some oil."

Dylan and Steve lifted the heater and lugged it toward the loading dock. They were soaking wet. It was pouring rain. And the mosquitoes were out in full force.

Wyatt limped behind them carrying the gym bag. He shook the water out of his hair. "I'm wet," he announced.

C. Todd Hartwell saluted them and said, "Wish me luck. I'm off."

The oilman disappeared around the front of the building. After a few minutes, his face appeared inside the glass windows of the service entrance and he buzzed them inside with the key he'd gotten from Bo Harlan's secretary.

The four guys ambled into the service elevator and made their way to the penthouse floor.

Inside the elevator, Wyatt began to unhook his belt and take his jeans off.

"You're changing in here?" C. Todd asked.

"Faster this way," Wyatt said.

He kicked off his tennis shoes, dropped his jeans, and stripped off his shirt.

"You're making fun of my threads and you're wearing tighty-whities?" Steve asked, pointing at Wyatt's underwear.

Wyatt grunted. It was difficult for him to change while standing on his prosthetic leg, so he sat down cross-legged on the elevator floor. Unzipping the gym bag, he pulled out a silver jumpsuit. He pulled it on one leg at a time, shimmied the suit up his body, and zipped the hood down over his head.

"You look like Dustin Hoffman in that movie about the plague," C. Todd said.

"*Outbreak*," Steve said. "That movie blew ass."

Dylan tried not to crack a smile. These were his partners in crime. Siskel and Ebert.

The elevators doors whooshed open and Dylan, C. Todd, and Steve hoisted the huge heater down the hallway. Wyatt—in his space suit—limped behind them. They checked around the hallways constantly, to make sure no one was around. But the building seemed empty at this hour. Houston's best and brightest weren't known for working Saturdays.

"Welcome to Titan Energy, boys," C. Todd Hartwell said, as they reached the office suite.

C. Todd Hartwell swiped the key across the slit in the door and smiled when he heard the click.

"Ta-da." C. Todd swept open the door and the four men streamed into the inner sanctum.

Dylan glanced around. Bo Harlan's office furniture was big and expensive. There were huge leather couches in the waiting room, along with real oil paintings on the wall. A bronze sculpture of a life-sized eagle rose up from the large mahogany entryway table.

The boardroom was even more exquisite, and Dylan sucked in his breath. He'd read somewhere that the conference table had been hewn from a single piece of virgin Canadian maple.

C. Todd Hartwell let out a low whistle as the four men made their way past the floor-to-ceiling windows with expansive views of the Houston skyline.

"Prime real estate," he sniffed.

"Which one is Harlan's office?" Wyatt asked. His voice was muffled behind the Mylar suit.

C. Todd Hartwell pointed down a long hallway lined with cubicles. "The big swinging dick suite on the end," he said.

The doorway at the end of the hall was closed tight. Wyatt pointed to a tiny red light that was making a small arc on the carpet outside the office.

"Don't get too close," he warned. "Or you'll trip the sensor."

Steve and Dylan set the heater down on the floor.

"Over here," the oilman said, pointing to a plug in the wall.

Dylan plugged in the heater and cranked it up. The key to the whole operation was to raise the heat slowly, so that the alarm wouldn't detect a change in body temperature when Wyatt approached it. The Mylar suit was to keep Wyatt's body heat from triggering the alarm as he worked to dismantle it.

The heater started churning out hot air. Steve wiped his brow, took off his pimp hat, and used it to fan his face.

"What now?" he asked.

"We wait," Dylan said.

After ten minutes, the heat inside the hall was unbearable. Dylan was drenched with sweat. He looked down and saw that his shirt was soaking. He mopped his brow and pushed his wet hair out of his face. A mosquito had gone to town on his wrist, and Dylan saw five red welts inflamed on his skin.

The three other guys looked just as miserable. They were all sopping wet from the rain and now drenched in sweat from the heat.

Wyatt pulled a thermometer out of the gym bag and checked the temperature. "We're ready."

"Good luck, brother." He and Wyatt bumped fists.

Dylan, Steve, and C. Todd watched as Wyatt limped toward Bo Harlan's door. He moved slowly, as if gravity was weighing him down. After each step, he'd pause and check the thermometer before taking another step.

Dylan glanced behind him to make sure no one was coming. It would be just their luck for some random employee to show up on a Saturday evening to check his e-mail or something.

Wyatt had nearly reached the end of the hallway. He approached the alarm site and checked the thermometer again.

As if on cue, Bo Harlan's door swung wide open, and the hallway was flooded with a bright white light.

"Oh holler out!" Steve shouted.

A piercing scream erupted, a woman's scream; and Dylan watched as Wyatt reacted. His brother jumped in fright and then pivoted on his heel to run, but his prosthetic foot got stuck on the carpet and he pitched forward onto his face.

Dylan stared in disbelief down the hallway as the woman who'd just come out of Bo Harlan's office let out another rip-roaring scream.

What on earth . . .

Thirty-eight

Kat's face was contorted in fear as she stared at the man in the silver bio-tech suit who'd just fallen on his face.

"You better run! I'm calling the police!" she screeched, kicking the man over and over again in the ribs.

"Oh Jesus Lord Almighty," C. Todd Hartwell muttered.

Kat looked up. Her mouth dropped open in recognition as she realized that Dylan was trying to hide behind Steve.

"*Dylan. Charles. Grant.*" Kat's voice boomed. "*What on God's green earth . . .*"

"You in trouble now, dawg," Steve said, snickering.

Dylan scuffed his shoe along the carpet. He'd been caught in a lie. And not just a little lie—this one was a doozy.

But maybe it was his turn to be angry. After all, what the heck was Kat doing inside Bo Harlan's office!

Dylan crossed his arms over his broad chest. "I guess I could ask you the same question."

Wyatt rolled over on the floor and said, "Jesus, Kathleen. You about killed me with that super ninja karate kick."

Kat stared at Wyatt lying on the floor in the silver Mylar suit. "Wyatt! Is that you? Why are you wearing that ridiculous costume? And why is it so hot in here?" She glanced down the hallway and spotted the heater. Then she pivoted around and looked at the alarm panel on the wall.

"I can't believe this," she said, shaking her head. She stared at Dylan, and her eyes were angry little needles. "Dylan, what have you gotten your brother into?"

"Me! Hell, Kathleen. Wyatt owes half a million bucks to these guys in Vegas! I didn't drag him here."

"This is about money?" Kat snapped. She crossed her arms over her chest and began tapping her foot now. The death tap. It scared the crap out of Wyatt, and he scrambled to his feet and stood in front of her, looking sheepish and ashamed.

"Bo Harlan's got a map that he stole from me," C. Todd Hartwell announced. "And I want it back."

Kat checked her watch. "Well, he'll be here in . . . oh, I don't know . . . let's say five minutes, so maybe you should ask him yourself. Instead of trying to break into his office like a bunch of thieves! You should be ashamed!"

"*Us!*" Dylan said. "What about you, Kathleen? Just what the *hell* are you doing here?"

"Language," Kat said, in a firm tone.

"Sorry," Dylan grumbled.

Steve started to giggle.

"I'm helping Shelby Lynn Pierce redecorate Bo's office. They left about twenty minutes ago to pick up sandwiches so I assume they'll be back any minute now."

"We're fucked," Steve said, glancing wildly around the office.

"I'm not leaving without my map," C. Todd Hartwell announced.

"What map?" Kat asked.

"Nothing you'd understand," C. Todd said.

"Let me guess. A seismic shoot of some land you want to drill," Kat said, matter-of-fact.

C. Todd turned to Dylan. "She's good." The oilman began to march toward Bo Harlan's office.

Kat stood and blocked the office door, her arms crossed over her chest. "You will not be stealing anything from this office, C. Todd. Sorry, but I guess you'll have to find your own way to drill for oil."

"Whose side is she on, brother?" C. Todd asked Dylan.

"Let's get outta here," Dylan replied. He walked to the wall outlet and unplugged the heater. When he glanced up at Kat, he saw that she was fuming. Gosh, he'd never seen her act *this* mad.

She was staring at him as if she wanted to break off their engagement. This was not good. Not good at all.

At that moment, Dylan heard voices coming from the lobby of Titan Energy.

"Shhhh. They're back!" C. Todd hissed.

"Hide!" Kat commanded them.

Dylan sprang into action. He and Steve grabbed the heater and pushed it under a desk.

"Where to?" Wyatt whispered, clutching his gym bag to his chest.

Kat pointed to a coat closet. "In there! Fast!"

The four guys raced toward the closet. The problem was, it was barely big enough to hold them. So they had to squeeze in. Two by two. Dylan was facing C. Todd Hartwell. Wyatt was facing Steve. Each guy was nose to nose, with their groins pressed up against each other.

"This is gay!" Steve hissed.

Kat slammed the closet doors.

Dylan could hear Kat's voice just outside the doorway. "I hope you remembered my potato chips," she was saying.

Bo Harlan and Shelby Lynn were laughing about something. In fact, they sounded like they were having a ball.

"Why is it so hot in here?" came a man's voice that Dylan recognized as Wild Bo Harlan's.

He heard Kat giggle. "I think you feel hot, Bo, because you're standing next to Shelby."

Dylan clenched his teeth together. Kat was now saving him. He didn't like this one bit.

The smell inside the closet was a cross between dead rat and stale gym clothes. Dylan attempted to hold his breath. Steve was wearing ten pounds of bad cologne; C. Todd reeked of whiskey; and everyone had bad BO.

Dylan was staring straight at C. Todd who was staring straight back at him. He noticed that C. Todd was about a half-inch taller than he, and wondered if it was the shoes. But he remembered C. Todd was wearing flip-flops.

Steve and Wyatt were also staring at each other. Wyatt towered over Steve in his silver space-looking suit, and Steve had somehow managed to race to the closet with his pimp hat cocked sideways on his head. Dylan glanced at C. Todd and saw that the oilman was trying to restrain a laugh. The ridiculousness of their predicament soon dawned on each of them.

Wyatt in his silver Mylar suit.

Steve with his pimp hat cocked sideways on his head.

It was painful. The four of them squeezed in, trying not to make a sound.

C. Todd started to snicker. Dylan started hiccupping to keep from laughing. Steve and Wyatt glared at them, which made C. Todd and Dylan start to laugh even more.

Dylan heard Kathleen ushering Bo Harlan and Shelby Lynn hurriedly into Bo's office. He heard the door shut loudly, and figured that it was time to make their getaway.

"Time to bounce!" Steve said.

Dylan swung the closet door open and peeked out. Bo Harlan's office door was shut. He waved for the guys to follow him. They tumbled out of the closet and hurried toward the reception area.

"Wait!" Steve whispered. "What about the heater?"

"Leave it!" Dylan hissed.

A man's voice sounded loudly behind them. It was Bo Harlan coming out of his office, with Shelby Lynn and Kat in tow. Dylan raced for the front door of the Titan offices. Wyatt was limping quickly, trying to make it as fast as he could, but his leg gave out and he tumbled to the carpet. Dylan turned and raced toward his brother. He crouched in front of Wyatt and said, "Piggyback." Wyatt jumped onto his brother's back, and Dylan huffed toward the door. The four guys slipped out into the hall.

They bounded into the service elevator and stabbed the button for the bottom floor. All four of them were breathless, sweaty, snorting, and laughing their heads off.

Steve and Wyatt high-fived each other.

"I don't know what y'all are celebratin'," C. Todd grumbled. "We didn't get the map."

"At least we're not going to jail, dawg," Steve said.

The four guys swept out the back door and into the loading dock. They spotted Achmed about a half block away and chased him down. Achmed edged the Hummer over on the curb and waited as they climbed in.

"What happened?" he asked.

"Nothing," Dylan said. "Except we lost a thousand-dollar heater."

"Sorry." Achmed shrugged. "But I still get paid, right?"

"Just drive, Abdul," C. Todd commanded.

Dylan rested his head on the seat rest. He realized that without the map, he and Wyatt were up the proverbial shit's creek. And now Kat was pissed off at him, too.

He had to devise another plan. Something to help rescue Wyatt. With Felix and his goons on their heels for five hundred thousand dollars, there wasn't much time.

Thirty-nine

Wyatt and Dylan sat on the couch, looking like a pair of schoolboys who'd just gotten caught flinging spitballs.

Kat stood in front of them, her hands on her hips. She was wearing her "Malibu Is for Lovers" T-shirt, and she wasn't smiling. "You've been summoned," she said, in an ominous tone.

"Summoned where?" Wyatt asked.

Dylan elbowed his brother in the ribs. "Why'd you have to live in Vegas in the first place!"

"Stop it, Dylan!" Wyatt pushed Dylan on the couch. The two brothers got into a little struggling match, so Kat had to resort to last remedies.

She began to tap her foot . . . tap . . . tap . . . tap.

Dylan and Wyatt stopped wrestling, and stopped breathing altogether.

"Aunt Lucinda wants to see both of you," Kat said.

"Oh brother," Wyatt said.

"C'mon, Kat," Dylan pleaded.

Kat held up her hand. "No ifs, ands, or buts. She wants to see both of you right now. And I told her we'd be on our way."

"I don't want to go," Wyatt grumbled. He reached out and grabbed a can of Dr Pepper off the coffee table.

"Me neither," Dylan said.

"I don't care what you want," Kat said. "You're going!"

"You're not the boss of me," Wyatt said, taking a chug from his soda.

"Grow up, Wyatt," Kat said, and then regretted saying it because Wyatt looked stung. He stared up at her from the couch with those beautiful blue eyes of his, reminding her of a sad little puppy.

It was time to change her tone of voice, and her tactics. "Put your shoes on, Wyatt," Kat said, picking up Wyatt's tennis shoes and dropping them at his feet.

"Lucinda spent all day making you her ribs and special dunking sauce that you love. I don't think it's fair to keep her waiting, do you?"

Wyatt's ears literally perked up. He bent down and tied his shoes on. "Did you hear that, Dylan? Lucinda's making her ribs."

"It's a trick," Dylan replied. He grabbed the key to the condo and held open the door.

"I'm sorry, babe," he whispered, as Kat passed by him.

"You better be," she snapped.

Kat knew that Dylan was sorry. She knew that he hadn't meant to lie. And she knew that Dylan was under pressure to pay off Wyatt's debt.

But still. Breaking into Bo Harlan's office, and risking a felony charge. That was pretty bad.

Forty

The three of them piled into the truck and set off for the Cullen King mansion. Dylan steered the truck down Kirby Drive and turned right onto the winding streets of River Oaks. They reached Lazy Lane where the houses were big and set back from the street. These were the types of grand estates surrounded by gates and guard shacks and thick privacy hedges.

Dylan pulled up to one of the gates and pressed the buzzer. A bevy of landscaping trucks was parked outside, and Dylan watched as the landscapers took to chopping down a dead live oak tree and putting it inside a wood shredder.

Lucinda's voice came on the buzzer.

"Let me guess. It's Jesse James," she said, over the microphone.

Dylan clenched his teeth. This wasn't going to be fun.

The gate swung open in a wide arc and Dylan pulled the truck up to the front of the house.

It was not your typical white colonial, or even your French chateau or Spanish Mediterranean. No. Cullen Davis King had built his home using a renowned architect from Chicago. The house was entirely unique, with sweeping windows and angles that took one's breath away. It was as if the house did not have a single straight line, but was instead a series of warm flowing curves.

Aunt Lucinda was standing on the front porch wearing a flowery Hawaiian muumuu. She wore purple sandals, a matching purple necklace, wrist bangles, and dangly earrings that looked like they were crafted from some type of indigenous island shell.

"Aloha, pretty girl," she said, grabbing Kathleen by her shoulders and kissing her on the forehead.

"Well, well, look who we have here," Lucinda said, crossing her arms over her wide barrel of a chest. Dylan and Wyatt walked cautiously toward her, as if they were afraid she would bite.

"If it ain't the Rough Riders," she said. "Come here, you." She held her arms out to hug Wyatt.

Wyatt limped over to Aunt Lucinda. She grabbed him in a big bear hug, and they rocked back and forth a moment. Then Lucinda let Wyatt go. She took a good look at him and then gave him a sharp whap across the top of his head.

"What on earth were you thinking, child?"

Wyatt stared at his shoes and scuffed his good leg across the pavement. "I dunno," he said sheepishly.

"And you!" Lucinda pointed her finger at Dylan. "What have you gotten your brother into?"

Great, Dylan thought. *Here it goes again.* As the older brother, he had always borne responsibility for Wyatt. Since they didn't have much of a father figure growing up, it'd been up to Dylan to care for his younger brother. Now that Wyatt was a grown man, things still hadn't changed.

And of course, Wyatt wouldn't rescue him. He wouldn't say, *Wait a second, I'm the person who moved to Vegas and gambled away a half million bucks.*

Nope. When it came to Aunt Lucinda, the rule was fairly straightforward.

Every man for himself, Dylan thought.

Wyatt plunged his hands into his jeans pockets. He looked over at Dylan and shrugged.

Hmph! Typical.

Lucinda eyed Dylan. "Come here and show your aunt some love," she said. Dylan trudged over to her. She grabbed him in a strong bear hug, and shook him back and forth. Aunt Lucinda smelled good, like pie, and her bracelets jangled on her wrist.

She grabbed Dylan by the shoulders and stared him hard in the eye. "You little devil, you should be ashamed of yo'self," she said, rapping him on the top of his head, just like she'd rapped Wyatt.

He knew that was coming.

"Well, don't just stand there. Come on in." Lucinda waved them inside. "Don't worry. I hid all my jewelry," she said, as a little joke.

Kathleen broke into a small smile.

Dylan came up behind Kat and tried to encircle his arm around her waist, but she smacked his hand away.

"Body off limits," she announced.

Dylan grunted. "You're being unfair."

"Am I?" She swiveled around and stared up into his eyes.

Dylan glanced at Kat's hand and saw that she was still wearing the ring. He knew she'd already shown it to Aunt Lucinda because Kat's former nanny hadn't made a fuss. And a ring like that wouldn't go unnoticed by Aunt Lucinda—who noticed everything.

The interior of the house was just as Dylan remembered it.

With the decor chosen by Kat's mother, who'd been known in Houston circles as having an eye for French antiques. The house was warm, despite the museum-quality furniture, chandeliers, and ornate carpets covering the parquet wood floors.

Lucinda waved them into a small sunroom off the side of the kitchen. There, Dylan saw that she'd set up a generous spread, Lucinda-style.

There was barbecue sausage and ribs and chicken along with cole slaw, fresh corn, Caesar salad, and Lucinda's famous home-made rolls slabbed with warm butter.

"Wooo eee. Chow time," Wyatt said, rubbing his palms together.

"Before we eat, I'd like for Dylan to say the blessing," Lucinda said, shooting Dylan a stern look.

Dylan sighed and bit his bottom lip. "If we could all grab hands," he said. The four of them stood in a circle and held each other's hands. Dylan took this opportunity to grab on to Kat's hand and squeeze. She didn't squeeze back, but she didn't let go, either.

"Let's bow our heads," Dylan said, and they all bowed their heads.

Dylan closed his eyes. He stood in silence for a moment, and then he blurted out:

"Dear Lord,

"Thank you for this food. Thank you for giving us the blessing of each other's company. And please watch over the children and families in the hospital, especially the children who are struggling. We need a miracle, Lord, so we hope you're listening. Thank you. Amen."

"Amen," everyone chimed in.

As Dylan said this last part, he squeezed Kat's hand. This time, she squeezed back.

Dylan's heart swelled in his chest. He bent over and kissed Kat on the top of her head and whispered, "I'm sorry, Kathleen."

She stared up into his eyes. "I know."

They were back. He knew this. And she'd forgiven him.

"I guess congratulations are in order," Aunt Lucinda said, as she dipped out a heaping spoonful of mashed potatoes onto Wyatt's plate.

Wyatt licked some of Lucinda's special barbecue sauce off the edge of his thumb. "Delicious, Aunt Lou," he said.

Aunt Lucinda waved her hand as if to say, *It ain't nothin', honey*.

Wyatt plopped down at the table and dug into his food. "When are you two lovebirds tying the knot?" he asked. "I assume I've got best man duties."

Dylan reached over and grabbed Kathleen's hand. "We have some planning to do," he said.

Kat stuck a fork into the side of Lucinda's homemade peach cobbler. "Aunt Lucinda and I have been discussing it," she said, "and we thought we could have the wedding right here. In Pa Pa's house."

Aunt Lucinda clapped her large hands and squealed. "It will be the most beautiful wedding ever, child!" She turned to Dylan. "What do you think, Jesse James?"

Dylan set his fork down. "Here? In this house?"

Lucinda swiveled around in her chair. "And what's wrong with this house?" she boomed.

"Nothing, Lou. It's just that . . . I don't know. I guess I've always felt . . ." Dylan trailed off.

Now Lucinda was standing up and leaning over the table. She was lopping a heaping spoonful of ham and peas onto Wyatt's plate, and her bangles jingled on her wrist.

"What happened? Devil got your tongue? Out with it," Lucinda commanded, heaving back down into her chair.

An awkward silence descended over the sunroom, and even Wyatt stopped chewing his rib midway through.

"You've always felt what?" Kat said, softly.

Terrific, Dylan thought. He'd stepped in it now. How could he explain that even in death, Cullen Davis King was still larger than life, an iconic figure in Texas history and the oil business that Dylan had tried so hard to break into.

How could he explain that a wedding in the very home of Cullen Davis King would attract so many bystanders, so many curious folks who wanted to see where the King himself had lived, breathed, and died.

Hell. He didn't want to turn his wedding to Kathleen into a damned sporting event. But he couldn't say this, could he? So Dylan chose the next best thing.

"I've always felt . . . like a guest."

"I've got a solution," Lucinda said, slapping her palms on the table and causing everyone to jump. "Why don't you take your new fiancé for a tour of your granddaddy's house, child?"

"Good idea. Come on!" Kat said.

Dylan stood from his chair and Kat grabbed on to his hand and began to tug him toward the living room. "You coming?" he asked Wyatt.

His brother looked up from his plate, his face covered in barbecue sauce. "I'm eating," he said.

"Good boy," Lucinda said, nodding her approval, and rubbing Wyatt on his shoulder.

Kat dragged Dylan into the living room, the dining room, the den, and the master bedroom where Cullen Davis King had died—and which still remained unlived in—as Lucinda preferred to sleep in the nanny's quarters where she'd spent forty years.

Dylan had seen the house before, but this was back when Cullen King was alive. And he'd been a young man on pins and needles. Now that Lucinda lived there alone, whenever Dylan and Kat visited, they usually stayed inside the sunroom or the kitchen. There had never been any reason to stray from the areas that Lucinda considered her home.

It was almost as if Lucinda kept the other areas cordoned off just as they'd been when Kathleen's grandfather was alive, in tribute to him.

"You're gonna love Pa Pa's study," Kat said, pulling Dylan into a beautiful room adorned with an ornately carved desk, a Tiffany lamp, and chairs. The entire room was paneled in a golden-hued wood, including the ceiling—in the center of which was painted a fresco, like the kind you see in Italian churches.

There was a fireplace and lots of books on the shelves, and English paintings of horses and fox hunts on the walls.

"Wow," Dylan said, under his breath.

Kat squeezed his hand. "This is where Pa Pa spent most of his time when he was home. We knew not to disturb him when he was in here working. Even Mother knew not to cross that threshold," Kat said, pointing to the doorway that led into Cullen Davis King's private study.

Dylan surveyed the framed photos on the bookshelves and on the massive desk. They showed Cullen Davis King in his element. Out in the oil fields of Texas, grinning broadly with his rig men, his geologists, his land men. All of them covered in dust and grease and looking as if they owned the damned world.

Something stirred inside Dylan. He realized that it wasn't envy, or greed, or any of the other ills that plagued young men of ambition. No. What Dylan felt was awe. Genuine awe.

Dylan wanted to be this man. He wanted to be as great as this man had been. Or else his life wasn't worth living.

Suddenly he was ashamed. Ashamed of how he'd behaved. Ashamed of trying to break into Bo Harlan's office to steal seismic data.

This wasn't how great men became great. This was how mediocre men got by.

Dylan realized that he would have to take risks. But not the types of risks that led to possible criminal charges and jail time. He'd have to take calculated risks, just as Cullen Davis King had done.

"I need a moment alone, hon," he whispered.

Kathleen nodded as if she understood. She left Dylan standing inside her grandfather's study. He heard her footsteps clicking down the hallway, back to the sunroom where Lucinda and Wyatt were surely starting in on dessert.

Dylan walked around to the desk and sat down. In the very chair where Cullen Davis King had sat. He stared across the room and considered his destiny.

He knew enough about the oil business to stake his own claim. He'd grown up around oilmen. He'd gone to law school, taken all the oil and gas classes that were offered, and passed the Texas State Bar exam. Before taking his fateful job at Enron, Dylan had interviewed with a bunch of firms. But the jobs at the big energy companies were not easy to get, and no one would hire the son of Butch Grant. Dylan had already tried that humiliating routine.

Dylan ran his hand across the top of the desk. The wood felt smooth under his palm, as if it had been freshly oiled.

Without thinking, he tugged open the middle desk drawer. He wasn't being nosy; it just felt like habit. Inside the drawer lay a few pens, some paper clips, a blank pad of paper, some loose pocket change, and a photograph.

Dylan picked up the photo and stared down at it.

It showed just a single thing—a stake that had been hammered into the ground. Dylan turned the photo over in his hand, and as he read the handwriting on the back, the hair on his arms stood up. In Cullen Davis King's own scrawl, it said: "Tangled Spur Mineral Interests, #1."

Dylan sucked in his breath. It couldn't be true, could it?

Here. In this photograph. In front of Dylan's eyes . . . was what he'd always suspected.

Forty-one

"Round up the troops," Dylan ordered Wyatt. Ever since finding the photograph inside Cullen King's desk, he'd spent the past three weeks poring over data inside the offices of the Texas Railroad Commission.

Every single oil well in Texas was regulated and had to be recorded at the commission. And in order to penetrate the reams of data, you had to know what you were looking for. While he was in law school, Dylan had spent a few summers working for a land man out in Brazos County. So the maps and oil logs and well permitting inside the offices didn't look like mumbo-jumbo to him.

After two hundred hours of digging through dusty files, Dylan had hit pay dirt. Cullen Davis King had recorded a well that he'd platted on August 27. This meant that he'd staked an area for the hole, and intended to drill it.

Except he never had.

Dylan remembered back to the funeral. It had been early September. Aunt Lucinda had woken up one day and found Kathleen's grandfather dead in his bed. The doctors ruled that he'd suffered a massive heart attack. The stink of it was . . . no one knew whether Lucinda had actually woken up beside the aging oil magnate, but this was the rumor.

Kathleen wanted to believe that her grandfather had gone out with a bang. She wanted it to be true that Lucinda was sleeping next to him when he died. She couldn't bear to think that he'd been alone. And everyone knew that Lucinda had been madly in love with Cullen Davis King for years. Since even before Kathleen had been born.

Dylan figured that Cullen King had died before telling anyone about the drill site. And the reason the secret had been kept for so long—the reason Cullen King hadn't told his usual business partners—was that this well had been *on his own* land. He'd wanted to drill it himself, with his own crew, as a matter of pride.

Dylan hummed quietly to himself as Wyatt made the phone calls to summon the troops.

An hour later, C. Todd Hartwell was behind the wheel of his Hummer. Dylan was in the passenger seat, and Wyatt and Steve were in the back.

They were headed to Tangled Spur, and each of them had packed their ranch necessities. Dylan had brought binoculars. Wyatt had packed his deer rifle to take down a wild boar. C. Todd Hartwell had brought a cooler full of beer, two bottles of whiskey, ice, and a bunch of plastic cups. Steve had brought sunscreen and an Evian spritzer for his face.

"You're high-maintenance, man," Wyatt had chuckled, clapping Steve on the shoulder.

"I get dehydrated," Steve had said, spritzing his face. Mr. Louisiana was sporting head-to-toe camouflage, and stingray cowboy boots.

"Nice outfit, Super Fly," C. Todd Hartwell muttered.

Steve said, "Thanks, dawg," and left it at that.

Dylan pointed out the location of Tangled Spur on a map, and C. Todd Hartwell gunned the Hummer out of the front parking entrance of the Royal Arms.

Wyatt cracked his window to drown out the overpowering scent of Steve's cologne.

They sped down the highway listening to a radio station playing "Sounds of the Eighties."

Madonna, Tears for Fears, Wham!, Frankie Goes to Hollywood, and even Van Halen's "Hot for Teacher."

When Prince came on with "When Doves Cry," Steve shouted, "Crank it up!"

About two hours into the trip, they stopped off at Whataburger and ordered three Whataburgers with cheese and one Whatachick'n with bacon for Steve. Wyatt ordered two fries for himself and a large Dr Pepper.

C. Todd Hartwell produced a bottle of whiskey from inside his Windbreaker and used it to top off his Coke.

He offered it around the table, but Dylan, Wyatt, and Steve declined. "Shit dawg, it's only ten A.M.," Steve said, checking his big gold watch.

"You shouldn't be driving. Let me take over," Dylan offered.

C. Todd Hartwell laughed and took a swig from his fountain drink. "I drive better with the medicine," he said. "Trust me."

Dylan excused himself from the table and went outside to call Kat. She was at the hospital with Diego's parents, and had spent the night there last night. Dylan had already shown her the photograph and told her his plan to look for oil on Tangled Spur. She'd said, "Go for it, babe."

"How far out are you?" she asked, as Dylan stood on the sidewalk outside the Whataburger.

"I expect we'll get there around noon," Dylan said, scraping his boot along the pavement. "How's it going . . . over there?" he asked hesitantly.

He heard Kathleen sniffle, and he clutched the phone tightly in his hand.

"We're holding up," she replied. "But it's *just so hard.*"

"I know, hon," Dylan said, softly. He hated to think of Kat inside that hospital room, watching that poor boy die, but this was what she'd chosen. This was what she referred to as her "life calling." So the least he could do was be supportive.

Diego's parents had called in all their relatives, and they were holding a twenty-four-hour prayer vigil over Diego's bedside. Kathleen had been invited to join them, and of course, she'd accepted.

"When this is all over," Dylan said, "I'd like to start planning our wedding."

"I've been thinking about it," Kat said. "Maybe we shouldn't have some big to-do at Pa Pa's house. Maybe we should just run off and elope. Like to Paris or Italy or Mexico or something."

"Whatever you want, hon," Dylan said. "It's your day."

"We really don't have the money for a big wedding, anyway," Kat said.

Dylan sucked in his breath.

"That's not what I meant," she said immediately. "It's just that we've got to focus on paying off Wyatt's debt first."

"No. *Wyatt* needs to focus on paying off *Wyatt's* debt," Dylan said. He glanced inside the Whataburger windows just in time to see his younger brother taking a huge bite from his cheeseburger. Grease and ketchup ran down Wyatt's chin, and he wiped it off with a glob of napkins.

Dylan rolled his eyes. "Look, hon. I'm going to make things right. You've gotta have faith."

"I do," Kat said. "And I love you, munchkin."

"Love you, too," Dylan said. He didn't like being called a "munchkin," but sometimes there was no rhyme or reason for Kat's pet names.

"Call me later?" she asked.

"You bet."

He clicked the phone off, sighed deeply, and felt a hand on his shoulder. It was Wyatt.

"Felix called me yesterday," he said.

"And?"

"And he wants his money."

"No shit, Sherlock. What did you tell him?"

"I told him we were drilling this big daddy-o, monster of all monster wells, and that it would take at least six more weeks."

Dylan scowled and shook his head.

"What's wrong with that?" Wyatt asked.

"All I have is a photograph and a log report from the railroad commission," Dylan said. "That's pretty far from this monster well you're talking about. I mean, Jesus brother! I'm working off a hunch. We haven't even found the drill site yet. And even if we do, we could drill a dry hole!"

Wyatt crossed his arms over his broad chest and flashed Dylan his movie star smile. "Won't happen," he said.

"Let me guess. This is what you folks on the West Coast call 'channeling positive energy,'" Dylan said dryly.

Wyatt threw his head back up at the sky and laughed. "You know what your problem is, brother? Here you are, on the phone with Kat, telling her to have faith. And you don't have any faith of your own!"

"What are you trying to say?" Dylan asked.

Wyatt shook Dylan by the shoulders. "I'm saying it's time to have faith!"

Forty-two

"Never in my entire career," Dr. Levin was saying, "have I seen anything this remarkable."

Kat had been the first to notice it. Diego's eyelids were fluttering. And then his hand moved a little bit. Then he opened his eyes fully. He blinked a few times and tugged at Kathleen's hand.

She'd rushed down the hall to Dr. Levin's office and called him to Diego's bedside. But Diego was unconscious again by the time the doctor arrived.

"It could be his reflexes," Dr. Levin said, after examining the boy from head to toe.

"Can we do another brain scan?" Kat asked.

"Sure. But I don't know what the point would be."

Diego's mother had begun to cry. She'd never stopped crying, actually. It's just that she cried so much, sometimes the tears dried up and she'd cry without them. This time, the tears ran down her face in rolling wet streams. Diego's father passed her the box of Kleenex from his lap.

"Please, Dr. Levin," Kat said. She looked him in the eye and he finally nodded and said, "Okay."

Kat helped the nurse roll Diego's stretcher into the PET scan imaging room. She helped lift Diego's body and transfer him onto the lab table. The nurse placed the catheter that would administer the contrast dye into Diego's bloodstream.

Once he'd been properly prepped, Diego was rolled inside the machine to get his brain scan.

The PET scan took about three hours, and Kat waited at the nursing station the entire time for the results. Dr. Levin had requested that the report come back "stat."

"What is stat?" Kat had asked.

"From the Latin word *statinum*," Dr. Levin said, "meaning immediately."

Kathleen waited for the results and prayed. She prayed for Diego Ramirez, for his family, for his future. She told God that it didn't matter whether she had any children of her own, *But please, Lord, please just spare this one child.*

The radiology report came back within hours. Dr. Levin motioned for Kat to follow him into his office. He stood by the window shaking his head.

"Never in my career . . ." he kept repeating over and over.

At that moment, Kathleen knew it was time to smile.

"Tell me," she prompted.

"Diego's brain tumor is in remission. The cancer isn't spreading as we originally thought. He's actually doing quite well."

Kathleen clapped her hands and squealed. She ran toward Dr. Levin and gave him a hug. He smelled like hospital soap and coffee.

"I knew it!"

Dr. Levin raised his hand up like a stop sign to settle her down. "We're not out of the woods yet. Diego's infection is serious and he's having difficulty breathing."

"He's a fighter," Kat said. "He's going to make it."

"That's the spirit," Dr. Levin chuckled. "Please send in Diego's parents. I would like to show them these scans."

Kat swept back into Diego's room and summoned his parents to Dr. Levin's office. She translated for Dr. Levin as he pointed out the spots on the scan which showed Diego's tumor. "There is no flare-up," Dr. Levin was saying, which was difficult for Kat to translate, but she managed to get the point across.

As soon as they were finished, Kat walked back to Diego's room and was not surprised to see that the little boy's eyes were open again. He spotted Kat coming into the room and he tried pointing his finger to his favorite book.

"You want me to read to you. Of course I will!" Kat swooned. She grabbed the *Tales of the Unicorn Land* book off the windowsill, cracked it open, and began to read:

Uli Unicorn's Magic Dust

Wilma the waterwitch
And her 25 black
Cats lived in a
Cave near the Smiling Pond.
Wilma was the dark cloud
Of the Unicorn Land.
Every time Wilma became
Angry, she went into
A screaming tantrum.
She screeched, fell on

The ground, waved her
Arms about, then
She cast a dark spell
And made it rain.
A day, a week, or sometimes longer!
Her black cats spit, yowled, and
Fought. All the noise
Scared the children of the
Unicorn Land. They would cover
Their ears and hide.
One day, poor old Wilberforce, the
Cross-eyed snake who saw
Double, accidentally bumped
Into Wilma. She went into
Her usual screaming fit.
Uli Unicorn had reached the
End of his patience with
Wilma.
He grabbed Wilma and
Her 25 cats and sprinkled them
With Magic dust.
They slept
Soundly for 24 hours.
When Wilma awoke, she
Smiled and was pleasant to
Everyone.
The cats
Played with each other and
Purred constantly.
From that day on, Wilma never
Had another tantrum.
Thus peace and happiness

Were again restored to
The Land.
Thanks to Uli Unicorn's
Magic Dust.

When Kat was finished reading the story, she placed her hand on Diego's forehead. It was warm, but she thought his temperature was coming down. She had the nurse check his vital sign monitor.

"He's doing good," the nurse said.

Kat smiled down at Diego and saw that his eyes were looking back at her. They were bright and strong. She felt a surge of warmth spread through her body. It was such a good feeling to discover that this child might have a chance. And it put her life into perspective. The work she did for her foundation. The money she'd raised. The goals she'd set. They no longer seemed frivolous. Kat envisioned children's cancer hospitals, just like this, all over the country. And even a cure for cancer, which would be the best news yet.

"You're a brave strong boy, Diego," she whispered into the child's ear.

Forty-three

Dylan swept the binoculars across the broad expanse of ranch land. C. Todd Hartwell maneuvered the Hummer across the gravel roads circling the Tangled Spur.

"Looks like we're gonna have to do this on foot," Dylan said. They'd already circled the ranch twice, and Dylan hadn't seen any stakes sticking up from the ground. He knew the stake could've come loose if the dirt around it got wet, or muddy, or for a whole host of reasons. And it could be lying in the tall grasses, hidden by cactus or brush. If this was the case, it would take him forever to find the drill site.

C. Todd Hartwell parked the Hummer, and the four guys climbed out. Wyatt propped his deer rifle up on his shoulder. "Let's get it on."

Steve rubbed sunscreen all over his face, donned a white Panama hat, and turned his collar up around the neck. He looked ridiculous in the camouflage, but Dylan knew better than to make fun of Mr. Louisiana's outfit.

C. Todd Hartwell took a swig from the whiskey bottle and

burst out with *"Let's get ready to rumble!"* as if he were announcing a WWE wrestling match.

The four guys fanned out across the land and began their treks.
The Texas landscape was harsh and unforgiving. Especially when
the sun was high in the sky and the temperature in the nineties.
On his shoulder, Dylan carried a CamelBak filled with water.

It was a fool's errand to try and hike the ranch without the ap-
propriate gear. Water, sunscreen, snake boots, and walkie-talkie
radios so they could get in touch with one another.

Texas terrain could kill people, and often did.

Over the next few hours, they'd each covered a few hundred
acres. Dylan hiked quickly toward the Wishing Rock, in the area
where he and Kat had first spotted the bubbling crude. If Cullen
Davis King knew about the surface minerals, this could've possibly clued him in to the idea of a sea of oil flowing underneath
his feet.

Dylan knew that the key was to first pump out all of the oil
first—which existed on a shallower level—before reaching the
big payload, the deep natural gas underneath.

He made his way toward the stream and spotted the Wishing
Rock in the distance. For some reason, his intuition told him he
was getting close. Dylan closed his eyes a moment and wiped
sweat from his brow. Wyatt was right. He had to have faith.

He trudged through the grasses and undergrowth, whacking
at the hanging brush and tree limbs with a small workman's machete. It was tough going, but he finally reached the hole.

Dylan heard a shotgun blast in the distance and realized that
Wyatt was close by. He reached for his radio.

"Hey brother, don't shoot me accidentally on purpose," he said.

Wyatt chuckled into the receiver. "The hog got away, but he
didn't get far. He's wounded."

"Are you tracking him?" Dylan asked.

"Yep."

"Well, you're supposed to be looking for the stake."

"Really? I forgot."

"Smart ass," Dylan grumbled. He knew that Wyatt's talents were much better served taking down a hog than searching for a drill site. While he'd always been an excellent shot, Wyatt was never one to notice "details."

His younger brother would probably step right over the stake and not realize it, Dylan thought, with a smile.

He radioed Steve and C. Todd Hartwell to check their progress.

"Any luck?" Dylan asked, into the radio.

"I saw some birds fucking," C. Todd said. "But that's been the highlight."

"You're a sick sonofabitch," Steve's voice sounded on the line.

"You have no idea," C. Todd replied.

"Back to work," Dylan said.

"Ay ay, Captain."

This was from Wyatt.

Dylan rolled his eyes and put the radio back in his pack. He was hot. Hot, tired, frustrated, and sick of this shit. *Something's gotta give,* he thought.

He raised the machete over his head and whacked at the bush in front of him. It was hard to take down so Dylan kicked it, and then decided to climb right over the top of the thing. He was cursing as he realized his hands were covered with burrs and pickers. And that he was going to have to pry them out of his raw skin one by one. He'd also been bit by a ton of mosquitoes and quite possibly a few ticks.

Great, Dylan thought. This little sojourn was going to give him Lyme disease. He was just about to throw up his hands and forget the whole thing.

And that's when he saw it.

Poking out of the dirt. A stake that had been hammered into the ground. Just like in the photograph.

Dylan felt his heart rise up into his throat. It was here! The drill site. Right near the stream. Right near the bubbling hole that he'd discovered.

Dylan rushed forward and checked the stake for any signs of markings. But if they'd once been there, they were long gone—having been stripped away by the elements. The stake was bare, and held not a single marking. But Dylan felt in his gut that this had to be it.

As he reached for his radio, Dylan paused. He wanted to take this moment to thank the Lord, or whoever had presented him with this gift. This opportunity. Dylan realized that the only person he wanted to share the good news with . . . was Kat.

He'd have to call her as soon as he reached an area with good cell phone reception. Until then, he needed to share the news with his makeshift "crew." They weren't professional in the least, but heck. They were all he had.

Dylan grabbed his hand radio. "I found it!" he blurted into the receiver. "Come look!"

Wyatt's voice came on immediately. "See, brother. I told you to have faith."

Forty-four

Kat felt like a scarecrow. Her arms were raised in the air, and she was waiting patiently as the Korean alterations lady at the Bridal Boutique pinned the dress all around her. Kat was standing on a small platform in front of a wide wall filled with mirrors. She felt ridiculous posing in the bouffant white dress, but Shelby Lynn Pierce had insisted that Kat buy a *new* wedding dress—not some "old rag" from Twice Around Texas.

"That dress is the bomb, honey," Shelby Lynn said as she circled around Kat, her expert eyes measuring Kat up and down.

"Who's the designer?" Kat asked.

"Oscar de la Renta," Shelby Lynn said.

"Who's that?"

Shelby Lynn glanced over at Aunt Lucinda sitting in the corner of the fitting room. Lucinda was drinking one of the Bridal Boutique's mango fruit punch cocktails out of a champagne flute.

"She's hopeless, Lucinda," Shelby Lynn said.

Aunt Lucinda raised her glass, smiled a tipsy, lopsided smile, and said, "Don't blame me, chile. I ain't her mama."

Shelby Lynn threw her head back in the air, and they both laughed at that one. Kat's mother had been one of the most fashionable women in Houston society, and had been voted into the Best Dressed Hall of Fame from *Houston High Society* magazine. It was a wonder that her only daughter was now questioning the likes of certain fashion designers.

"Let me see that killer rock of yours again," Shelby Lynn said, pouncing on Kathleen's hand.

"You may want to put on your sunglasses so you don't get blinded," Lucinda said.

Kat flashed her ring finger so Shelby could admire the antique Kashmir sapphire.

"I'm thrilled with it," Kat said.

"Who wouldn't be?" Shelby cooed. "And now for the finishing touches . . ."

Kat stood still as Shelby Lynn picked up a veil and attempted to arrange it on Kat's head.

"The train flows out behind you like this," Shelby Lynn said, straightening out the train behind the dress.

"Well?" Lucinda asked. "What do you think, Cinderella?"

Kat stared at herself in the mirror and bunched up her lips in a pout. It looked like a giant cream puff had exploded all over her. Granted, the shantung and lace and beading were exquisite, and the train fell perfectly down the small of her back and across the floor, but still.

Kat raised the veil up over her head. "This isn't me," she said.

Shelby Lynn Pierce shot her a look. "You are not buying your wedding dress at a thrift store and that is final," she said.

"Luu-cindaa," Kat whined, staring back at her old nanny for help.

Lucinda downed the rest of her champagne glass. "Don't look at me, child. I'm just here for the alcohol," she tittered.

Kat realized that Lucinda was toasted. Her warm chocolate brown eyes were even a little shiny.

"You're buzzed." Kat giggled.

Lucinda never drank anything except hot tea. So this was a nice change.

"I thought this was a party," Lucinda said, waving her empty champagne flute in the air.

"It is. And we're going to do it right," Shelby Lynn chirped. She sent the saleslady off to bring them another round of mango fruit juice cocktails "with a kick."

"How about a dress that's simple?" Kat asked. She was trying to struggle her way out of the wedding dress, but something had gotten caught in her hair and she was stuck.

"Let me help you with that, silly buns." Kat felt Shelby expertly jerking the dress this way and that, until it came off over the top of Kat's head. A wave of relief washed over her. She was back to panties and bra and feeling free as a bird again.

"You're too thin," Aunt Lucinda said. "We need to put some meat on those bones."

Shelby Lynn whirled around with her hands on her slim hips. She was model-thin herself, with a perfect figure from many hours spent in the Houstonian gym and spa, and some guessed the plastic surgery suite of Dr. Franklin Prose.

"I wish I were too thin," she said.

Lucinda, who'd always been fifty pounds overweight, just rolled her eyes.

"You're perfect, dear," Lucinda trilled, flapping her hand at Shelby as if to say, *And everybody knows it.*

Shelby broke out into a broad smile. "Oh stop it, Luce. I'm not perfect by any means."

Kat smiled to herself. Both Lucinda and Shelby Lynn knew the score. Lucinda knew that Shelby Lynn thought of herself as having the body to die for—which she did. And Shelby Lynn knew that Lucinda was blowing smoke up her ass.

The saleslady arrived and swirled around with a platter of fresh champagne cocktails. She'd also brought a small dish of tasty-looking petits fours.

"Oh, don't mind if do!" Lucinda said. She grabbed the whole plate and set it on her lap.

The saleslady raised her eyebrows and shot Lucinda a quizzical look.

"Don't worry. These little birds won't want any," Lucinda said, popping one of the pastries in her mouth.

"I don't eat sugar on Mondays," Shelby Lynn said.

"I'm still full from breakfast," Kat piped up.

Lucinda eyed the saleslady. "See. What did I tell ya."

Kat looked at the rack of dresses in the corner of the fitting room. "I think I need something less flouncy," she said. "I'm thinking of a long white gown, no train, no veil."

"Cinderella wants something sleek and classic with a little bit of sexy hoochie mama thrown in," Lucinda said, downing her champagne.

"I have just the thing," the saleslady said. She swooped across the rack of dresses and said, "Aha! Here we go."

Kat held her breath as the woman held up a gorgeous long white silk gown with a swooping dropped back.

The dress looked modern and sleek, and exactly what Kat imagined.

"I love it!" Kat squealed, and clapped her hands.

"I can already tell this one's a keeper," Lucinda said.

"Ooh la la! Super chic! The designer is Alexander McQueen," Shelby Lynn said, checking the label on the dress.

"Who's that?" Kat asked, causing everyone in the fitting room to laugh. Even Aunt Lucinda, who watched E! Entertainment television religiously, and hosted her church group's Academy Awards chicken dinner each year, knew who the various fashion designers were.

Kat marveled at herself in the mirror. The dress made her waiflike figure appear curvaceous. She felt emboldened by the dress, as if she'd suddenly transformed into an old-time Hollywood star. Ingrid Bergman herself would've approved.

Kat desperately wanted to ask the saleslady how much the dress cost, but since Shelby Lynn was there, she decided against it.

"How much for the dress?" Lucinda blurted out, as if reading Kathleen's mind.

"It was originally thirty-eight hundred, but we've marked it down half off because it's last season," the saleslady replied.

"Fabulous," Shelby Lynn said. "She'll take it."

Kat realized that she didn't have anywhere near this amount in her savings. She'd just paid the rent, bought groceries, and mailed checks to pay off the monthly balances on her and Dylan's credit card bills—without his knowledge.

"I'll think about it." Kat sighed, pulling the dress up over her head. She'd find a used wedding dress for a few hundred bucks at any thrift store in town.

"Ring it up," Lucinda chimed in, motioning toward the saleslady. She was waving a champagne flute in one hand and her credit card in the other. As she stood from her chair, the plate of half-eaten petits fours fell from her lap and dumped onto the floor.

"Whoopsy-daisy, I've done crazy!" Lucinda giggled.

"Oh my gosh, I think she's toast," Shelby Lynn said.

"Lucinda. I can't let you do that," Kat said, in a serious tone. She was not allowing her former nanny to pay for her wedding dress.

"This is my engagement gift, chile," Lucinda said, stumbling toward Kathleen to give her a hug.

"No," Kat said. "It's too much."

"I'll split it with you, Luce," Shelby piped up. She pulled an AmEx black card from her small green crocodile clutch and handed it to the saleswoman.

"You guys, I can buy my own dress," Kat said stubbornly, crossing her arms over her chest.

"Honey, you may be able to fool all the other women in this town, but I know for a fact you don't have a penny to your name because you gave all your money away like some kind of Sister Teresa," Shelby Lynn said.

"*Mother* Teresa," Lucinda corrected her.

"Sister, mother, whatever," Shelby Lynn continued. "Why do you think I keep donating so much to your foundation, Kathleen? It's because you do more than anyone, silly." She was giving Kat a look that said, *Who are you trying to fool?*

Kat was momentarily stunned. She had no idea that Shelby Lynn was well aware of her dirty little secret number one, and yet still remained a good friend.

"Well, Shelby Lynn. Now that you know my dirty little secret," Kat said, "I guess you should also know that I'm barren. I can't have children." .

Shelby Lynn shot Lucinda a quick glance. "I know. Lucinda told me."

"*Lucinda!*"

"Accident." Lucinda shrugged.

Kat shook her head back and forth. If there was one thing she'd learned from her mother, it was that there was no such thing as secrets.

"Don't be mad," Shelby Lynn said. "We want to help you, because you're always helping everyone else. I mean, look what you did for me and my self-esteem by introducing me to Bo Harlan. I couldn't have asked for a better man to help get me out of this divorce funk."

"We want to help you, child," Lucinda said softly. "But you're as stubborn as your granddad ever was."

"There's nothing you can do," Kat mumbled. "I'm getting married, and I'm happy for that. But I'll never be able to have children."

"Never say never," Shelby Lynn said, wagging her finger. "My brother is the best fertility doctor in New York and he makes miracles happen."

Kat took a deep breath and thought about Diego. About how he'd almost died. About his three brain surgeries, his collapsed lung, and his dangerous infection. About all the trials he'd suffered in his short, young life.

If this young child could pull through with a miracle, perhaps she should have more faith.

"I guess this means we're going to New York City," Kat said.

"We already booked your appointment," Lucinda said, shooting Shelby Lynn a mischievous wink.

The two women both started giggling, watching Kat standing in her bra and panties on the small fitting room platform, holding an empty champagne flute in her hand and looking entirely stunned.

"You look like the shocked version of Aphrodite," Shelby Lynn said.

Kat broke out into a smile. "You two partners in crime can buy my dress after all."

Shelby turned to Lucinda, and both women raised their hands up in the air and slapped a high five.

Forty-five

Dylan had been drinking. Not drinking, drinking. Like his old man used to do. But enough to where he felt sloppy.

Wyatt had arranged a birthday dinner bash for Steve at La Dolce Vita Pizzeria, and he and C. Todd Hartwell were ordering rounds of shots as if they were back in college again. They'd decided on silly shots—like Sex on the Beaches, and Lemon Drops, and Buttery Nipples, and each time they ordered them, they ordered a second round for the sexy bartender gals as well. That way, everyone was getting nice and hammered.

Dylan had drunk four glasses of Chianti and eaten an entire pepperoni pizza. But the liquor was doing a number on his stomach. He felt like having fun for a change. So he joined into the festivities and ordered a round of Sambuca—"to make you puke-a." Which made everyone roar with laughter. He wished that Kat could've joined them but she was doing what she called "wedding stuff" with the girls.

As he threw back his Sambuca and felt the burn in his throat, Dylan realized that he was enjoying himself for the first time since hearing the news of Butch Grant's death. Since *dealing with* the aftershocks of Butch Grant's death.

Plus, things were looking up. He and Kat were getting married. And he'd found the stake on the ranch. Sure, it was too soon to celebrate. *But heck*, Dylan thought, *how often did Steve from Louisiana turn thirty-seven?*

Staying true to form, Steve was wearing what he called his "Supa Fly birthday suit." A purple suit with large white pinstripes. White patent leather loafers. A white hat cocked sideways on his head. And gold . . . everywhere. Gold watch, gold rings on his fingers, gold chains around his neck.

"You realize that you're a short-ass white guy!" Wyatt roared, clapping Steve on the shoulder.

"And you're a dumb, one-legged sonofabitch!" Steve replied.

"Hey, I've gotta news flash, Justin Timberlake! You're not in the NBA!" Wyatt roared.

"Ladies, this man thinks he's Tom Cruise!" Steve shouted to the girls behind the bar. "Check out the ladies' man over here. Straight off the plane from Las Vegas. Aren't we lucky to have him in our podunk little city."

Steve pointed at Wyatt, and Wyatt rolled his hand a few times and took a bow. They both broke down laughing at their tremendous brand of put-down comedy.

Dylan grabbed another shot off the bar and smiled. For some reason, his younger brother and Steve had bonded the way men do—over offensive jokes and physical shoulder slapping.

C. Todd Hartwell was swaying near a bunch of stools, looking like he was about to keel over.

"Gimme another round of shrinks!" he slurred.

One of the bartenders shook her head and pointed across the bar at her manager. "You're cut off. Sorry, hon," she said.

"This is *bull crap!*" C. Todd said. He was precariously close to falling over, and Dylan thought this was tremendously funny.

Wyatt and Steve started pounding on the bar and chanting, "*Bull crap . . . bull crap . . . bull crap . . .*" over and over, until the manager came over and threatened to call the police if they didn't settle down.

"Fuck the *po . . . lice!*" Steve rapped, as if he were Tupac, which sent everyone into stitches.

Dylan was laughing so hard he nearly threw up. The four guys tumbled out into the parking lot and tried to hail a passing taxi.

There was no way any of them were driving. Not in this condition. And not in Texas. Where Mothers Against Drunk Driving had made a DUI akin to a death sentence.

Before Dylan could recognize the black sedan parked a few feet away from them, it was too late.

Dylan's eyes were adjusting to the night sky when he felt the first punch land squarely across his face.

He, Steve, Wyatt, and C. Todd Hartwell were attacked from either side by four men in suits.

Dylan tried to punch his way to freedom, but the hits were coming from all angles and he felt himself going down. Something heavy landed on his arm, and he realized it was a baseball bat. Dylan felt no pain at first, until he fell to the cement. Then the pain rocketed across his arms and chest.

He felt the kicks to his ribs, abdomen, and groin. And he vomited up his pizza.

"*Felix!*" he gurgled. "*I have your cash!*"

Suddenly the kicks stopped coming. Dylan coughed and scanned the parking lot for any signs of Felix. Wyatt, Steve, and C. Todd Hartwell were writhing around on the cement, groaning in pain.

Felix appeared over Dylan's head, his gold tooth protruding

from his permanent sneer. A pave diamond–encrusted skull necklace dangled from his neck. "I told you not to make me come back here," he snapped.

"Sorry," Dylan grumbled. "Look. I've got your money. Give me a week."

"No more time," Felix said. "I'm out of patience, my friend."

"We've got something better than cash," Wyatt piped up. Dylan turned and glared at his brother. He saw that Wyatt had gotten the worst of the beating. His nose looked broken and his eyes were both swollen.

Dylan shook his head vigorously back and forth, trying to signal for Wyatt to *Please shut up!* But his brother just wrangled on ahead.

"Ah, the younger brother speaks out," Felix said in a snide tone. "What's better than cash?"

"Oil," Wyatt groaned.

"I see," Felix said. He circled around Wyatt while his men kept guard, their baseball bats propped firmly up against their shoulders.

"We're drilling a monster well," Wyatt sputtered.

Dylan dropped his head into his hands. Luckily, C. Todd Hartwell had passed out from the combination of alcohol and ass kicking, and was snoring loudly on the pavement. Otherwise, he probably would've kicked Wyatt's ass himself.

Steve was watching Felix—like a snake watches a hyena. Mr. Louisiana shot up off the pavement and grabbed Felix by the throat.

"Tell your guys to *back off, dawg!*" Steve commanded, squeezing Felix's throat until the bookie actually yelped.

Felix motioned for his men to step away.

Dylan held his breath. He knew that Steve worked with some

shady characters back in New Orleans, and so Felix was quite possibly a dead man.

"My friend over here told you you'd get your money in a week. I suggest you wait a week," Steve hissed into Felix's ear. "You understand?"

Felix nodded.

Steve released the bookie's throat and watched as he gasped for air. "You'll be all right, just *breathe*," Steve said, patting Felix on the back as if he were burping a baby.

Felix stared at Wyatt and then back at Dylan.

"You need investors for this oil thing?" he choked.

"No." Dylan wiped blood from his cheek.

It was funny, really. As soon as the words "oil well" came into play, everyone wanted in on the deal.

"What if I forgive the entire loan in exchange for a piece of it?" Felix asked.

"Could be a dry hole," Dylan said, hoisting himself up off the pavement. "And then you wouldn't make shit."

"What if it isn't a dry hole?" Felix asked.

Dylan wiped his hands against his jeans. Felix wasn't dumb, that was for sure.

"You'd make ten times your money. Possibly more."

"What are the odds?" Felix asked.

Dylan smirked. Mr. Vegas was now asking about the odds.

"Five to one."

"Okay," Felix said. "It's a deal. Have your lawyer fax me the documents tomorrow."

Spoken like a true businessman, Dylan mused.

"Done," Dylan said. The bookie stretched out his hand. "Does this mean we have a gentlemen's agreement?" he asked, flashing Dylan his gold tooth.

Dylan pointed over to C. Todd Hartwell, who was still lying on the pavement passed out cold. "Sure, Felix. But do you think your guys can help us move our buddy off the pavement?"

Felix snapped his fingers, and his men bolted into action.

They struggled to pick up C. Todd, flagged down a passing taxi, and carried him like he was in a parade.

Forty-six

Dylan rolled over in bed and groaned. Kat threw her arm around him and held him tight against her body.

"You okay, honey buns?" she whispered.

Dylan grunted and let out a loud snore.

Kat kissed her fiancé on his bruised shoulder. His body was warm and his skin covered in sweat. A few hours earlier, he and Wyatt had dragged themselves back to the apartment looking battered, bruised, and drunk.

Boys will be boys, Kat thought.

She'd heated up a can of chicken noodle soup and forced them to drink the broth before they both collapsed. Wyatt crashed on the couch, and Dylan stumbled into the bedroom.

She'd been surprised to see Dylan in that condition because he'd never been one to overindulge in alcohol. He'd always felt extra cautious about drinking, because of the childhood he'd endured. Kat had met Butch Grant only a few times, and each time it hadn't been a good experience.

Once, when she and Dylan had been in high school, Dylan's

father had even attempted to grope her. Kat had never mentioned this to Dylan, or the fact that she'd promptly kicked the senior Mr. Grant in his knee and called him a "perv."

Some secrets were meant to be kept. There was no reason to fuel the fire, in Kat's opinion. Especially since Dylan was already suspicious of Butch Grant's behavior.

Kat tousled Dylan's wet hair. Her fiancé seemed particularly stressed about their financial situation, the impending wedding, and the possibility of drilling a dry hole on Tangled Spur.

She lay in bed with the lights out and considered her options. She wanted to become more involved in Dylan's work. More educated about oil and gas in general. Although her mother would've considered this to be the eighth deadly sin.

Never involve yourself in your husband's business affairs, her mama had always told her, *unless you want to be treated like a secretary.*

Kat figured she could involve herself just fine, as long as she played the right role. That of visiting dignitary. Perhaps she could use the foundation dinner as a platform to get inside the deal flow. Kat didn't want to be the last to know information, especially since it was her Pa Pa's property that was being drilled.

It's time to get off the sidelines, Kat thought as she fluffed up the pillow underneath her head.

It's time to be inside the loop.

Forty-seven

Jonathan Whipley sat across the conference table from Dylan. The doughnut heir was wearing his usual crisp suit and tie combo that looked like a million bucks, and made Dylan want to head straight for Neiman Marcus.

Mr. Doughnut was staring down at the photograph of the stake in the ground.

"So you want me to invest in this deal?" he asked, in his posh, Ivy League voice.

"That's correct," Dylan said.

C. Todd Hartwell had already contributed a small cash infusion from his other investors, but Dylan still needed the big fish. Someone to write a monster check that would take them over the goal line. Jonathan Whipley was just that fish.

"But you don't have any seismic data?" Jonathan asked.

"Nope." Dylan blinked a few times and rubbed his temples with his thumbs.

"So you have no real proof that the minerals are below ground?"

Dylan tapped the photograph on the conference table. "This photograph is the proof. I also found a well log at the railroad commission showing that Cullen King intended to drill his own land before he died."

Jonathan Whipley leaned back in his chair. He took a sip from his coffee and shot Dylan a dubious look. "You have no clue whether the stake you found on Tangled Spur is the same stake that's in the photo. You're essentially asking me to fund a project which is half-cocked in its inception."

Dylan sucked in his breath and stood from his chair. Jonathan Whipley was calling his idea "half-cocked."

Stay calm, he thought.

"I'm getting coffee. Anyone want one?" Dylan asked around the table, as he walked to the coffee machine.

"I'm good," C. Todd Hartwell replied. He'd already had a shot of whiskey this morning, and Dylan knew this because he could smell it on the oilman's breath from a mile away.

Dylan wanted to start his own oil company; he didn't want to deal with investors and this dirty art of fund-raising. And yet he had to make his *big push*. The one big score that would put his name on the map.

Dylan glanced around the conference table. He needed this motley cast of characters. He needed C. Todd Hartwell's industry connections; Jonathan Whipley's money; Steve and his Louisiana crew to operate the rig; hell, he even needed Kat's permission to drill her granddad's land. The only person Dylan didn't "need" was Wyatt. But Wyatt would be included because Wyatt—by sheer kismet—always managed to get himself inserted in the action.

Dylan pushed the button on the coffee machine, inserted a Styrofoam cup under the dispenser, and planned his next move.

Jonathan Whipley might not want to gamble on this venture, he knew, so Dylan was bringing in his Secret Weapon. The one person in the world who could get *anyone* to write a check.

Just as the coffee machine stopped whirring, Kat bustled into the conference room like a woman on a mission. She was wearing all white and beige. Like some fund-raising fairy.

"Hello beautiful men," she chirped. "Sorry I'm late."

Kat gave Dylan a little sideways wink. She was right on time, and she knew it. Taking a seat at the head of the conference table like she owned the place, she folded her hands calmly and turned her attention toward Jonathan Whipley.

"And who do we have here?" she said, flitting her eyelashes.

Jonathan Whipley cleared his throat and glanced at the other men around the table, who seemed unfazed by Kat's arrival.

"I live in the building," Jonathan said.

Kat looked at Jonathan and blinked.

Dylan knew that his fiancée was doing her actress impression. The one she'd learned from her mother.

"Kathleen King," Kat said, as a matter of introduction. "I don't believe we've met."

She extended her slim hand, and Jonathan Whipley nearly tripped over himself trying to reach it.

"Jonathan Whipley," he said, grabbing Kat's hand and pumping up and down.

Nervous as a jackrabbit, Dylan thought. He tried not to smile. He was glad that Mr. Million Bucks had shed his cool, calm persona and was falling all over himself.

"Whipley?" Kat asked, pressing her hand primly to her chest. "Don't tell me you're related to Kinkaid Whipley?"

Jonathan Whipley broke out into a smile. "She's my wife."

"Oh goodness. That must be such a treat."

"And how do you know her?"

"Why, Jonathan. Your wife runs my favorite shop in town."

"Don't tell me you buy your clothes at Twice Around Texas?" Jonathan asked, looking skeptical.

"Do I ever!" Kat trilled. "I adore vintage!" Kat stood from her chair and modeled the crisp white pants and beige top she was wearing. "This outfit *was a steal*," she whispered, as if telling Jonathan a state secret.

Jonathan admired Kat's outfit and nodded his head approvingly. "When Kinkaid told me she wanted to manage a vintage clothing shop, I just didn't get it," he said. "But the children are off at school and I think she got bored sitting home all day. It became a nice change of pace for her. And my wife loved it so much that we ended up buying the store from the old owner. He was ready to retire, and so we took over the whole place."

"You're joking!" Kat said. "So you and your wife own my favorite clothing boutique in the *whole wide world*?" she asked, in her sweet-as-pie tone.

"Looks that way," Jonathan said.

"I don't believe you," Kat said, playfully tapping Jonathan on the arm as if he were fooling with her.

"Believe it," Jonathan said. He bucked out his chest as much as someone from Harvard could buck out his chest, and looked pleased with himself.

"Then I must get together with your wife!" Kat exclaimed, clapping her hands a bit. "I was planning on having a little fashion show at my Annual Foundation Dinner, and I wanted the theme to be vintage fashion. Do you think your wife would be interested in arranging the clothes for my event?"

"For the King Foundation Dinner?" Jonathan Whipley asked. He tugged at the knot in his tie and cleared his throat.

Dylan noticed that the doughnut heir seemed to have stopped breathing.

Kat was in full swing now and had Jonathan's undivided attention. "So you've heard of my little dinner?" she asked.

Jonathan Whipley grinned. "Who hasn't?"

Kathleen broke out into a smile as if she were surprised that Jonathan Whipley was keenly aware of the most famous fundraising dinner in Texas.

"You're too sweet," she said, rapping his arm again. "So. The details. Every year, we do this private little dinner to raise money for the children's hospital, and this year I thought it would be fun to have a fashion show. If Kinkaid wanted to dress the models, I think it would be great marketing, don't you agree?"

"Definitely," Jonathan said. "How nice of you to think of her."

"Oh, it's completely selfish on my part. I just love the clothes," Kat said.

Jonathan looked like he'd just won the keys to a brand-new Ferrari. Dylan imagined the doughnut heir rushing upstairs to the penthouse floor and announcing to his wife that he'd scored her a fashion show at the King Foundation Dinner.

"If you want, I could also provide some specialty doughnuts or crepes for desert," Jonathan piped up. The doughnut heir was in full giving mode now. He sliced his arm through the air as if he were announcing a game show. "You know our motto, don't you?"

Kat opened her mouth and sang the commercial in pitch-perfect tone: *"Whipley's will 'Whip Up' something special for your special event . . ."*

"You have a fantastic voice," Jonathan said. "We should hire you to do all of our commercials."

"Aren't you a dear!" Kat trilled.

She reached over and placed her hand on top of Jonathan's. "I'm tickled to death that you're joining us on this little oil venture, *Jonathan*. It's going to be such a hoot."

Dylan watched his fiancée in amazement. She spoke of a massive drilling project as if it was an afternoon spent beside a swimming pool. A trifle.

"Pa Pa would've been so pleased to know that such a fine group of men were involved in this project," Kat said, beaming at all the men around the conference table.

Jonathan Whipley swung around toward Dylan. "Count me in," he said. "I'll wire the money this week, no problem."

"Great," Dylan said. He carried his coffee over to the conference table and took a seat next to Kat. She'd done a fine job with Jonathan Whipley, and now it was time for her to leave the room.

Dylan glanced over at Kat, but she'd taken a notepad out of her purse and was flipping it open as if she were a reporter.

She looked over at him and tapped her pen against the notepad. "I'm ready when you are," she said.

Dylan gulped back his coffee and managed to scald his tongue. "We're about to start the meeting, hon," he said, "and I bet the details will bore you to death."

"Oh, don't mind me," Kat cooed. She beamed a winning smile at each of the men around the table. "Y'all don't mind if I stay, do you?" she asked.

"We'd be honored to have you," Wyatt piped up, because he didn't know any better.

"Make yourself at home, sista," Steve said.

"Why the hell not?" C. Todd Hartwell said magnanimously, as he shot Kat his usual I-wish-I-could-have-sex-with-you look.

"I'm just happy to be here myself," Jonathan Whipley said.

Dylan gritted his teeth. He didn't plan on Kat staying for the entire meeting. What had gotten into her all of a sudden? Why did she want to spend three hours going over the fine-line details of an oil and gas deal?

Just then, he felt a soft hand glide over the top of his wrist. Kat was staring at him. "You don't mind if I stay, do you, dear?" she asked.

"If you want to stay, stay," Dylan said. "But I think you're gonna be bored to tears."

Kat scribbled out a little note on her notepad and thrust it over to Dylan. He picked up the piece of paper and read it quietly to himself.

> *Thank you for your concern, Dylan Charles Grant.*
> *But I'll be the judge of that.*

Dylan took a deep breath. Kat would be Kat. There was no point arguing with her once she'd made up her mind. He stood from the table and began passing around a chart outlining the drilling costs associated with the venture.

To drill a hole was no small feat. Preparing a drill site required many steps. First, Dylan would need to hire various contractors to clear and level the land around the drill site, build an access road, make water available, and dig a pit to serve as a waste protector. Then, Dylan's contractors would move in the rig and the other necessary equipment. Once the rig was in position over the conductor hole, the drilling would begin to create the surface hole.

There was no such thing as "taking a break" once drilling began. The rig would be in constant motion twenty-four hours a day, seven days a week straight, and the drilling crew would man their posts in twelve-hour-on/ twelve-hour-off shifts.

Once the drill rig reached final depth, Dylan's geologist would determine whether there was enough oil and gas to proceed with the most expensive part of the drilling process—the completion. If the hole ended up being "dry," then Dylan would order the drilling contractor to plug it up and abandon the project. And all money would be lost.

Part of drilling for oil was skill; the other part was luck. And Dylan needed all the luck he could manage.

As he stood beside Kat, he leaned down to her ear and whispered, "Check out who I named this well after."

He watched as Kat studied the report—at the top was her name in large bold letters.

KAT #1 DRILLING PROSPECT

"You're naming the well after me?" Kat whispered.

"Of course, hon. You're my best luck charm," Dylan replied. He knew he shouldn't kiss her on top of her head. He didn't want to show affection in the meeting—not in front of the guys. But he couldn't help it.

Dylan crossed his fingers that no one was paying attention. He leaned down and quickly kissed Kat on top of her head, inhaling the scent of her apricot shampoo.

"Oh Lord. Get a room," C. Todd Hartwell said, rolling his eyes.

Forty-eight

Sailors and baseball players were notorious for being superstitious. That's why sailors named their boats *Serendipity*, or *Godspeed*. And why baseball players kissed their bats before stepping up to the plate.

But sailors and baseball players had nothing on wildcatters. Dylan knew that Houston oilmen were the most superstitious group of people on the planet. Some would wear lucky amulets around their wrists or special cuff links; some would refrain from drinking alcohol or having sex during the drilling process in sort of a servitude to the drilling gods; and one wildcatter in particular, by the name of C. Todd Hartwell, would eat only Cheerios for breakfast, lunch, and dinner while a drilling rig was at a site.

For Dylan, his luck was inextricably tied to naming the oil prospect after the one woman whom he loved more than anyone. He'd decided to wear his lucky T-shirt, the one with the screaming eagle emblazoned across the chest, for good measure. He'd owned the T-shirt since college, and even though it sported a few tatty holes around the seams, Dylan had always felt the shirt brought him an extra dose of good energy.

The Tangled Spur Ranch was located in South Texas in an area that had constantly given the big oil companies a headache. First, the soil was too soft, which made drilling a challenge. Soft soil could cause the rig to tilt, and possibly collapse or snap in half if the pressure became too great.

This would be a catastrophic event for most oil companies, which didn't dare risk losing the equipment, and even possibly the lives of rig workers working on the platform during a collapse.

The ranch was paved with gravel roads, but the area where Dylan had found the stake—the drill site—was about five hundred yards from the nearest paved road. So a new road that could sustain the heavy equipment had to be paved across Kathleen's land.

Dylan shielded his eyes from the sun, watching the bulldozers and load trucks clearing land and pouring concrete. His meeting with the geologist was on schedule, and he gunned the truck's accelerator until he made it to the mobile command center.

From the outside, the command center resembled a sleek silver mobile home—nothing spectacular. But as Dylan stepped inside the command unit, he was surrounded by panels of computer imaging rivaling NASA.

Drilling deep into the earth's surface was akin to plunging the darkest depths of the ocean or sending a rocket into space. It required massive amounts of real-time computer imaging and analysis to determine all the variable factors—from well depth to water content to the massive drill that would break through the layers of shale and rock.

Dylan had always gotten excited upon entering a mobile

command center. In the past, he'd been a small player on the stage. Like a guy in a sporting arena happy to get a seat inside the VIP box. But this time, *he* was in charge. This was *his* show. *His* VIP box.

Dylan wiped his hands against his jeans and spotted the Golden Buddha. His real name was Einrich Von Hearn, and it was rumored that he'd emigrated from Germany in the late 1990s. Now the famed geologist spent most of his time scouring the fields of East Texas for oil underneath the surface. He'd been nicknamed "the Golden Buddha" because of his notorious record for producing great wells.

The Golden Buddha's stats were volleyed back and forth like football scores. He'd been credited with discovering more than fifty new oil fields, including the Bartlett Shale, which had just made the record books with its sizable million barrels a day production.

Dylan had hired the best because he needed the best. And the Golden Buddha wouldn't attach himself to any project he deemed "unworthy." Dylan was giving him a percentage of the well if it "made hole," and even if it ended up dry, Einrich Von Hearn still stood to make a quarter million dollars' salary for his six weeks of work.

"Ah hallo, Meester Grant," Einrich said as Dylan strode toward him. The two men shook hands, and Dylan noticed how much the geologist resembled Santa Claus. His hair was a shock of white, and he sported a bushy white beard and eyebrows.

Dylan couldn't determine the geologist's age, but from the crinkles sprouting across his forehead and the laugh lines near his eyes, he guessed Einrich was somewhere in the neighborhood of sixty-five.

"How are we making out?" Dylan asked. He'd been requesting constant status reports that he then disseminated to C. Todd

Hartwell, Steve, and, of course, Mr. Deep Pockets, Jonathan Whipley.

Einrich sailed his hand across the air as if drawing an imaginary line. "We are sailing in good wind, but too early for good news!" he boomed.

Dylan couldn't help but chuckle. In the oil and gas business, delays were de rigueur, and patience a virtue. Einrich probably thought of Dylan as being a bit too in-his-face. Perhaps it was best to leave the Golden Buddha alone inside the mobile command center—doing what he did best.

"How deep are we?" Dylan asked, glancing at one of the computer monitors.

"Fourteen thousand feet and counting!" Einrich crowed. He clapped his hands together sharply, causing Dylan to jump.

"Two thousand feet more and *bam*!" Einrich clapped. "We have our answer!"

"I'll keep my fingers crossed," Dylan said.

"No need for fingers of the crossing!" Einrich hooted, grabbing Dylan by the shoulders and giving him a small shake.

"It will be as it shall be!"

Ah, Dylan thought. *So this is why he's called "the Golden Buddha."*

"So you're telling me the path to enlightenment is right outside this window, hey Einrich?" Dylan smiled, motioning out the window of the mobile command unit to the giant drilling rig that sat like a rocket ship in front of them.

"Exact!" Einrich said, whipping his finger through the air like a maestro at the symphony.

"I guess I didn't need to wear my lucky T-shirt, then?" Dylan pointed to his shirt.

"Not so nice shirt, I agree." Einrich laughed and poked Dylan in the arm. "This shirt good for boy, not for man."

Dylan glanced down at the eagle emblazoned across his chest and realized he did look foolish. Who was he trying to be? Kurt Cobain? Bono? The rock star of the oil and gas industry?

"Next time, I'll wear my Speedo," Dylan promised.

The Golden Buddha tugged at his white beard and guffawed up at the ceiling.

Forty-nine

Shelby Lynn Pierce and Bo Harlan were officially "an item," according to Holly Drash, the gossip columnist at *PaperCity* magazine.

The pair had been spotted dining in a private corner booth at Café Annie, and according to one of the waiters on duty that night, Bo Harlan had given Shelby Lynn an orange Hermès gift bag—the contents of which could only be guessed, but many surmised that he'd given her the gold and white crocodile clutch from the new fall line that she'd been seen carrying everywhere.

This crocodile clutch was now perched in a prominent position on the table next to Kathleen.

"I love your handbag," Kat said.

Shelby Lynn smiled coyly, leaned over, and planted a kiss on Bo Harlan's ruddy cheek. "Bo has impeccable taste for a man."

Kathleen smiled and raised her wineglass in a silent toast to Wild Bo Harlan. She was sitting at the head of the tasting table that had been arranged by the French caterers she was about to hire for the Annual Foundation Dinner. The goal was to taste every item on the menu to determine which would be the best for serving at the biggest fund-raising dinner of the year.

Shelby Lynn had suggested a cheese course consisting of Brie, blue, and "the other stinky one."

Kat knew that more than half the women at her event wouldn't dare touch a piece of cheese, so she countered with tureens of tomato consommé, the warm pear salad, followed by a sorbet palate cleanser, and possible entrees of duck au jus, veal, or chicken paillard.

Bo Harlan was focusing on tasting all the deserts and was deftly gobbling up the chocolate mousse with raspberry sauce. He looked thrilled when Shelby Lynn stuck out her pink tongue and licked chocolate off the tip of his nose.

Aunt Lucinda was polishing off the bread basket and commenting favorably on "the butter."

"It's not margarine, it's real butter," she announced, dunking her bread into the butter plate and sipping her Earl Grey tea. She was wearing her island wrist bangles, which jangled each time she moved her arm.

Kinkaid Whipley was drowning herself in wine. She'd "tasted" six out of the nine bottles. But instead of pouring herself the typical tasting portions, she'd gone ahead and filled her glass each time.

Kat had recently befriended Jonathan Whipley's wife inside the small gym at the Royal Arms, and the two had bonded instantly.

Kat was pleased when Kinkaid Whipley turned out to be down-to-earth, funny as heck, and a little on the chubby side for Houston society standards. The doughnut heir's wife was a solid size twelve, and Kat was thrilled to see that she wasn't one of those plastic surgery stick figures.

Kinkaid Whipley spoke with a heavy East Coast accent, and when she said things like "water," it sounded like "wooder."

She also called Shelby Lynn "fatso," which was an obvious joke, and everyone except Shelby Lynn thought it was hugely funny.

Shelby Lynn Pierce looked dazzling in her outfit du jour—a knee-length gold and white Pucci dress, and gold Jimmy Choo stilettos. Around her neck, she wore a diamond and gold choker that looked like it was straight out of a Sotheby's catalogue.

Shelby Lynn picked at her salad plate and scraped the goat cheese to the side. "I don't know why they need to dump so much cheese on these salads." She wrinkled her nose and pushed the plate away.

"For a woman so dead-set on wanting a cheese course, you sure do hate cheese," Kinkaid Whipley said, raising her wine-glass and gulping back another large "sip."

"Salads are supposed to be healthy," Shelby Lynn said. "Otherwise it's not salad."

"Do you eat ranch?" Kinkaid asked, taking another swig of wine. "Ranch dressing has more calories than cheese."

"Duh," Shelby Lynn said, drumming her perfectly manicured nails on the tabletop.

"Ladies, ladies. Be nice," Bo Harlan instructed, running his hand through the white streak in his hair.

Kathleen knew that the oilman was thrilled to be invited into the mix, especially as the only man at the tasting table. As if his opinion about the caramel sauce was of top importance.

"You women *sure are* feisty when it comes to your society dinners," he said, throwing his arm over Shelby's thin shoulders.

"If you can't beat 'em, join 'em," Shelby Lynn said, kissing Bo again.

"So tell me, Bo," Kathleen said, plucking a strawberry off one of the desert plates. "What makes you such a fine poker player?"

Bo Harlan's face lit up and he sat back in his chair and crossed his burly arms over his chest. "Well, ladies. It's like this," he said. "You've gotta know when to hold 'em. And know when to fold 'em."

"You think we're stupid, don't you?" Kathleen asked.

Shelby Lynn plugged her manicured finger into Bo Harlan's chest. "I want you to know that the best poker player I've ever seen is sitting right here at this table. And it *ain't you.*"

Bo Harlan's eyebrow curled up. "And who might this mysterious card shark be, my dear?"

Shelby Lynn pointed her finger across the table at Aunt Lucinda, who was quietly minding her business and munching her bread.

"Don't you be pointing at me, child," Lucinda said, through a mouthful of bread. "Kathleen is way better than this old lady."

Shelby Lynn swung around in her chair. "I didn't know you played cards, Kat?"

"I used to play with Pa Pa." Kat shrugged.

"You up for a quick game?" Bo Harlan asked. He pushed the plates out of the way and pulled a deck of cards from his jacket pocket.

"I don't know, Bo. I heard you cheat," Kat said, and then giggled a bit to make it seem as though it weren't true.

"Person who told you that was a person who lost fair and square and can't stand the reality of it," Bo Harlan drawled as he expertly shuffled the deck.

"Who's in?" he asked abruptly.

"Wait a sec. Don't we have to bet on something?" Kinkaid Whipley asked. She squirmed in her chair. Grabbing one of the wine bottles off the table, she poured herself another generous "taste."

"We can play for fun. Or we can play for quarters," Bo Harlan said, pulling some coins from his pocket and dropping them on the table.

"I don't think so, Bo. Who do you think you're dealing with? A bunch of scared little girls?" Shelby Lynn said. She took off her diamond stud earrings and her huge diamond cocktail ring and set them on the table. "Count me in," she said, giving Bo Harlan a killer femme fatale look.

Kathleen smiled to herself. Some women were vixens and some were damsels. Shelby Lynn Pierce was definitely the former. She had more Sharon Stone in her than anyone, which was why Tate the Cheater had been shunned by Houston society and had fled to Florida or Cabo with his Asian mistress.

Kinkaid Whipley pulled a checkbook from her purse and ripped off a blank check. "My husband's going to kill me," she said.

Bo Harlan glanced over at the Duchess. "You in or you out?" he asked.

Lucinda waved her hand as if shooing a fly. "I don't have blank checks or diamond earrings."

"How about a year of home-cooked meals, Lucinda?" Shelby Lynn suggested.

Kinkaid Whipley rubbed her palms together. "Ooh, I would love to win a year of home-cooked dinners. Then I could lie to Jonathan and tell him I cooked them myself!"

Bo Harlan shrugged his bullish shoulders. "Why not?"

He turned to Kathleen. "And what are you betting, Ms. King?"

Kathleen paused. "If you win, I'll let you cochair the annual dinner and put your name on it. So the dinner will be known as the 'King-Harlan Annual Dinner.'"

Bo Harlan smiled broadly and bucked out his chest. "You sure you want to do that? You're changing history, here."

Kathleen reached over, took the cards from Bo's hand, and shuffled them like a Vegas dealer. Bo watched in amazement as she flicked the cards around the table quickly to each of the women. Lastly she turned to Bo and said, "And what might you want to bet, *my dear*?"

"I don't know, Kathleen. Is there anything you want?" Bo asked, winking at her.

Kat knew the oilman was just trying to be flirty in front of Shelby Lynn. She had planned this little card game from start to finish, so her response was quick.

"I want the Clarissa #7," Kat said, looking Bo Harlan straight in the eye.

"So that's what this is about. Your boyfriend sent you to do his dirty work?"

Kathleen dealt Bo his cards. "He doesn't know a thing."

"Look. I don't blame Grant Junior for being burned up over this, but his daddy lost that oil well to me a long time ago, and real men don't shirk their gambling debts," Bo Harlan announced. He picked up his cards, organized them into a fan, and surveyed the hand he was dealt.

"You know as well as I do that Butch Grant suffered from problems," Kathleen said.

"Problems he created," Bo Harlan huffed.

"There's no denying that," Kathleen said. "But the Clarissa #7 has sentimental value."

"Ain't that sweet. I swear you women would go so much farther on this planet if you remembered the main principle in business."

"What's that?"

"It all comes down to money, honey."

"You don't look as if you're hurting for money, honey," Kathleen said.

"Who says I had to be hurting?"

Kathleen chewed on her bottom lip. "Perhaps I don't know the main principles of business, but I do know when right is right, and wrong is wrong."

"You're in over your head, Kathleen. But I have to admit, you're one courageous broad."

Kathleen smiled sweetly at Bo Harlan. "Just shut up and play cards," she said.

Fifty

Since Kat was spending the afternoon at her tasting lunch, Dylan decided to hit the links. He, Wyatt, Steve, and C. Todd Hartwell rolled to the seventh hole in their golf cart. It was one of those picture-perfect Texas days, the sturdy sky filled with puffy white clouds. A cool breeze swept past Dylan's cheeks as he jumped out of the cart and headed for the green.

He was wearing his favorite golf outfit—the red shirt preferred by Tiger Woods, along with tan pants and his white golf shoes. Wyatt was wearing shorts, which was odd because he usually preferred to cover up his prosthetic leg. C. Todd Hartwell was wearing flip-flops instead of golf shoes, and an Astros World Series baseball cap.

Steve, well . . .

When Steve had first arrived at the golf course, it took every ounce of Dylan's self-control to keep from laughing. Mr. Louisiana was sporting what could only be described as "the Artist Formerly Known as Prince Golfing Outfit." Bold white pinstripes ran everywhere across his royal purple golfing clothes. His golf shoes were gold. His necklaces were gold. He was wearing a white beret turned backward on his head, and huge white sunglasses with rhinestones on the rims. His golf clubs were custom made, and he hoisted a custom white and purple golf bag that matched his outfit to a T.

"Here comes Fancy Fart," Wyatt had said.

Dylan had punched his brother hard in the arm to shut him up.

"You gonna stand there and make love to it, or you gonna swing?" C. Todd Hartwell said.

Dylan pulled his driver from the golf bag and stepped up to the tee box. He arched backward and hit a beautiful swing, watching the ball sail two hundred and fifty yards past the sand trap and bounce onto the green.

"Killer shot, man," C. Todd Hartwell mused. The oilman had been drinking beer since they'd arrived at the Plattsville County golf course, and now his breath smelled heavily of Michelob.

"This golf course blows ass," Steve muttered as he stepped up to the tee box.

He's right. Dylan surveyed the rocks and weeds strewn over the course. The Plattsville County course wasn't fancy like the well-manicured clubs in Houston, but Dylan had chosen it based on proximity.

He wanted to remain close to Tangled Spur, and while the course wasn't in spitting distance, it was just a few miles from the drill site.

Dylan waited as the other men took their shots. Wyatt was terrible at golf because he couldn't concentrate. But Dylan's younger brother plied the men with funny stories of all the hot Vegas chicks he'd "bagged."

The four men were having a grand ol' time. They drove the cart to the clubhouse, which was really just a hot dog cart, and ordered a round of dogs and cold beer. C. Todd Hartwell produced a box of Cheerios from his golf bag.

"Got milk?" he asked the guy working the hot dog cart.

"Water, beer, and soda," the man replied.

"I'll take a Dr Pepper," C. Todd said. He popped open the soda can and ate the Cheerios dry from the box.

"You on a diet, dawg?" Steve asked, scratching the chest hair creeping out of his shirt.

"Don't ask an oilman about his drill routine," C. Todd said. He and Dylan both shot each other knowing looks. They'd both been in the oil business long enough to know that superstitions—even in the form of eating Cheerios—were a respected art form.

Dylan squeezed mustard onto his dog and took a bite. His cell phone buzzed in his pocket, and he realized it was the Golden Buddha.

Not good, he thought as he held the phone to his ear.

"We are having some difficulties!" Einrich Von Hearn was shouting into the receiver.

In the background, Dylan could hear a loud whirring noise— the sound of heavy machinery pushing its limits.

"I'll be there in a jiff!" Dylan shouted, as a large, booming sound came over the phone line.

"Too late!" Einrich shouted as the phone went dead.

Dylan dropped his hot dog. He ran to the edge of the golf course and stared in the direction of the Tangled Spur Ranch. In the distance, he caught a plume of smoke rising into the air.

"Motherfucker," he murmured.

The other men followed his gaze.

C. Todd Hartwell dropped his box of Cheerios, stomped on it, then kicked it hard across the ground.

"We're lost. Ain't we?" he said.

Dylan gritted his teeth. He could kill himself for not wearing his lucky eagle T-shirt—even if he did look like a rock star wannabe.

"Let's go find out," he said.

Fifty-one

The poker game was going on its fifth hour. Shelby Lynn Pierce had lost her diamond stud earrings and cocktail ring to Bo Harlan, but he'd promptly given them back to her as "a gift." She'd allowed the oilman to slip the ring on her finger, and then proceeded to kiss him full on the mouth in a lusty, wet kiss that only Shelby Lynn could pull off.

Kinkaid Whipley was too drunk to continue and had pushed in her markers early. She'd ripped up her blank check in front of everyone and said, "Not today, chumps."

She and Shelby Lynn Pierce were now giggling and drinking wine in the corner of the room while Kat and Lucinda gave Bo Harlan a run for his money.

Kat knew Lucinda and Bo were the best players at the table—better than she. Although her Pa Pa had taught her a few tricks of the craft, Bo Harlan was formidable. The oilman didn't flinch whenever he was dealt a hand. His body language was cool, calm, and calculated. He sweated constantly so this couldn't be attributed to a bad set of cards, but his eyes remained nonchalant and expressionless.

Aunt Lucinda winked at Kathleen because if either of them won, it wouldn't matter much. They'd just trade-up at the end.

The key was beating Bo.

Kat surveyed the cards in her hand. It was dangerous to go out with a pair of queens, but this was all she had.

She felt Bo Harlan's eyes on her. The oilman was serious as death when it came to his card games, and no matter how much Shelby Lynn Pierce teased him, he didn't stray from his cards.

Kathleen wanted to win back Dylan's oil well. She wanted it so badly she could envision it in her mind, but as soon as she set her cards down, she realized she'd made a grave mistake.

Bo Harlan's expression changed. He set his cards down, and Kat saw that he'd beaten her with the wild card.

"Sorry, babe," he said, looking pleased with himself. "I guess this means we're calling it the 'King-Harlan Annual Dinner.'"

"Stop it, Bo. Don't be ridiculous," Shelby Lynn said from across the room.

"No, Shelby. He's right." Kathleen swallowed hard. "Fair is fair and he beat me." She felt a pit growing in her stomach and spreading up her spine. She'd tried to do the right thing, but now what?

Kat felt the bile rise up in her throat, and she had to swallow hard to keep from throwing up.

"Not so fast, Mr. Harlan," Lucinda piped up.

Kathleen glanced over at the Duchess and watched with wide eyes as Lucinda spread out her cards in a fan across the table.

Bo Harlan's eyes widened and his face went ash gray.

"Well I'll be a sonofabitch," he whispered.

Lucinda's hand was all aces.

Kathleen sighed deeply. She clapped her hands against her cheeks and mouthed the words "thank you" to Lucinda.

The Duchess clucked and turned her nose in the air.

"You thought you were gonna get yourself a year's supply of home cooking . . . well, think again, darlin'. This old lady's bones are starting to ache."

Shelby Lynn tapped her fingernails against the table. "See, Bo. I told you Lucinda would wipe your ass."

"You sure did," Bo Harlan breathed.

At least he's big enough to admit he lost, Kat thought.

"So let me guess how this works, Lucinda. I give you the Clarissa #7 and you pass it right on over to her," Bo said, thumbing his big thumb toward Kathleen.

"Oh, don't you mess with me," Lucinda scolded. She motioned to Kathleen. "Kids are getting married, and I think an oil well makes a fine wedding gift, what do you think?" she said, shooting Bo her famous better-leave-well-enough-alone eyes.

Bo Harlan looked ruffled. Sweat dripped down his forehead, and the deep purple pallor of his skin looked as if he'd run a marathon. He licked his lips, grabbed a mini quiche off one of the platters, and stuffed it in his mouth.

"Hell, what's one less oil lease . . . I've got a ton of 'em," Bo huffed, standing from his chair. "Ladies, it's been a pleasure," he said.

Kathleen was amazed when the chubby oilman strode over to Shelby Lynn Pierce, grabbed her tightly around the waist, and gave her a dance dip.

"I've been searching for you all my life, beautiful," he said as Shelby Lynn hooted with laughter.

Kat could see that the scrappy oilman (who'd worked his way up from nothing) and the flawless and fabulously wealthy Shelby

Lynn Pierce had somehow, and magically, fallen madly in love. She was happy for her new friends.

Kathleen walked over to Lucinda. Her former nanny was drinking another pot of tea, with her pinky finger outstretched— as if she were royalty herself.

No one except Cullen Davis King and Kathleen Connor King knew who the real card shark was. It'd been Lucinda all along.

What Bo Harlan didn't realize was that Lucinda was carrying her own deck of cards in her purse. Lucinda always carried her own cards. She and Kat had planned the tasting menu and poker game down to every last detail. They didn't know for sure whether Lucinda could beat Bo Harlan. But Kathleen never lost faith.

She leaned down and squeezed Lucinda's shoulders. "You never cease to amaze," she said.

"Oh, child. Please." Lucinda crinkled her eyes.

"Pa Pa loved you," Kat whispered.

"Don't talk nonsense," Lucinda said, fluttering her hand.

Kat knew her former nanny would never admit to the long-standing love affair she'd had with Cullen Davis King. No one had ever suspected it. There'd never been even a whiff of a rumor.

But Kathleen knew it was Lucinda who'd woken up next to her grandfather the morning that he'd died. He'd possibly even said his last words to her. And this made Lucinda family.

"Dylan and Wyatt are going to be over the moon when they find out," Kathleen said.

Lucinda crinkled her eyes and patted Kathleen on the cheek. "I can't imagine a happier day."

Fifty-two

Watching a six-thousand-ton oil rig snap in half was not your average, run-of-the-mill event.

The crew chief was shouting out orders to the men racing in all directions. Dylan stared at the chaos surrounding the snapped rig. Smoke and flames rocketed up through the hole, and massive steel beams fell like boulders from the sky.

"At least no one's died," Wyatt said.

"Yeah, we're lucky," C. Todd said dryly. He'd snapped up a phone and was making a frantic call to the insurance company.

Dylan jogged toward the mobile command unit. He tore through the doorway and spotted Einrich Von Hearn. The Golden Buddha was sitting calmly in front of his panels of computer screens with his eyes closed.

"This is insane!" Dylan hissed. He knew that his geologist had been working a twelve-hour shift, but was he actually asleep? Dylan rushed over to his geologist and shook him hard on the shoulders. "Wake up!" he shouted.

"How could I sleep with all this booming?" Einrich said, his eyes snapping open. He tugged his white beard and shook his head.

"Tell me our options," Dylan said, dropping into an empty chair.

"The hole has much water," Einrich said, pulling at his beard. "We need to keep stirring so the earth doesn't collapse inside, and"—he motioned outside the windows to the snapped rig— "we need new drill."

Dylan dropped his head into his hands. He'd been working with a bare-bones budget as it was, and now he'd have to fund a new drilling rig?

"Impossible," he said through his teeth

"Insurance won't pay?" Einrich asked.

"Not for this," Dylan said. He'd taken a risk signing the contract. In order to save bundles of money—money that he didn't have—Dylan had assumed the risk of all liability.

This meant he was out.

"I have good news, believe it or not," Einrich said.

"Let's hear it."

The Golden Buddha punched some keys on his computer and pointed to the flat computer screen monitor on the wall. Dylan leaned forward and stared at what looked to be a huge stain on the seismic map in front of him.

He felt his stomach leap into his throat. "Don't tell me," he choked.

"We have found the field," Einrich said. "It is deep, deep. But we have found it."

"How . . . how much are we talking about, here?"

Einrich worked his lips feverishly trying to come up with the exact number. "This will be . . . biggest field discovery of my career." The geologist sighed.

"If we can tap it," Dylan breathed. He didn't want to get too excited. There was always a catch. Even if they found an ocean of gas, it didn't mean they could successfully extract it.

Dylan didn't want to be in the position of handing the reins over to one of the big dogs on the block. Like Shell or Exxon.

He wanted to maintain control. But how could he possibly come up with the money for a new rig?

C. Todd Hartwell's investors were tapped out. Jonathan Whipley had already written a huge check, and Dylan couldn't go back for more. Steve had committed for his company in Louisiana to do the expensive completion work once the well had been successfully drilled, which included getting the oil and gas "to market." And Wyatt relied solely on his charm and good looks.

Dylan considered whom he could ask for the money. A thought suddenly struck him, and he leaped from his chair.

She's going to kill me.

Fifty-three

"*No,*" Kat said. She crossed her arms over her chest and shot Dylan a stern look.

He dropped down onto his knees on the floor. "Please, hon."

"*No!*"

"How come?"

Kathleen glared at her fiancé. She now knew what all the fuss had been about. First, he'd taken her to Indika—her favorite Indian restaurant—a place that Dylan loathed because the spices gave him gas. Then he'd surprised her with a flower bouquet. When Kat had asked him the occasion, he'd replied, "Just because."

And now this. She should've known.

Dylan cupped her hands in his. He was staring up at her so sincerely it nearly melted her heart.

Damn, she thought. *He's good.*

"First of all, it's illegal," she said.

"Since when have you been big on technicalities?"

"Get off the floor. You don't need to beg like a dog," Kat in-structed. She began tapping her foot impatiently.

Dylan scrambled off the floor and stood in front of her. "Do you want me to do my naked dance?" he asked. He pulled off his shirt and began swinging it over his head.

Kat was not amused.

"I am not amused," she announced.

"Aw, c'mon, hon. Give a guy a break," Dylan grumbled. Before Kat knew what was happening, he'd grabbed her and thrown her on the bed.

She kicked at him as he struggled to lie on top of her.

"Easy, wild Kat," he said in that sultry voice that got her every time.

Kat pushed Dylan off her and propped up on her elbows. "Why do you have to steal money from *my* foundation?"

"Not steal," Dylan said, flicking his finger in the air. "*Borrow.*"

"And what if you drill a dry hole?" Kat pouted. "What then, Einstein?"

Dylan ignored her and swept his arm through the air. "You should've seen it, hon," he whistled. "It's huge. And it's right underneath your granddad's property. The property that *you now own.*"

"The first rule in oil and gas is never count your chickens before they're hatched," Kat said. She leaned forward and ruffled Dylan's hair.

"It's a risk, hon. I realize. But if anything happens, I promise I'll pay it back. To the last penny."

"And how do you intend to make this miracle happen?"

"I'll get a job." Dylan shrugged.

"You're not qualified," Kat said.

"Funny girl," Dylan said. He reached out and pinched Kat on her bottom.

She scooted away from him. Kat considered telling Dylan about the Clarissa #7, but Lucinda wanted it to be a wedding surprise. And there was no going against the Duchess.

Besides, Kat thought. *It's not enough money anyway.* Not for what Dylan wanted.

He'd asked to borrow a million dollars out of the King Family Foundation escrow account. If the oil well "produced," he'd pay back the money with interest. If the well didn't perform, Kat didn't know how he'd ever pay it back.

"I can't in good conscience," Kat said. She'd almost made up her mind when she spotted something. A teardrop. Falling from Dylan's right eye onto the bedsheets.

"Are you . . . ?" Kat asked, softly.

"Heck no!" Dylan said just as another tear hit the sheets.

"Oh my Lord! Dylan, you're crying!"

Kat rushed into the bathroom and grabbed some Kleenex. She leaped onto the bed and dabbed at Dylan's face, which was now streaked with tears.

"My dad is dead," Dylan said, as if recognizing this fact for the first time.

"I know, sweetheart."

"And I don't *want to ever* be a loser like him."

"You won't."

"How do you know?"

Kathleen stroked Dylan's hair, which was still damp from the shower. "Pa Pa always told me there were two kinds of people in this world. Givers and takers. And you're a giver. Look what you did for your mother, Dylan, while she was alive. You protected her. You cared for her. And look what you're doing for Wyatt. God knows where he'd be without you. Dead in a ditch somewhere. You're a caretaker, my love. You always have been."

Dylan snuggled his head against Kat's shoulder. She was probably a sucker. Her mother would've told her not to give in. But Kat couldn't help it.

"Just don't lose it," Kat murmured. "I could never forgive myself if that money didn't go toward the hospital."

"I promise," Dylan whispered. He kissed the sapphire ring on her finger and rolled on top of her. "Now let's make a baby," he said.

"You know I can't," Kat said.

Dylan stroked Kat's breasts and she suddenly felt warm all over. "Hell, hon. You're taking all the fun out of trying."

Fifty-four

The next morning, Dylan and Kat left early so they could make it to the bank right as it opened. Dylan pulled through the drive-through at Taco Bell and ordered them a round of breakfast taquitos and steaming hot coffees. Kat said she didn't want any and wasn't hungry, but Dylan held a taquito beneath her nose until she snatched it away from his grip and took a bite.

"Thadda girl." Dylan chuckled. Kathleen had always been a small eater, but sometimes it got ridiculous.

"These are sinful," she said, pulling another taquito from the greasy bag and crunching it between her teeth.

A few minutes later, Dylan swung the truck into the Bank of Houston parking lot.

He turned toward Kat. She was wearing a conservative navy skirt and white blouse buttoned to her neck, which made her look like a sexy librarian. Kat always dressed up for the bank, especially when she was about to withdraw a million-dollar cashier's check.

"Are you sure you're okay with this?" he asked

She shot him a look that said, *Don't push it.*

"Look, hon. Have I ever told you the story about Colonel Edwin Drake?"

"Who's that?" Kat asked. She'd turned her full attention toward Dylan and blinked a few times, before staring at him dead on with those eyes of hers.

"Well, the truth about Colonel Edwin Drake is that he wasn't actually a colonel. He made up the title to impress the townsfolk of Titusville, Pennsylvania, back in the 1850s."

"So?"

"So Edwin Drake came to this small town in Pennsylvania to drill for oil. Back then, the only way these wildcatters could figure out how to drill was the same way they drilled for water. But there were so many problems they ran into that Drake's investors kept running out of money. He had to keep borrowing more and more to keep drilling. Anyway, the costs got way out of hand and people started calling the project 'Drake's Folly.'"

"Let me guess, he struck oil and made everyone happy in the end," Kat said. She flipped down the visor and checked her face in the mirror.

"You got it, babe. On the very day that Drake got an order to cease his drilling operations, pay out all his remaining bills, and close up shop—he struck oil. They had gotten down to about seventy feet—Can you imagine? Seventy feet back then?—when they shined down some lights and saw oil floating in the hole."

"What happened next?"

"It was like the gold rush of the Wild West. Titusville, Pennsylvania, had been a quiet little farming area, but towns sprang up overnight and the whole area was covered in derricks. Pennsylvania supplied half of the world's oil until we discovered it here in East Texas in 1901."

Kat flipped up the visor and looked at Dylan. "Thank you,

Professor. That was very enlightening. Now, why don't you sit tight while I go get you your million dollars."

"Thank you, my lady."

Dylan watched Kat hop out of the truck and walk toward the bank. Before she entered the front doors, she reached her hand back and smacked her own ass.

Dylan rolled down his window. "Nice one, hon!"

He leaned back in the seat and considered what he was doing. If the well didn't produce, he'd be in trouble with Kathleen, with Felix, with Jonathan Whipley, and possibly with the law since he was borrowing money from a charitable escrow account and using it for personal purposes.

For a moment, Dylan closed his eyes and prayed. He prayed for positive energy, he prayed for the world to work out right, for things to center themselves. Most of all, he prayed for a miracle.

A moment later, he heard the passenger door click open. "Praying isn't going to help, Colonel," Kat said. She handed Dylan the cashier's check.

"What will help?" Dylan asked. He stared down at the million-dollar check.

"You."

"English, Kathleen. Please."

"Pa Pa used to spend day and night out at his drill sites," Kathleen said. "Even when he'd made all the money he could ever dream of, he still knew every detail of every little thing. You need to do the same. Otherwise, people might start calling it 'Dylan's Folly.'"

Dylan stared at his fiancée and realized he'd been dumber than dirt. What the hell had he been thinking? As if wearing a T-shirt with an eagle emblazoned on it was enough? Why had he been out on the golf course during the drilling? Cullen Davis King wouldn't be caught dead on a golf course during a drill.

Dylan thought about all the photographs he'd seen inside Cullen King's library. In the fields of East Texas—out in the nitty-gritty of it all—with his team. Why wasn't Dylan inside the mobile command unit at all times?

Dylan pounded his fist against the steering wheel.

"Don't get cross," Kathleen said.

"I'm excited, hon. You're as right as right can be. I'm gonna drop you off, head straight to the ranch, and you're not gonna see me till this thing's panned out."

"I'll miss you," Kat murmured.

"Don't worry, babe. You'll have a lifetime with me."

Kat rolled her eyes.

Dylan chuckled. He turned the keys in the ignition and roared out of the parking lot.

Fifty-five

Kat glanced around the plush first-class cabin of the Continental Boeing 777. A flight attendant was passing around champagne and orange juice mimosas on a small silver tray. Kat accepted the cocktail and drank it in two long gulps.

She'd never taken a girls-only trip before, and could barely contain her excitement. Spending the weekend in New York City with Shelby Lynn Pierce and Kinkaid Whipley was sure to be a riot.

Aunt Lucinda had canceled at the last minute due to some phantom "appointment" she swore she couldn't break. Kathleen had raced over to the house and begged her to join them, but Lucinda was deathly afraid of flying. Kat had offered to drug her with Xanax and drag her on the plane anyway, but Lucinda put up a hollering fight.

So Kat let it go.

She and Shelby Lynn and Kinkaid would probably drive Lucinda nuts anyway.

Kat took a sip from her champagne glass and giggled. New York City! What a hoot!

Shelby Lynn Pierce had wanted to take the Pierce family jet, but apparently it was "in the shop." The multimillion-dollar Gulfstream needed repairs to its navigation system, and Shelby Lynn cursed the plane as if it were a lemon she'd just driven off the car lot.

"Damned thing won't start," she'd joked, stepping onto the Continental aircraft and sniffing the air as if it were poison.

Kathleen had suggested purchasing coach class seats she found on sale at Expedia, but Kinkaid and Shelby Lynn insisted on upgrading using their miles. Kathleen realized that they'd upgraded her, too, using miles from one of their accounts.

God bless my friends, she thought, as the plane accelerated down the runway and took off.

Their plan was not to have a plan.

"I know New York like a stripper knows a fat cat," Kinkaid Whipley said. She'd put her finger against her lips and said, "Shhhh. I'm originally from South Jersey but don't tell anyone."

Shelby Lynn Pierce said, "I slept with a guy from New Jersey once. He smelled like pork sausage."

She pulled a black satin eye mask down over her eyes. "Ladies, I need my beauty rest if we're going to hit the ground running," she announced.

Kinkaid Whipley said, "Go to sleep, fatso," and they all laughed.

A few hours later, the three women were whizzing around Manhattan in the back of a yellow taxi. Kinkaid Whipley took them to the new "in" shops on the Lower East Side around Rivington Street.

Kathleen bought rhinestone hair barrettes in the shape of butterflies.

Kinkaid Whipley bought a leather motorcycle jacket from a boutique called Dykes with Bikes.

Shelby Lynn Pierce clutched her orange lizard Birkin bag tightly under her arm, stuck her nose in the air, and said, "I'll wait for Madison Avenue, thank you very much." Houston's most famous Pierce was wearing head-to-toe black—black turtleneck, tight black pants, and high-heel black boots. She looked sleek and stylish and just off the runway.

"I only wear black in New York," she explained.

They decided to grab pastrami sandwiches from Katz's deli, and while they were sitting at one of the tables, Kinkaid Whipley reenacted the Meg Ryan orgasm scene from *When Harry Met Sally*.

Later, they checked into the Four Seasons Hotel, where Jonathan Whipley had a corporate account, and proceeded to get nice and buzzed in the downstairs bar.

When a group of men approached and offered to buy drinks, Shelby Lynn Pierce pointed to Kinkaid Whipley and said, "Stand back. She's got a bomb!"

The women laughed a lot, strolled around the city until midnight, ate sushi at a little place in the West Village, and then collapsed back at their hotel suite.

The next morning, Kathleen woke early and got dressed. She didn't want to disturb Kinkaid or Shelby Lynn, who were sleeping as if in a coma, and so she quietly exited the room and made her way to the doctor's office.

Shelby Lynn's brother had set up his fertility clinic right smack-dab in the middle of where New York society women felt the most comfortable. Sixty-eighth and Park—next to all the best salons and the bagel shop that charged nine dollars a pop for a "schmear" of homemade cream cheese.

Kathleen walked briskly up Fifth Avenue past Central Park,

and then turned onto Sixty-eighth. The air was crisp around the park and she suddenly missed Dylan. How romantic it would be to spend a few days with him in NYC, she thought.

Stepping inside the office, Kathleen thought she was in the wrong place. Rather than a drab waiting room, Dr. Pierce's office resembled a chic recording studio at a hot new record label. The walls were adorned with large framed black and white vintage posters of Jimi Hendrix, the Stones, the Beatles, and Bob Dylan.

The waiting room looked like it had been designed by Ian Schrager—with fashionable white leather sofas, white lacquer tables filled with the latest magazines, and a small side bar with juices, fresh pastries, and an espresso machine.

"I'm here for my nine A.M. with Dr. Pierce," Kathleen said, stepping up to the appointment desk.

The woman behind the desk passed her a clipboard. Kathleen signed herself in, filled out all the necessary paperwork, and took a seat in the empty waiting room. She was glad to see that she was the first patient of the morning.

Within minutes, a nurse called her into the back. Kathleen stripped off her jeans, put on the hospital gown, and waited. Her entire body was shaking suddenly, and she felt cold. She'd brought a folder with all of her previous medical records, CAT scans, and her most recent blood tests. She opened the folder and stared down at her most recent scan. The cyst looked like a small white egg. She'd had surgery to remove it, but there was still scar tissue.

Dr. Pierce stepped inside the room, and Kathleen could immediately see the resemblance. He was tall, slim, and smooth as butter—just like Shelby. And he held himself with the same poise and confidence possessed by the entire Pierce clan.

"Kathleen King, it's a pleasure," he said in a deep voice, shaking Kathleen's hand.

Kathleen squirmed on the examination table. Dr. Pierce was so handsome, he reminded her of one of those soap opera doctors on afternoon TV.

Oh Lord help me, she thought, as Shelby Lynn's brother proceeded to examine her. Kat felt cold all over and her skin was covered in goose bumps.

"Just relax," Dr. Pierce said sexily, reaching his hand underneath her gown.

"I hope you're gay." Kathleen giggled as he dug his hands into her abdomen and felt for the cyst.

Dr. Pierce laughed and said. "Worse. Happily married."

"How many kids?"

"Five."

Dr. Pierce pointed across the room at a photograph. His five children smiling in bathing suits on the beach. His wife in the background trying to herd them together for the shot.

"Lucky," Kathleen said. "Lucky, lucky, lucky."

Dr. Pierce gave her a serious look and sat down on a small stool. "I'm not going to lie to you, Kathleen. This is going to be a tough road."

"Will I have to take shots?"

Dr. Pierce nodded. "Twice a day." He tapped the top of his thigh. "Right here, in your thigh. Do you think you can do that?"

Kathleen crinkled her nose. "I've never given myself a shot."

"Do you have someone who can do it for you?"

Kathleen thought of Dylan fainting the time he'd tried to put in contact lenses.

"I think it's better if I learn it myself," she said. She'd spent so much time at her own hospital, administering a shot to herself couldn't be that difficult. If she had trouble, Dr. Levin was always there to help.

"Good. I want you to start immediately. There's a new medication on the market. They're calling it the 'fertility miracle drug.'"

"I like the sound of that."

Dr. Pierce slapped his hands against his legs and stood up. "Just remember, in order for this to work, you've got to focus on your cycle—the times of the month when you're most likely to get pregnant. I'm going to send you off with an ovulation kit—it's not difficult—it's just like an over-the-counter pregnancy test that you buy in the pharmacy."

"Dr. Pierce?"

"Yes, Kathleen?"

"What are my chances?"

"I don't like statistics. If this doesn't work, we can explore other options."

"Like a surrogate?" Kathleen asked. She wondered what it was like to use a surrogate mother. To entrust another woman with your own biological baby.

"This is one option, certainly."

"Why can't I be normal?" Kathleen sighed.

"Sometimes it's a good thing." Dr. Pierce chuckled. "And besides, any friend of my sister is certainly *not normal*."

Kathleen smiled and shook Dr. Pierce's outstretched hand.

"Why all the rock star posters?" she asked as he opened the door to the examination room.

"I always wanted to be John Lennon," he said, clicking the door shut behind him.

Fifty-six

Around eight o'clock that evening, Shelby Lynn insisted on having dinner at "Chips," which was Cipriani on Fifty-ninth and Fifth.

Kathleen wore her favorite little black dress and strappy high heels; Shelby Lynn Pierce wore a stunning floor-length forest green gown with a jade choker around her neck and jade bracelets running up the length of her arms; Kinkaid Whipley wore her new motorcycle jacket over a pair of black suede pants.

The three women scored a table near the "action" at the bar, and ordered salads for appetizers and steaks for entrees. They drank an entire bottle of Chardonnay, and when a group of men at a nearby cocktail table sent them a round of Bellinis, Shelby Lynn raised her glass and hooted, "Thanks for the drink, but I was looking for sex."

The women drank and laughed and gossiped in that kind, cautious way that women tend to do. About halfway into her steak, Kinkaid Whipley whipped around toward Kathleen and admired her engagement ring.

"When's the big day?" she asked, gulping back the last of the Bellini in her glass.

Kathleen curled a strand of hair around her ear. "It's a surprise."

"C'mon, Kathleen! You big sneak! Share the wealth. When are you two doing the deed?" Kinkaid pressed.

"You'll see," Kathleen said, allowing a glimmer of a smile to creep past her lips.

After many restless nights, she and Dylan had finally figured out the perfect wedding arrangements. It would be unlike anything anyone had ever seen, or would ever expect. When Lucinda suggested holding the wedding reception in the Cullen King mansion, Dylan confided in Kathleen that he didn't like the idea.

"I want this to be *our special day*, hon," he'd said. "Not some circus filled with gawkers wanting to see where your grandfather used to live."

Kathleen realized that Dylan had a point. While he was alive, her grandfather had never allowed people in his home, never hosted parties, and had been a mystery among the Houston socialite crowd. His aloofness made the notion of attending his granddaughter's wedding inside his home all the more tantalizing, and Dylan admitted to Kathleen that he didn't want their wedding to have that type of draw. Even after her grandfather's death, Dylan had rarely set foot inside the mansion himself—except to have brunch with Lucinda in the kitchen or out on the sun patio. It was as if the mansion was not a living, breathing home but was instead a Parthenon—a mausoleum in memory of this great man, Lucinda being its sole caretaker.

Kathleen breathed through her nose and wished Kinkaid Whipley would drop the subject. Everyone would find out soon enough about the wedding plans.

Shelby Lynn and Kinkaid shot each other a look, and Shelby Lynn grabbed Kathleen's hand and said, "What's with all the mystery, Kit Kat?"

"Believe me, Shelby Lynn. You'll find out soon enough."

Shelby Lynn clapped her hands against her cheeks. "You know I hate surprises, darling. My husband surprised me with that little prostitute of his. I'm surprise-scarred for life."

"But you used to *love* surprises," Kat said. "I thought Bo was a surprise. Falling in love with him the way you did . . ."

Shelby Lynn stared down at the table. "Bo is a good man," she said slowly. "I don't know. Maybe I'm looking for replacement love. Someone to fill the void."

Kinkaid Whipley polished off the rest of her steak and set her knife down with a loud clack. "I've seen the way that man looks at you," she said. "As if you hung the moon."

"I could certainly do worse," Shelby Lynn said.

"All the good ones are married or gay." Kinkaid Whipley nodded. "Believe me, I thank my lucky stars that Jonathan and I met back in college."

Kathleen smiled to herself and though about Dylan. He was certainly a catch.

She wondered how things were progressing at the drill site.

The waiter swirled around the table and produced delicate chocolate soufflés for dessert, and glasses of ice wine. When Shelby Lynn Pierce reached over and dipped her fork in one of the soufflés, Kinkaid Whipley said, "Stop stealing my soufflé, fatty."

Kathleen giggled. She relaxed her shoulders and allowed herself to breathe. A moment later, her cell phone buzzed in her purse.

"Let me guess," Shelby Lynn said, popping a teeny bite of chocolate in her mouth. "It's el Jefe."

Kathleen pulled her phone from the purse and was pleased

to see Dylan's number pop up. He'd programmed her phone to read, "Dylan Grant, your Master and Commander," every time he called.

"Hi babe," Kathleen cooed into the phone. It had been weeks since Dylan left for the ranch, and she felt a knot in her stomach at the sound of his voice.

"Are you girls having fun?" he asked, right off the bat.

Kathleen gripped the phone in her hand. She was having a phenomenal time, but she didn't want to mention her doctor's appointment.

"We're having a blast," Kat said, winking across the table at Shelby Lynn and Kinkaid. "In fact, we've met some lovely men across the bar who persist in sending us rounds of drinks."

"Sounds like I need to jump the next plane to New York and open up a can of Texas whoop ass," Dylan said, which caused Kathleen to laugh.

"How are things down there?" she asked cautiously.

"Well, Einrich and Wyatt can tuck down more barbecue than anyone I've ever seen. I swear they each leveled a rack of ribs last night."

"What about the drilling?" Kathleen asked. She didn't want to sound *too brazen*, but this was *her land*, after all.

"It's right on track, hon. We're keeping our fingers crossed."

"Can you be more specific?"

"Aw, hell Kathleen. An oil well is like a woman. You don't *really* get to know her until you sleep with her."

Kathleen smiled and felt her heart soar in her chest.

"You sound just like Pa Pa," she said. She knew this was the highest compliment she could pay Dylan.

He paused a moment. And then his voice came on the line.

"Thank you, hon," he said softly. "That means a lot."

Kathleen hung up the phone and stared at her two friends. "My fiancé is now, officially, a wildcatter," she announced.

"God. Bless. Texas." Shelby Lynn drawled, raising her glass in the air.

The three women raised their glasses and clinked a toast. Kathleen summoned the waiter and reached in her purse to pay for the check. It was the least she could do for such supportive friends. And especially for Shelby Lynn—who'd set up the doctor's appointment with her brother. This debt, Kathleen knew, she could never repay.

When the waiter brought the check, he announced that it had already been taken care of over the phone by a Mr. Bo Harlan from Houston, Texas.

"Oh brother," Shelby Lynn said, drumming her fingernails against the table.

"You're in trouble now, girlfriend," Kinkaid Whipley said.

Kathleen flung her napkin across the table at Shelby Lynn. "You better hurry up with that divorce so you can get remarried, fatty," she said, and everyone laughed.

Fifty-seven

The oil business was all about delays. Delays and risk. It took a steel stomach to embroil oneself in the nitty-gritty, the ins and outs, the dirty details. Ever since he'd arrived at the ranch, Dylan had been popping an hourly Tums.

He knew full well that the flash-in-the-pan, overnight success stories were bogus. Any oilman who recounted how he'd made the big one, the big gusher, without any problems was a braggart and a liar. It was the same as those Boston whaling men, and all their big fish stories. Men would be men. But in the oil business, exaggeration often meant staggering losses.

Dylan didn't want to get his hopes up. He'd pinned everything on a single well. Common sense dictated that it was better to spread risk among many different wells, but this was a luxury Dylan didn't have. He was playing a high-stakes game. It was all or nothing.

Inside the mobile command unit, Dylan stood side by side with Einrich Von Hearn. The Golden Buddha scanned his computer monitors by the minute, tugging on his white beard. Dylan stared out the windows of the high-tech RV. The drill site was laid out in front of him. He watched the men working the platform covered in sweat and dirt, and Dylan knew how they felt.

He'd been "in the country" for weeks on end, and he stank of insect repellent and stale beer. The mobile home where he and Wyatt were spending their nights had only two minutes' worth of hot water, so they took turns showering.

Wyatt spent his days trolling the remote areas of the ranch, taking potshots with his rifle out the Toyota's driver's side window. A week ago, he'd killed a wild boar, strung it up with cable wire, skinned it whole, and served the fresh meat over a spit fire to all the men at the drill site.

Wyatt was always everyone's hero.

Dylan sat down next to Einrich. He was sweating, and he pulled the packet of Tums from his pocket and popped the last one in his mouth. Besides the constant stomachache and the smell of his own BO, he felt good about spending day and night at the rig. He wasn't just a bystander, but had taken a major working role alongside his geologist and the engineers on site. He even spent time with the supervisors barking out orders for the roughnecks.

When one of the field hands had failed his weekly drug test, Dylan had fired the man on the spot. This wasn't a place for the restless and lackadaisical, he figured.

Each man on the team had to work in concert with the others. There was no room for hotheads or troublemakers. And roughnecks weren't known for their charming personalities. Dylan's job was to keep the drill site running smooth, and everyone in check.

So far, there hadn't been any major personality clashes or scuffles. Not like on the offshore rigs out in the Gulf of Mexico, where the men were stuck on platforms in the middle of all that churning blue sea, which tended to make them crazier than the onshore drilling hands.

If anything, it was the heat, the mosquitoes, the twenty-four hours of streaming bright white lights surrounding the rig, and the constant hammering of the drill bit looming all through the day and night that could make a person crazy.

Dylan had worked the night shift—the "vampire shift"— for three straight weeks, because Einrich Von Hearn liked his beauty rest.

He sucked on the Tums and rubbed his eyelids. Even with Kathleen's infusion of cash, Dylan was still over budget. One of the drill parts had gotten too hot and nearly exploded, so he'd been forced to order a new one and wait for the repair. In desperation, he'd taken out a loan from the community bank in the small town of Plattsville in order to divvy out last week's paychecks. He'd fudged on all the loan documents, and was praying that he wouldn't end up in jail.

Dylan felt a large thud on his shoulder, and realized it was Einrich. His geologist had clapped him on the back, and was beaming at him with his expressive, twinkly eyes.

"*Look, look!*" he boomed, pointing at one of the computer screens.

Dylan tried not to flinch. He'd gotten used to Einrich shouting all his sentences. The geologist had long since lost his hearing. Spending so many years next to the screeching drills had robbed the Golden Buddha of his ears.

"We made it to sixteen thousand!" Einrich shouted.

"Good deal," Dylan said.

One thousand feet to go, he thought, *and then we'll know for sure.*

"You must leave and take break! You look like walking dead man!" Einrich yelled in Dylan's ear.

"I want to be here for the last thousand feet," Dylan grumbled. He wanted to remain at the drill site, but Saturday night was right around the corner. And he and Kathleen had already made their big plan. A plan that couldn't be broken.

"Do not worries!" Einrich boomed, clapping Dylan on the shoulder once more. "You stay, you go! Does not matter. It will be as *it will be!*"

Dylan exhaled slowly. The geologist was right. There was nothing left for him here. Nothing left except to wait.

Dylan shook Einrich's outstretched hand and stepped outside the mobile command unit into the sun. Wyatt was standing next to the Toyota truck. His younger brother was wearing a wide-brimmed cowboy hat and sunglasses. He was smoking a cigar.

"You ready, big brother?" he asked, puffing a ring of smoke into the air.

Dylan strode toward the pickup and kicked the dirt with the toe of his boot.

"Ready as ever," he said.

The two brothers climbed into the truck and set off for Houston.

Fifty-eight

Kathleen couldn't believe the big day had finally arrived. The King Foundation Annual Dinner promised to be a lavish affair with all the bells and whistles. The evening would begin with champagne and cocktails, along with strolling violinists from the Houston Symphony playing Chopin in unison. Then Kathleen's guests would be summoned into the main dining room, which was lit by thousands of tiny white candles. The tables were trimmed with white tablecloths with antique silver place settings bearing the King family crest.

Kathleen had spent hours with the florist to create the perfect table centerpieces. Hand-tied, all white floral bouquets overflowing with calla lilies, stephanotis, and Vendela roses.

At the behest of Shelby Lynn Pierce, the six-course French dinner would actually be seven, as it included a cheese course. For the wine pairings, Kathleen had worked directly with a sommelier and wine merchant to have specialty vintages flown in from St. Emilion. The wine pairing with each course reflected a different family-owned vineyard in France, and was not available for sale in the United States. For the main course, Kathleen had selected a newly released Pomerol that no one except the vintner and his French sommelier had ever tasted.

In the center of the dining room, a beautiful white stage had been arranged for the fashion show featuring Kinkaid Whipley's "vintage couture." Afterward, Walton Riley and the Riley Big Band would take the stage and proceed to play from their Grammy Award–winning album. The night would end with dancing and Whipley's specialty chocolate crepes. Kathleen had also ordered a four-tiered white Italian cream cake from Let Them Eat Cake!, the best event bakery in Houston.

Kathleen did a final walk-through of the space and realized that she couldn't have planned for a more magical evening. The setting took her breath away, and she leaned toward one of the tables and smelled the fragrant flowers. Closing her eyes, she said a silent prayer.

This would be the most special evening of her life. And she wanted it to be perfect. At the head table, she'd seated Jonathan and Kinkaid Whipley, Shelby Lynn Pierce and Bo Harlan, Dr. Levin and his wife, and her and Dylan. Wyatt was bringing "the woman of his dreams," which was Aunt Lucinda, of course.

Kathleen checked the clock on the wall. The Annual Foundation Dinner started in less than an hour.

I'm late! she thought. She'd lost track of time. She hurried toward the bank of elevators that would whisk her up to the hotel suite that she'd reserved for the night. When she finally reached the hotel room, Dylan was nowhere to be found.

"*Dylan!*" Kathleen shouted.

"In here, hon," came the reply.

Kathleen found him inside the bathroom putting on his tux. She beamed at her fiancé. He looked dynamite in the penguin suit, with his dark hair slicked back and his broad shoulders filling out the jacket perfectly. He was wearing a white bow tie and matching white pocket scarf.

"Hon, I swear you'd be late to your own birthday party," Dylan quipped, straightening his bow tie in the mirror.

Kathleen giggled and took her dress out of the hang-up bag. She held it up for Dylan to see.

He whistled through his teeth. "Some dress," he remarked.

"You can't watch me while I'm getting ready," Kathleen said, tapping her foot against the bathroom tile. "Those are the rules."

Dylan saluted her as if she were in the military. "Yes, ma'am. If you need me for anything, you know where I'll be," he said, walking into the living room of the suite and plopping down onto the sofa. Kathleen heard him flick on the television and click over to the Golf Channel.

Kat raced around the bathroom like a madwoman. She pulled her dress over her head, hopping up and down to get it over her waist. Reaching back to the tiny string she'd affixed to the zipper, she was able to zip the dress all the way up her back. Then she took the white headpiece made with seed pearls and tiny fresh white flowers and placed it on her head. Sweeping a sheer lip gloss across her lips, Kathleen admired herself in the mirror.

"*Dylan!*" she called out to the next room.

"You ready?"

"I'm ready," she said.

Dylan's head popped around the bathroom door. "You look beautiful," he breathed. "You nervous?"

Kathleen smiled. *Not one speck*, she thought.

Fifty-nine

The cocktail hour had come and gone, but Kathleen and Dylan were nowhere to be found. Houston society had been ushered inside the main dining room and taken their seats. Everyone was waiting for Kathleen Connor King—the mistress of ceremonies—to take the stage. Usually Kathleen took the stage and proceeded to thank everyone for their generous support of the children's hospital. A brief slide show revealing the strides made by the foundation in attempting to cure pediatric cancer was typically shown prior to the food being served. But this year, Kathleen was nowhere to be found.

"Where are they?" Shelby Lynn whispered across the table to Kinkaid Whipley, as an awkward silence descended upon the room.

Shelby Lynn was wearing a strapless pink silk gown that she'd bought in Milan, along with a pink diamond ring the size of Ecuador.

"How would I know?" Kinkaid said, adjusting the strap on her dress. She glanced around the dining room. "I don't see them. They're both MIA."

"C'mon, ladies. Give me a break," Wyatt drawled. "Dylan and Kat haven't seen each other in months. They're probably up in their hotel room playing a famous little game called 'Find the Sausage.'"

"Nice image, child," Lucinda said, patting Wyatt on his knee.

"I knew you'd appreciate that, Luce," Wyatt joked, shooting Lucinda his superstar smile.

"Don't you be looking at me like that! I'll smack those fancy blue eyes right out of yo' head," Lucinda said, rapping Wyatt against the side of his head.

Bo Harlan threw his head back and laughed. "If you think that stings, son, you should try playing her in poker."

Wyatt stared hard across the table at Bo Harlan. "I guess you'd know a thing or two about that," he snapped.

"Easy, Wyatt," Shelby Lynn said, flicking a single warning finger in the air.

Lucinda patted Wyatt on his knee. "Be nice, child," she whispered. "There's more to this story than meets the eye."

Wyatt swung around toward Lucinda and leaned in to her ear. "I can't believe Kat seated him at our table! What was she thinking?"

"Be patient, child. You may have a few surprises in store." Lucinda winked.

Suddenly the doors to the dining room swept open, and a chorus of singers and orchestra musicians flooded the room. The music grew louder as the singers streamed around the tables, plying everyone with a pop version of "Amazing Grace." They snapped their fingers to the beat and encouraged people to sing along with them, while the musicians played around each table.

"What on earth?" Jonathan Whipley asked.

Kinkaid shrugged her shoulders. "Heck if I know."

Bo Harlan turned toward Shelby Lynn Pierce. "This ought to be good," he said.

A collective gasp was heard from around the room as people spotted Dylan and Kathleen.

The bride wore a floor-length white gown. Instead of a veil, she'd tucked a flower garland decorated with white seed pearls around her head. In her hands, she carried a small, tight bouquet of fresh white roses.

The groom looked dashing in his black tuxedo, with the single small bud white rose pinned to his lapel.

Both Kathleen and Dylan were grinning from ear to ear. They swept through the center of the room arm-in-arm, and walked toward the stage. As they passed the head table with their "family," seated at it, Wyatt stood up and began to clap.

Dylan's younger brother had tears streaming down his face, and the rest of the audience followed him and stood, too.

A master of ceremonies approached the microphone and asked everyone in the audience to please be seated and bow their heads in prayer.

Kathleen and Dylan gave each other a knowing smile as they approached the minister on stage. They turned toward each other, clasped each other's hands, and began to recite their vows . . .

"Kathleen," Dylan began in a solid voice . . .

"You are the woman I was meant to marry. You are the only woman I have ever loved. You have been the constant light in my life. My center. My sun. I want to be with you always, until death do us part. I promise to love, respect, and take care of you until my dying day. I am yours, to the very depths of my soul.

"I am yours, Kathleen."

Kathleen allowed a single teardrop to dot her cheek. She wasn't wearing makeup, so it didn't matter much. She clasped

Dylan's hand in hers and rolled a small silver ring onto his wedding finger.

"With this ring, I thee wed," she said quietly.

The minister raised his arms in the air and said, "I now pronounce you husband and wife. You may kiss the bride."

Dylan leaned forward and gave Kat a gentle peck on the lips. But it wasn't enough. He grabbed her around the waist, pulled her close into his arms, and laid a big, memorable smooch on her.

Kat smiled at her new husband and said. "Way to go, Prince Charming."

She and Dylan turned toward the audience and waved to everyone as the minister announced, "May I present to you the newly married couple . . . Mr. Dylan Charles Grant and Mrs. Kathleen Connor King."

Everyone in the dining room jumped to their feet and applauded loudly. Kathleen and Dylan turned to each other and beamed. A few weeks ago, they'd determined that the Annual Foundation Dinner was the perfect setting for their surprise wedding. Their dear friends and "family" would be there, and no one would have to make a big fuss. There would be no gifts, no bridal registry, no groomsmen or bridesmaids—none of the traditional pomp and circumstance.

It was perfect. Just as they'd wanted it.

Dylan and Kathleen walked around the tables and greeted all their guests, who couldn't hide their shocked faces. C. Todd Hartwell and Steve, who'd been invited at the last minute by Kat, shouted out, "Congratulations!" as Dylan passed by their table.

When Dylan reached the head table, he and Wyatt clutched each other in a deep bear hug. Both brothers let the tears fall freely.

Shelby Lynn and Kinkaid gave Kathleen the thumbs-up, and

there was not a single dry eye at the entire table. Even Bo Harlan's traditional poker face was streaked with tears.

It had been a meaningful event, a beautiful experience.

Kathleen walked toward the stage once again, and the audience took their seats and quieted down.

She stood in front of the microphone, dressed in her wedding gown, and glanced around at everyone inside the dining room.

A smile lit up her face.

"Before we get started with this year's King Family Foundation Dinner, I have a surprise for you," she began . . . which caused everyone in the room to burst out laughing.

Kathleen waited for the laughter to subside before continuing.

"I can't imagine a greater wedding gift," she said, "than that of your generous support. Thank you for coming this evening and for being part of this special day. I want you to know how much I appreciate your year after year support of the King Family Foundation. The Pediatric Cancer Hospital is the reason we are here," Kathleen said. She motioned toward a table near the stage. "And on that note, I'd like to welcome Diego Ramirez and his family to this event. Diego was a patient at the hospital just a few short months ago. And I'm happy to say he's a survivor." Kathleen smiled at Diego and his parents.

The audience burst out clapping, and Kathleen waited until they'd finished.

"Your contribution makes a profound difference in the lives of children, and I would like to recognize one person in particular who raised the bar this year by donating a half-million dollars. And that person is Bo Harlan," Kathleen said, motioning toward Bo Harlan.

The stocky oilman stood in his seat and took a small bow.

Dylan and Wyatt gave each other a look, but Lucinda and Shelby Lynn shot them the evil eye, and they both settled down.

"I would also like to thank Dr. Victor Levin for his ongoing service to the hospital. Dr. Levin is more than a doctor. He is a visionary, and a personal family friend. Thank you, Dr. Levin, for your continuous service."

Dr. Levin nodded toward Kathleen, and his wife patted him jovially on the shoulder.

"And finally, I would like to say how fortunate Dylan and I are to have you join us on this special day. We chose this dinner as the site for our wedding because we could think of no better gift than the gift of friends and family. And the gift you've given to the Pediatric Cancer Hospital is the best wedding present a couple could ever ask for. Thank you once again. Thank you . . ."

Kathleen smiled broadly and walked off the stage to the sound of a thunderous standing ovation.

When she reached the main table, Dylan swooped her up in his arms and planted a big, fat kiss on her lips.

"Nice one, brother," Wyatt said. He stood and raised a toast to the new bride and groom. Everyone in the dining room raised their glasses and toasted the newly married couple in unison, and shouted, "Hear, hear!"

Sixty

Dylan requested for the band to play, "What a Wonderful World," by Louis Armstrong.

He sang softly in Kat's ear as he swung her around the dance floor. He felt Kat's head resting on his shoulder. *Kathleen. His wife.* And Dylan couldn't feel more proud.

When the song lyrics got to *"I hear babies crying, I watch them grow . . ."* Kathleen stared into Dylan's eyes.

"We have to escape," she said suddenly.

Dylan nodded and took her by the hand. "Where to?"

"How about the room?"

"C'mon, hon. We can't duck out early from our own wedding. And from the biggest fund-raiser of the year. This is your big day."

Kathleen paused and worked her bottom lip, which meant she was thinking.

"How about we just sneak out to the pool for a few minutes?" Dylan could see that Kathleen needed a break. She'd been float-ing around tables and talking with all the guests nonstop. As was her style, she'd spent the past few hours being a gracious hostess and more than gracious bride. She'd even read a few pages from the *Tales of the Unicorn Land* book to Diego—which his mother now carried in her diaper bag everywhere she went. With Diego on her lap, and since she was wearing the wedding dress, Kathleen had looked like an angel.

Dylan had never seen such a vision, and he closed his eyes and implanted the image in his brain so he would be able to recall it for the rest of his days.

Kathleen's voice had become hoarse from too much talking. "I guess the pool will work," she said.

Dylan guided his new bride off the dance floor. They tried to sneak out to the back doors that led to the hotel pool.

Wyatt spotted them and rushed over. "Hey! Where are you guys sneaking off to?"

Kathleen smiled at her brother-in-law. "Can't a bride get a few moments alone with her new husband?"

"Sure, Kathleen. But I was kind of wondering what was up with Bo Harlan. I mean, I know he wrote that big check, and he's dating Shelby Lynn, but I just don't get it."

Kathleen pointed at Lucinda, who was on the dance floor leading a crowd of people in the electric slide.

"I think the fine woman dancing over there in the purple dress can enlighten you."

Dylan clapped his brother on the shoulder. "You're never going to believe this, brother, but Lucinda beat Bo Harlan in poker. And you'll never guess what she won . . ."

Wyatt broke into a wide grin. He spun around, ran to the dance floor, and picked Lucinda off her feet. She screeched with laughter and whacked him repeatedly over the head.

"Those two are a pair," Kat said.

"Let's get out of here before anyone else sees us," Dylan said.

He pushed open the door leading out to the pool and hustled Kat through it.

"Damn! Closed," Dylan grumbled, as he saw the sign announcing the pool closure time at ten P.M. The entire area was pitch black, save for the pool lights underneath the water.

"Since when did the rules ever *stop you*?" Kathleen asked, shooting Dylan a knowing look. "I seem to recall a recent breaking and entering . . ."

Dylan shook his head. "You're never going to let me live this down, are you?"

"Not until you come clean with Bo Harlan," Kathleen said. "Besides, I think he'll get a kick out of it. Especially when he gets to know you."

"And why would I want to align myself with him?"

"Because you're in the business now," Kathleen teased. "That makes you *one of them*."

Dylan chuckled and followed Kat as she led him to a small pool shack filled with lawn chairs and pool equipment. "So. Where are you taking me, 007?" Dylan asked, stepping inside the shack, which smelled like musty chlorine.

Before he knew what was happening, Kathleen had pulled up her wedding dress and was flashing him what could only be described as Commando Bride.

"Please tell me you wore panties during our ceremony," Dylan breathed.

"Duh. I just took them off in the bathroom," Kat said. She pointed toward a rusty lawn chair that didn't look comfortable, in Dylan's opinion.

"This is not how I pictured our wedding night," he said.

Kathleen laughed. "I just took the test."

"What test?"

"You know. *The* test."

"You mean the baby-making test?" Dylan asked playfully. He knew that Kat was diligently taking her shots every day, and the ovulation tests which told her whether she was "in the zone."

He took Kathleen's hand and led her toward the lawn chair. She slipped the white wedding dress up over her head, threw it over the back of the chair, and lay down stark naked against the rusty chair.

Dylan felt himself getting aroused.

"A man's gotta do what a—"

"Save it," Kathleen instructed him, as she kicked off one of her white shoes. She was still wearing the wedding flowers in her hair, and looked like some kind of bohemian Hawaiian princess.

"My Lord, woman. You take my breath away," Dylan said. He unzipped his pants and let them drop down to his ankles. Then he hopped over to the lawn chair and leaped on top of Kathleen, who was now in stitches with laughter.

"I'm bringing sexy back," he said, winking at her. He put his hands on her breasts and stroked them softly until she arched her back. Then he climbed on top of her and slid himself inside.

"Oh, sweetheart," Kathleen moaned as Dylan moved up and down inside her.

"I love you, wife," Dylan breathed.

He didn't need to wait for the hotel in Galveston. The one he'd booked for a special super-saver rate because that was all the money he had left. He'd have to take her on a "real" honeymoon some other time. Until then, they'd have to wait.

Dylan's thrusts grew faster and faster, and Kathleen cried out in pleasure. She squeezed her thighs underneath him, and Dylan felt her wetness all over. He couldn't hold it much longer so he said, "C'mon, babe. C'mon . . ."

Kathleen threw her head back, closed her eyes, and moaned.

Dylan thrust deep inside her and moaned along with her.

When they were both finished, they lay side by side, panting and out of breath.

Dylan kissed Kat's fingers one by one. "I think we won't have any problems making that baby," he said.

Kathleen felt a strange stirring inside herself. It lasted for only a split second, but her woman's intuition was strong. She'd never felt anything like this before.

"I hope you're right," she whispered. "But I guess we should get back to our wedding duties."

"We're staying right here. Right where we are," Dylan said. He held tightly on to Kathleen's small hand, and they both stared up out the glass roof of the pool shed to the stars outside.

They realized they'd both fallen asleep in each other's arms when a loud rapping sound at the door startled them awake.

"Oh!" Kat exclaimed. "We fell asleep!"

Dylan sat up with a start and realized that his pants were still puddled around his ankles.

"Just a minute!" he shouted. The rapping at the pool shed door grew louder. He whirled around toward Kat and helped her pull the wedding dress back over her head.

"It's Wyatt," came a voice through the door.

"Go away," Dylan said.

"And C. Todd. And Steve."

"Go away, all of you," Dylan said.

"And Einrich!" another voice boomed.

Dylan jumped up and rushed toward the door. Gripping the knob, he wrenched the door open and saw his younger brother, C. Todd Hartwell, and Steve, standing alongside the white-bearded Golden Buddha.

"We made a good well!" Wyatt shouted, raising his arms in the air like Rocky Balboa.

"More than good!" Einrich screamed.

Dylan pivoted on his heel to tell Kathleen, but she'd come up behind him and was already standing at his side.

"We did it!" Wyatt shouted. He, C. Todd Hartwell, Steve, and Einrich Von Hearn began jumping up and down, doing a little dance, as if they were football players who'd just scored a touchdown.

Dylan squeezed his wife's hand as the tears came to his eyes.

"*You did it*, Colonel Drake," she whispered.

Dylan turned and stared at his beautiful wife. He grabbed her in his arms and kissed her long and hard.

"Aw, heck, Kathleen," he said, wiping a tear from her face. "Even a blind squirrel finds an acorn once in a while."

A⁺

**AUTHOR
INSIGHTS,
EXTRAS, &
MORE...**

**FROM
JO
BARRETT
AND
AVON A**

THE GLAMOROUS (hiccup!) LIFE OF JO BARRETT

I own a ranch, don't you?

Before you send the hate mail, let me start out by saying that I'm a Texan. You may not think it to look at me. Sometimes I wear scarves tied tightly about the neck. Or flat, sensible shoes during the day. The big tip-off—I don't wear makeup at the gym. Yes, I have the "East Coast" thing down to a T. And I should. After all, I've spent the past twelve years hopping around New York and Boston and Washington, D.C. Let's put it this way. When I order a bagel and "schmear" in Houston, Texas, they still look at me kind of funny.

But even after all my East Coasting, I *love* Texas. And Texans, too, for that matter.

I love, for example, that Texans drink Red Bull before going to see Joel Osteen. (Helps the hangover.)

I love that Texans say neat phrases like: "Grandma may look old but she's gonna keep on keepin' on."

And I *love* that Texans have ranches. Ah, the smell of a patent leather Manolo Blahnik setting foot on a ranch.

So I guess you're wondering where the hate mail part comes in. Okay, here goes . . .

Some people are using the word "ranch" much too liberally.

Let me give you an example. A few weeks ago, I was invited to attend a certain "ranch" party.

Wow, a ranch party, I thought. *This should be a hoot!*

I quickly pulled out my black leather weekender bag and packed all the Western wear at my disposal, which consisted of

1. My cowboy boots—hand-stitched Lucchese—hey, this ain't my first rodeo, folks.
2. Jeans—the tight, slutty ones—perfect for a ranch party! I mean, what if Mr. Right is a cowboy?
3. A hat purchased from the Beretta gun store in Maryland—it's an old hat, back from my staffer days when I used to work on Capitol Hill. (P.S. Please don't ask why I happened to be in the Beretta gun store in Maryland.)
4. Mosquito repellent.
5. A digital camera—me as Georgia O'Keeffe, taking landscape and flower shots of the "ranch."

The invitation suggested an evening with a fire pit and a real barbecue and horseback riding.

A ranch party!

Now, correct me if I'm wrong. In my mind, the word "ranch" evokes a certain image. An image of a large—to very large—to sickeningly large tract of acreage. On this tract of land, there should be all manner of wild animals, like rattlesnakes and doves and wild hogs. There should be game fencing, and hunting vehicles, and a lovely limestone house done up in that chic Texas hill country style—complete with deer trophies over the fireplace mantel.

Driving out to the "ranch," I was greeted, instead, by a cottage. A cottage with a barbecue pit in the back, a quaint little swimming pool, and a *pony for children*.

"Is this . . . *the ranch*?" I sputtered, hoping that I'd gotten the wrong house, the wrong town, the wrong invitation.

"Yes, we just bought it last year! Tammy is thrilled because she gets to grow her own tomatoes!"

I remember swallowing hard. In the kitchen, there was a bag of Doritos. A blessing from God, I assume.

Everyone else at the "ranch party" was wearing regular clothes. Meanwhile, with my skintight jeans, boots, and hat, I was doing my best Dolly Parton, *Best Little Whorehouse* impression.

People stared. I tipped my hat, "Howdy, folks!" and ate Doritos like it was my last meal.

Some ranch, I thought. *This is more like a ranch-ette. Or ranch-ini. But it's no ranch, ranch.*

So, please. I beg of you. The next time you leave for your quaint little country house on fifteen cute acres, please do not say: "Tammy and I are takin' the kids out to the ranch this weekend. We're throwing a party on Saturday. Wanna come?"

Instead, why not call a spade a spade. "Tammy and I are takin' the kids out to our *country* house this weekend. It sits on fifteen acres in the country and we love it because we can barbecue."

The word "ranch" does not mean "house with extra big backyard." Granted, there are some large backyards in Texas. But, I ask you . . .

When did Texans become the type of people who drive a Toyota Tercel but carry a key ring that says, "Hey! My other car is a Porsche!"

I love your dress! And could you please pass the Bazooka?

Dear Ladies Who Lunch,

I love gum. Gum is playful, and I feel like a kid when I'm chewing it. I'll admit that as I'm writing this, I'm plowing through a pack of Dentyne Ice, Arctic Chill.

I never used to chew gum until a few years ago, when I noticed hordes of thin, gorgeous Texas women chewing a lot of gum. That's when it hit me. Gum . . . is actually a meal supplement. That's right. You heard it here first, folks. Gum is the best dieting tool around.

I mean, why else would all these fabulous Texas women be chewing gum all the time? Like, literally, all day long? It's because gum is better than Atkins, and Weight Watchers, and those awful protein smoothie shakes that taste like cement.

Gum, I realized, is the key to being thin.

Let me give you an example. Let's say you've just worked out at the gym for two hours. You've done the treadmill, the stair stepper, and a round of weights. You are sweaty, fatigued, and feeling pretty good about yourself for burning all those calories.

At this point, you can either go for a cheeseburger, fries, and a Diet Coke (remember you're trying to lose weight, here) or you can opt for a nice, refreshing slice of gum. Ahhh, the joys of sliding a thin little wafer-sized slice of gum into your mouth. And then chewing on it for the next six to eight hours, until the hunger pains subside.

I typically opt for the cheeseburger. But these thin, gorgeous Texas broads—I have a sneaking suspicion they're reaching into their purses for that dainty, sugar-free pack of Orbitz.

And yet, despite the obvious merits of bubble gum (blowing big fat bubbles that get stuck on your face), there is one place where you should never, ever, not in a million years, pop a slice of Big Red. Or Wrigley's Spearmint. Or Freshen Up.

And this place, of course, is the Black Tie Affair. Gowns and gum don't mix, ladies. In fact, watching a Texas woman wearing a ten-thousand-dollar custom-ordered Naeem Khan clinging to her perfectly sculpted figure while smacking on a piece of gum is enough for me to send the dogs after her. And that's putting it mildly.

So why do I find myself at these black tie affairs, with gorgeous, perfectly sculpted women popping their gum? I mean, can't someone tell these ladies that everyone else ordered the burger?

Have fear. The world is ending.

Have you turned on the news lately? Me neither. Actually, this isn't true. I've become shamelessly addicted to CNN. And to the doom and gloom that the actors (oops! I mean "newscasters") are hurling our way.

For example, the other evening, I tuned into Anderson Pooper on CNN. Now, I realize that his real name is Anderson Cooper. I realize that his mother was Gloria Vanderbilt, and that many women find him attractive despite his awkward leprechaun ears and premature gray hair. (I mean, what's with the little boy grin and the gray hair, Anderson? You're freaking me out.)

I also realize that he is one of the few news anchors who look good in Prada. Hey, but I digress.

Within thirty seconds of flipping on "the Pooper," I was barraged with floods, hurricanes, tornadoes, political scandals, and missing child reports.

And the look on the Pooper's face after his report? It's almost as if he was enjoying it. To peddle fear is great power, isn't it?

To add further insult to injury, the next "report" focused on— and I bet you can guess—the *oil crisis*!

That's right, people. Apparently, we are embroiled in a full-on, balls to the wall, *oil crisis*!

As I'm sure you've noticed when filling up your tank, gas costs more these days. But this is not where it ends. *The oil crisis affects every industry in our lives.*

According to Anderson Pooper, the *oil crisis* is responsible for all of the following:

1. Airlines on the brink of bankruptcy.
2. Soaring food prices at your local grocery store.
3. The economy in shambles.
4. A real estate meltdown.
5. Angelina Jolie's decision to send Pax to public school.

It's gotten so bad, that Anderson Pooper said—and I quote:

"Americans are now being forced to choose whether to *fill up their gas tank OR PUT FOOD ON THE TABLE.*"

Wait. Stop the press, Anderson. Are you telling me that Americans are choosing whether to drive their cars *or eat*? I don't buy it. I mean, c'mon. I just saw a four-year-old talking on a cell phone.

Will someone please pass the Chardonnay?

Dear Kind Readers,

I'm a red wine drinker. I tend to stray away from the hard stuff because I morph into Faye Dunaway in Barfly. *P.S. For those of you over the age of thirty-five, do you remember the tagline from that film?*

"Some people never go crazy. What truly horrible lives they must lead."

Oh, it's perfection.

But I digress. Let's get back to the red wine. I've recently been invited to several parties. And not just your average, run-of-the-mill shindigs. I'm not talking about a barbecue in the backyard, dog jumping in the pool, kids screaming for ice cream type of bash. Nope. These are the real deal. The big enchiladas of parties. The savoir faire's of fetes.

Imagine valets in red jackets parking your car, a golf cart sweeping you up to your host's front door, where you are greeted by a waif-like Heidi Klum bearing a tray of champagne flutes. And that's just the entrance.

Inside, the decorations include the likes of flower bouquets fit for a royal wedding, candles large enough to light Ecuador, and mini-quiches served from domed English platters.

The guests are fashionable types. You know these people. Hey, you may even be one *of these people. Flitting around in the latest high heel mini-boots. Waving to your similarly clad, gorgeous, mini-booted friends.*

Meanwhile, I've shown up in a perfectly respectable outfit.

And yet, I've missed the hot trend. The "this season must-have." The slouchy mini-boot.

Let's face it. I may as well be wearing parachute pants and Kaepas. Ah, such are the trials and tribulations of the glamorous life.

I wind my way toward my only salvation—the bar. And there is the bartender, shaking fun little cocktails for everyone. Topping off champagne flutes. Smiling as if he owns the house—which he absolutely *does not*, by the way.

"What can I get you?" he asks, because this guy recognizes a fish out of water. It's as if I'm wearing a name tag that reads: Hi, I'm Jo. And I'm not wearing mini-boots.

"I'm easy," I say. "I'll have a glass of red wine, please."

The bartender shakes his head, grimly. I can tell he's about to deliver the bad news, like the captain of the Titanic.

"The host is only pouring Chardonnay this evening," he announces.

I stare at him, but he remains poker-faced.

"No red wine?" I ask.

He shrugs and looks at me with pitying eyes. I can tell he feels my pain, but he doesn't dare say a word. This bartender is one smart cookie. He knows where his bread is buttered, if you get my drift.

"How about a Gibsen?" he offers. "I make a mean martini."

"Can't," I say.

"How come?"

"I'm like Faye Dunaway."

He smiles. "Barfly, right?"

I immediately have a fleeting fantasy. The cute bartender and I are on a desert island drinking red wine out of huge goblets. We toast to the sun and the sand and to the fact that we are alone.

And no one is afraid that we'll stain anything.

I will now perform a trick called "The Balancing Act."

Hear ye! Hear ye! Come one, come all! It's The Greatest Show on Earth!

Watch as the Magical Splendini balances a cocktail plate in one hand and a fork in another!

Okay, party people. It's time to get down to business. Let's talk plates.

I've recently become aware of a frightening trend at parties: the advent of the itty-bitty cocktail plate. Now, I don't know who's to blame for this. The caterers? The hosts? The event planners? Oprah Winfrey?

Who came up with the idea of the diminutive party plate? A plate so microscopic, it requires a NASA engineer to determine whether it will fit a chicken skewer.

There is no room to set your fork on these plates, much less any food. You almost have to cup the plate in the palm of your hand while at the same time balancing your wine glass, your fork, your napkin, and your dignity.

Now, I'm not good at balancing acts. I don't work for Cirque du Soleil. And I've been known to trip over invisible "bumps" in the floor in broad daylight. So I ask you this question, dear ladies:

What is so offensive about providing guests with a regular dinner-sized plate? Is there a fear that *actual eating* will take place?

Of course, there are certain scenarios where the petite cocktail plate makes sense. Say, at a Weight Watchers convention. Or perhaps, at a large, thousand-person event where people are meant to "nibble," as opposed to "chow down."

In these instances, the miniature cocktail plates set the tone. The tone of: "Hey, folks. We're not serving a meal, here. These are just mini-quiches."

(P.S. And yet, there's always that one guy in the crowd, piling his plate as high as the Tower of Babel. *Uh, pardon me, Sir. This is not Luby's.*)

However, there are other times when a dinner-sized plate should be de rigueur. Like when you serve an entire fajita dinner complete with rice, beans, chips, and queso.

And now for my next trick! Come see the Magical Splendini as she attempts to eat a fajita without dripping cheese on her shoes!

Jo Barrett

Photo by Ashley Garmon

JO BARRETT is a graduate of the University of Texas at Austin and Georgetown Law School. Her previous novel, *The Men's Guide to the Women's Bathroom*, was optioned by CBS/Paramount Pictures with Hollywood actor Hugh Jackman's production company attached. Her second novel, *This Is How It Happened (Not a Love Story)*, is available in bookstores nationwide. Find out more at JoBarrettbooks.com.